P9-CDP-698

THE HEART TO KILL

A Literary Fiction Novel

Dorothy M. Place

Stephen F. Austin State University

For more information:
Stephen F. Austin State University Press
P.O. Box 13007 SFA Station
Nacogdoches, Texas 75962
sfapress@sfasu.edu
www.sfasu.edu/sfapress

Book design: Shaina Hawkins
Cover design: Shaina Hawkins
Distributed by Texas A&M Consortium
www.tamupress.com

LIBRARY OF CONGRESS CATALOGING-IN-PUBLICATION DATA
Place, Dorothy M.
The Heart to Kill/Dorothy M. Place

ISBN: 978-1-62288-129-1

To my daughter Marcella Place Sheehan
Who has been with me every step of the way.

But can you have the heart to kill your flesh and blood?

—*MEDEA*, Euripides

THE HEART TOKILL

Chapter One

$\mathcal{I}$t is frequently said that friends made in high school are seldom forgotten. But Sarah Wasser rarely thought of JoBeth Ruland. And why should she? After their high school graduation, each had set out on different trajectories: Sarah returned to Chicago for her undergraduate studies and then on to law school, while JoBeth remained in Eight Mile Junction, South Carolina, to marry and start a family.

Although they were separated by time and thousands of miles, JoBeth thrust herself back into Sarah's life that March night when Sarah returned from a full day of study and classes. Famished and headachy, she bypassed the annoying flash of the red light on the answering machine, shook out two aspirin, and headed for the fridge.

Ignoring the nagging reminders and the exam schedule taped onto the refrigerator door, she gazed at the picture of her black lab, Chewie, the consolation prize from her parents when the family moved south at the beginning of her sophomore year in high school. She blew an air kiss toward the picture, pulled a flyer from the door advertising the upcoming marathon, and tossed it into the trash. She hadn't trained for it, and wouldn't take time out of her study schedule to race if winning wasn't a possibility.

She grabbed a smoothie and the leftover half of the turkey sandwich purchased at the cafeteria the day before. It had been a bitch of a day. Her top standing in Bolinski's contracts class had been jeopardized when he called on her to discuss the law of obligations and she failed to fully summarize unjust enrichment. Alone in the kitchen, her face grew hot and her armpits prickled with sweat as she recalled his rant about the oversight that ended in a sustained look of sour disappointment, holding her afloat, ensuring that every student in the room had witnessed her undoing. Until now, he had seemed to favor her by calling on her to correct or improve upon the presentations of other students. She unscrewed the plastic cap on the smoothie and drank greedily. The blinking light on the telephone caught her eye; she walked into the living room and punched the play button. Two messages.

"This is Alfred Molitor's office," a woman's voice said. "He thanks you for your application for the summer's internship but is sorry to inform you that you were not one of the students selected for the position. If you have any questions…"

Sarah pressed the pause button. Her pulse soared and beat against her ear drums. Had she misunderstood? She bit her lip and pushed replay, listening long enough to confirm that Molitor had turned her down. She sank into the overstuffed chair and picked at its frayed upholstery. Her father had finagled that interview and, in his opinion, she was a shoo-in. He wouldn't take the news well. The internship fit in nicely with his plans for her to become a corporate attorney by combining a law degree with an MBA.

Her mind skittered about for excuses but, knowing her father, he'd question her until he latched onto something she did wrong, like not enough follow-up calls or relying on only one personal interview. As irritating as he sometimes was, she always relied on his judgment and worked hard not to disappoint him. She pulled a thread from the already tattered arm of the chair, nervously rolled it between her thumb and forefinger, and tried to suppress the growing panic that engulfed her stomach. No matter how she framed Molitor's decision, her father would see the outcome as her failure.

Two washouts in one day. Held up for ridicule by Bolinski and blown off by Molitor. She rested her forehead on her palm and, with the slim hope that the second call was from Molitor's office saying that it was all a mistake, she pressed the play button.

"Sarah." It was her mother's voice. "Call me as soon as you come in. Something terrible has happened."

What could be so terrible? Right now, she had enough problems. She wasn't in the mood to talk about a sweater shrunk in the dryer or a misplaced family heirloom. Anything her mother had to say would be too trivial for her to deal with. She finished off the smoothie and went back into the kitchen to throw the container into the recycle bin. It missed, bounced off the rim, and fell to the floor dribbling pink liquid as it rolled.

Substitution the coach called out. She was off the team. Shit, what a day.

The room chilled but she was reluctant to turn on the heat. It made her drowsy, and the dust mites blown through the ancient vents made her sneeze. A shower would help her think. She shed her clothes and turned the faucet. The pipes rattled their displeasure at having to force water through their crusty interior, and a spider clung to its web that twisted about in the small turbulences caused by the warming currents of air. She left it to its own devices. She hadn't killed one since she read *Charlotte's Web* in the third grade.

Afterwards, she lay on her bed and opened the contracts book, but her mother's distressed voice intruded and prevented her from concentrating. She rolled over and pushed the speed dial. Her mother answered.

"Oh, Sarah, I'm so glad you called." Her mother's voice was tight and caught several times. She coughed to clear her throat. "Something awful has happened to JoBeth."

"What happened?" Sarah impatiently toyed with the telephone cord, waiting for her mother to regain her composure. The cord stretched thin and retracted reminding her of a slinky.

"Her children are missing."

Sarah sprang to the edge of the bed. "Missing? When did that happen?"

"The night before last," her mother whispered.

"Speak up. I can hardly hear you. Where is JoBeth now?"

"The paper said she's with her parents."

"What else?"

"She left the children in her car in the Bi-Lo parking lot while she ran in to get a few groceries and, when she came out, the car and the kids were gone. Poor JoBeth. She must be out of her mind with worry."

"Casey and Daniel missing? What are the police doing about it?"

"The sheriff said they're putting everything into finding them. He says there's a good chance of getting them back, but I don't know."

"What's Dad saying?"

"Not much. Just says it's another poorly managed life gone wrong. You know your father."

After she hung up, Sarah shuffled to the window. Tears spilled onto her cheeks and wet the corners of her mouth; she licked them away with her tongue. She wasn't sure whether she was crying for JoBeth or for herself. The neon sign across the street advertising Lucy's Luscious Kitchen blurred as the narrow tubes that spelled out the restaurant's name melded together. Cars below honked their way past, and a group of female students in blue jeans and brightly colored vests bent their shoulders into the wind and chitchatted their way into Logo's Used Book Store. Sarah rapped on the window to chase away the pigeons roosting on the fire escape. "Paloma," she whispered bitterly. "Such a pretty Spanish word for such foul little beasts."

The call from her mother dredged up images that flooded Sarah's mind: JoBeth before the mirror in the girl's bathroom touching up her already too thick mascara; JoBeth gently working the snags in Sarah's long curly hair; JoBeth sunbathing at Fenton Lake, determined to tan her porcelain skin; JoBeth, a June bride happily marrying her Prince Charming; JoBeth in the maternity ward after a long labor, beaming and passing baby Daniel for Sarah to hold.

Although Sarah intended to contact her friend after her mother's call, she let the days slip by without phoning. She meant well, but the timing never seemed right. So much had happened since she and JoBeth had shared confidences. What could she say? Sorry? Of course she was sorry. How else could it be? But after that?

Besides, her life had been complicated by Molitor's decision. Her father might contact his college friend and discover that she hadn't been selected for the internship. It would be like him to do something like that—then demand an explanation, first from Molitor, then from his daughter. Humiliation prevented her from telling anyone, not even Marney Diggins, the friend with whom she shared a carrel in the law library. The secret wedged itself in her stomach, refusing to move. Time passed. The days became bunched into a wad of half-remembered busyness; the future wrapped in uncertainties and fears.

The second telephone call from Sarah's mother came less than two weeks after the first. It was a Saturday morning, and Sarah was listening to the radio as she folded laundry. Her mother began speaking before Sarah finished saying hello.

"JoBeth has been charged with murdering her children."

"Wait a minute," she said. Sarah turned down the radio. "Now, what did you say?"

"JoBeth *murdered* Daniel and Casey."

"Did you say murder? What are you talking about?"

"I saw it in today's paper. You should see the headlines—'Sheriff Charges Mother with Murder of Her Children.' The kids were found at the bottom of Fenton Lake, drowned."

"But you told me Daniel and Casey were missing. That JoBeth left them in the Bi-Lo parking lot, and when she came out they were gone. Now you're telling me they're dead?"

"She confessed."

"Confessed to what?"

"Here, let me read it. 'Mrs. Ruland confessed to taking the children to the lake that night, but says that's all she remembers.'"

"If she only remembers taking them to the lake, then how can they say she confessed to murder?"

"It says right here in the paper that there are no other suspects."

"Well, that doesn't mean anything. It's too soon to say that. Anyway, I don't believe it. I know JoBeth. She wouldn't have the heart to kill her children."

"I know, Sarah, but your dad says it doesn't look good for her."

Sometimes her father was too opinionated. "He hardly knows JoBeth," Sarah protested. "She adored those children. Where is she now?"

"In jail."

"They must have hired a lawyer. Why isn't she out on bail?"

"All I know is what's in the paper, and the paper hasn't reported anything about lawyers or bail. It only says that they're holding her in jail."

"Keep track of things, will you? Call me if anything turns up."

As the school term drew to a close, Sarah tried not to be distracted by the murders. She worked to regain her status in Bolinski's class without kissing ass. He'd catch onto that, wouldn't let her schmooze her way back into his good graces. Final exams were just four weeks away, and she was determined to begin her final year at the top of her class. That meant long study hours and little sleep.

Then, there was the problem of the coming summer. How to keep the news of Molitor's rejection from her father? She could sit in her apartment the entire summer break, pretending that she was happily at work. Or, she could tell him the truth. That meant she'd have to figure out some way to minimize her father's disappointment. But she couldn't bear telling him the truth. Couldn't bear the damage to her image of a daughter that always got it right.

Despite her efforts to concentrate on her studies, visions of JoBeth rolling her car into the lake with the children strapped into their seats crept into Sarah's mind. Did Daniel and Casey wake up at the first touch of cold water on their little legs, or did they mercifully remain asleep as the water filled the car and carried them to the muddy bottom? And

JoBeth. Did she quietly watch the car sink below the surface, or did she cry out in horror at what she had done? Sarah tried to push the horrific images away but, whenever her mind rested, her friend and the children moved through her thoughts as ghosts move about in places where they once spent their lives, gliding soundlessly about, materializing at unwanted times, invoking unwanted memories.

Sarah sank into a blue and grey melancholy. The world she had once been on top of was now an unfair and unforgiving place. Bolinski's class ended before she could redeem herself, and her inner voice repeated Molitor's rejection like a tape stuck on replay. Her rehearsed excuses about the lost internship sounded gratuitous. Dwelling on them was useless and depressing. And when not wrestling with the rejection, she became increasingly preoccupied with seeking an explanation for the murders. In law school, answers to legal problems were simply a matter of having enough patience to find a related case or a correct statute. But why a mother murders her children? The answer to that question couldn't be found in law books. Her search for answers remained unrewarded.

During the final weeks of the academic year, Sarah toyed with the notion of returning home for the summer break and finding work with JoBeth's defense team. If she put the right slant on it, there was an outside chance that she might convince her father that getting some criminal trial experience made her a better candidate for a job in some corporate legal department. As a bonus, she might find an explanation for JoBeth's behavior and, with some luck, be able to help her friend.

By the time Sarah entered the Celtic Knot Public House for the end-of-term celebration, the partying was well under way. The benches along the highly varnished tables were full, and fat pitchers of beer were being passed hand-over-hand up and down the long tables. Irish folk music could barely be heard above the noise, and a silent television was replaying a hurling match between Cork and Limerick Counties. Waiters in ankle-length white aprons, like the ones in pictures of Irish pubs popular in the 1900s, wrestled pitches of beers and trays of food between the crowded benches.

When Sarah located the table with her classmates, Marney scrunched over to make room. Her thick, bobbed hair was nearly the color of the pilsner they were drinking and hugged her head like a neatly fitting cap. Sarah pushed her unruly hair into place with a super clip and slid into the seat. The atmosphere in the pub vibrated with the raucous sounds of happy students, so much so that she and Marney had to raise their voices to be heard.

"You finally got here," Marney shouted. "We're way ahead of you."
She saluted Sarah with a half-empty mug of beer.

Sarah mumbled an excuse not meant to be heard. The Celtic Knot
wasn't her favorite place and she wasn't in the mood to party. The term
was over and, although she had been thinking of going home for the
summer, she still hadn't told her parents. The thought of calling them
hung heavily on her conscience and nurtured the lump in her stomach.

"When do you start your internship?" Marney asked. Then to the
waiter, "A quarter pounder and hold the mustard."

"Not ready," Sarah told the waiter when he asked for her order.
"I'm not staying in Evanston," she told Marney. "I'm going home for the
summer."

Cork made a goal. The students cheered. The two women watched as
the teams reformed for the face-off. It was raining, and the player's faces
were almost as muddy as their uniforms.

"Looks like a messy game," Sarah commented.

"What did you say about your internship?" Marney asked. "Did I
hear you right?" She took a sip of beer. "Going to eat something?"

Sarah reached for the menu. "You heard right. I'm going home for
the summer."

The Celtic script made the menu look very Irish but difficult to read.
She had said it aloud, told someone that she was going home. Her words
joined the other words spoken by the students, and settled among the
pitchers of beer, fish and chips, and hamburgers. Up until now, it had
been an idea, but at this moment, it became real. She had committed to
the idea of going home.

"You've got to be kidding. I thought that internship was your ticket
to a corporate job after law school. Isn't that what your father wants?"

Sarah shrugged. The waiter was hovering. She pointed toward Marney's
plate. "Same thing." She poured herself a beer.

"Why'd you change your mind?"

Sarah took a sip, and shook her head. The beer left a line of foam on
her upper lip.

"You've got a mustache," Marney laughed.

Sarah rubbed her thumb across her lip. The students roared again,
and Marney turned her attention to the television. Their exuberance irked
Sarah. It was just a game, no need to act as though it was a life-changing
event. She took out her compact and fussed with her eyebrows. They
were too bushy, needed to be plucked, but the thought of pulling out

those tiny hairs one at a time made her cringe.

The dish clattered as the waiter placed her order on the table. "Anything else?" he asked.

Sarah shook her head, and stared at the plate loaded with enough French fries to feed a troop of Boy Scouts. Catsup and grease oozed across the plate. Why had she ordered the damned thing? She took a bite of the hamburger, but her throat tightened, preventing her from swallowing. Too much meat. Her mind drifted, first to the mechanics of returning home for the summer, and then to JoBeth and the children.

Daniel would be in nursery school, probably the same serious little boy she remembered, thin and dark like his father, always at the fringe of things, happy to be playing alone with his Legos. He had been born when she was home for the Christmas break her freshman year at Chicago, and she remembered the nurse handing her the little bundle, so impossibly small. JoBeth always said that a bit of Sarah became part of her son's character that day. "He'll be just like you, Sarah," she had said. "Smart and ambitious."

By now, Casey's little Michelin Man legs would be propelling her around the apartment. The last time Sarah saw her she was an infant, chubby and blonde, nestling against his mother, eyeing the world with a mild curiosity. Sweet and soft, she favored JoBeth. Casey had reached out with her dimpled hand, and tightly clutched Sarah's fingers. Sarah's heart ached at the memory.

The evening after the end-of-term celebration she called home. Her mother answered. Sarah fiddled as she waited for her father to come to the phone, twisting a lock of hair around her finger. Several strands broke. She flicked them off, and watched as they floated to the floor.

"I'm coming home for the summer," she said when he answered.

"What do you mean coming home? What about your internship with Molitor?"

"I'd like to work with JoBeth's defense team instead. I hope you'll understand, Dad."

"You're telling me you're throwing your internship away?"

"At the time you suggested it, I thought working with Molitor was a good idea. But I changed my mind. I hope you're not disappointed."

"What about the MBA, and your plans to become a corporate lawyer?"

"Practicing corporate law is still on my radar. But this summer ..."

"Listen, I put my name on the line for you with Molitor, and you know how much my good name means to me. Besides, he and I go a long way back. This whole thing involves more than just business."

"I know and I'm sorry." She began to pace. The telephone cord stretched, pulled the phone off the table. Sarah jumped when it hit the floor, but her father didn't seem to hear the noise or the ringing sound that reverberated in her ears.

"Sorry isn't good enough."

"I'll make it up to you. You'll see," she pleaded. "Please ..."

"You haven't said anything to Molitor yet, have you?"

"Well, sort of."

"Look, I've done everything to make sure you'll be successful in life, and this internship was to be a big part of furthering your career. Give up that silly idea that you can change things for JoBeth. I want you to call Molitor and tell him you've reconsidered. Take care of it and call me back tomorrow. I'll be waiting. Don't let me down."

He hung up. The telephone buzzed in her ear. She was consumed by the urge to immediately call back and apologize. That's what she had always done when she displeased him. Apologized and did as he asked.

This time, she couldn't. The internship was a dead deal. If she told her father the truth, it would only transfer his disappointment from her giving up the internship to her failure to get it. The latter was far worse. Going home was the only way to solve the Molitor issue, and working with JoBeth's defense team, the only way to salvage her self-respect. And JoBeth? Perhaps the trial would reveal what had really happened. She replaced the telephone and pulled her suitcase from under her bed.

Chapter Two

Sarah pushed her way through the crowded bus station in Columbia, South Carolina, hurrying past the travelers surrounded by suitcases marked with colorful ribbons and boxes held together with strapping tape. The gritty smoke-filled room smelled of hamburgers and French fries. A disembodied voice announced bus arrivals and departures in a shower of unintelligible words that ricocheted off the walls and ceiling like errant ping pong balls.

She stopped at the sundries counter to purchase a bottle of water. When the vendor turned to ring up the sale, a bearded man, with a watch cap pulled low over his ears, scooped up the change left as payment on the pile of newspapers and melted into the press of bystanders. Sarah shrugged and stuffed the water bottle into her backpack, escaping the waiting room through a door that led to a garage full of idling busses. The smell of fried food gave way to exhaust fumes. She found the bus that would take her to Eight Mile Junction, climbed aboard and walked to the rear, dumped her backpack on the aisle seat, and slid past to the window.

The bus seats gave off a stagnant odor of clothing too long in the hamper, and the road film and dust on the window had been molded into brown squiggly streaks by a recent rain shower. She pushed the seat back and leaned her head against the glass only to be startled by a passing worker spraying the bus clean with a powerful stream of water. The resulting coolness on the window was calming.

Usually the bus trip from the airport in Columbia to Eight Mile Junction was tedious, but this time Sarah looked forward to having a few hours to think about her dilemma. Her father would be angry; she was certain of that. An apology alone wouldn't suffice, and he had already rejected the idea that working on JoBeth's defense team would change what he thought would be the inevitable outcome of the trial. If she simply didn't offer an excuse and stonewalled him, there was an outside chance he might come around, but that was risky. She had yet to best him in a contest of wills. He had to be convinced that criminal trial experience was an essential ingredient of any attorney's education, and he had to believe that the idea was his. Let him think he was managing the situation. She closed her eyes, and tried to conjure up a believable game plan, but her thoughts became clogged with memories of her high school friend.

Sarah first met JoBeth at Fenton Lake the summer her family moved from Deer Meadow, Illinois to Eight Mile Junction, a small town in the foothills of South Carolina's Appalachia. The relocation was engendered by her father's promotion to general manager of the GNL Manufacturing Company. Shortly after the announcement, her mother began packing and her father left to take on his new position. Sarah wrenched herself away from her friends at the Preston Academy for Girls and sullenly helped her mother prepare for the move. That was the summer before Sarah's sophomore year in high school.

One morning, a few weeks after they had settled into their new home, Sarah and her mother were at the breakfast table. Her mother, wearing her favorite blue duster, was reading the *Daily Journal* and sipping coffee while Sarah toyed with the uneaten sunny-side-up eggs on her plate.

"Sarah, dear, look at this." Her mother had held out the newspaper, pointing to the article she was reading. "There's a picnic for high school students at Fenton Lake. This may be a good chance to meet some kids your age before school starts."

It was only eight but already humid and uncomfortable. A ceiling fan sent ripples of air about the room with so little conviction that nothing moved despite its efforts. Sarah gathered her curly hair in her two hands, twisted it into a roll, and shot a clip thorough the thickest part. Several recalcitrant strands fell to the nape of her neck and stuck to her damp skin. She took the newspaper from her mother and, without looking at the article, began to fan her face and underarms.

"I don't want to meet kids my age."

"Sarah." Her mother's pale blue eyes pleaded with her daughter to cooperate.

"I'm only doing time until I go north for college. I'm not going to the lake for any party with a bunch of kids I don't know."

"What's this I'm hearing about a party at the lake?" Sam Wasser entered the kitchen. Sarah gave her father's pin-striped suit and vest a short-tempered glance. And those damn Buddy Holly look-alike glasses. Straight out of the fifties. Doesn't he know it's the 1990s?

He smiled and slid into the chair next to his daughter. "Good morning, Ellen," he nodded toward his wife. "Scrambled eggs this morning, no bacon, dry toast."

Ellen brushed her husband's forehead with a kiss, and busied herself preparing his breakfast. Sam patted his daughter's knee. She pushed his hand away and continued to fan herself.

"My little girl grumpy this morning?" he teased.

Sarah propped her feet up on the empty chair next to her and glared at the eggs trapped in a pool of solidifying butter. She threw her napkin over the plate so she didn't have to look into their glassy eyes or smell their pungent egginess.

"Your mother's right, you know," her father said. "I moved us here because of what the new job offered. You're here now; it's up to you to make something of it."

"I don't remember you asking me if I wanted to move." Sarah glanced sideways at her father, expecting to the chastised.

"Look how much more we have here than we did in Illinois," Sam continued as if Sarah hadn't spoken. "A bigger house. A housekeeper so your mother doesn't have to work so hard. And no long, snowy winters. That's a bonus, don't you think?"

Sarah had heard this kind of sweet talk before. He talked, but only about what was important to him. She reached down and scratched her ankle.

"There are more damn mosquitoes in this damn place than damn people."

"You know how I expect you to behave," Sam warned.

She nodded, reached over, and fingered the Jessamine her mother had brought in from the garden several days before. "The last of the spring blooms," her mother had announced cheerily when she brought them into the house. "Aren't they just lovely?"

The bright yellow flowers were fading but her mother, reluctant to discard them, kept changing the water and picking off the dead leaves to extend the life of the bouquet. Wasn't that just like her mother? Hold on a little longer and everything might turn out all right. Sarah had no patience with her mother's perpetual forbearance and her continual hope for a happy ending.

The cloying scent of the dying flowers added weight to the already oppressive air. Sarah, edgy and restless, shifted in her chair. Her annoyance with her father turned to anger with her mother. She wanted to blame her for everything; the move south, her pathetic willingness to nurture the dying flowers, wearing that damned blue duster every morning, always giving in, always keeping the peace.

Sarah tossed the newspaper in her father's direction and stormed upstairs to look for her bathing suit. Even when she rebelled, she always ended by giving in to his wishes. She may as well take the shortcut—don't argue—just do it.

After changing into her bathing suit and shorts, Sarah went out and opened the padlock on the double doors of the garage. As she pulled one of them open, it stuck on the broken cement. She kicked the door frame. A piece of molding splintered and fell to the driveway, exposing the bright red color of the cedar wood. She took a deep breath and lifted the door up and over the obstruction. There was another thing. At Deer Meadows, the garage had a door opener. She gave the door another kick, carefully aiming at the solid center.

She pushed her bicycle onto the street and set off toward the road that connected the town with the lake, a distance of about five miles. She estimated the number of times she would have to pedal across each sunny spot before she found relief in the next patch of shade. The game helped her ignore the glare of the sun and kept her mind off the sweat trickling down between her breasts, and soaking her back.

As she pedaled, a Chevy Silverado without a muffler roared its approach and, as it passed, the driver leaned out and yelled, "Hey, Sweet Thing, got an old man?" The dog in the passenger seat barked and spewed spittle. The driver stepped on the gas, leaving two neat ribbons of tread on the pavement.

"Asshole," she mumbled, searching for the next shady patch, counting the turns of the sprocket, and listening for vehicles coming from behind. What was her father thinking when he moved them to a place like this? Did he actually think she could be friends with people like that? She longed for her girlfriends at the Academy and vowed that, once high school was finished, she'd say good riddance to the South.

About a mile before the turnoff to the lake, a wooden shack covered with kudzu stood back from the road. Sarah had noticed it before and pitied the old building. She wondered how long it had endured the suffocating embrace of the vines and how long it would be before the patches of tin roof, the chimney, and the upstairs windows entirely disappeared under the invasion of tangled greenery. Despite the heat and the humidity, the fecundity of the engulfing vines made Sarah shiver. Like the old building, she was trapped.

Her legs ached from pedaling uphill so she was relieved when she saw the sign marking the turnoff to the lake. In spite of her earlier protest, the thought of a leisurely swim dissolved her foul mood. Perhaps her parents were right. She ought to reach out and make friends. And she'd better have some names. Her dad would be grilling her at dinner.

She rode into the parking lot and bent to lock her bike. As Sarah turned toward the lake, one of the students approached. She was barefoot, and her large breasts swayed as she stumbled over the sharp gravel. Her pudgy midsection bulged slightly over the bottom half of her bathing suit, and the pale, unblemished skin on her face and shoulders had been reddened by the sun. She appraised Sarah guilelessly. Sarah was reminded of one of the cherubs she had seen in a painting of mother and child: innocent, blissful, and completely unmindful of her ripened and sensual body.

"Hi," she called out, coming up close, so close Sarah could smell the greasy saltiness of the bag of chips in her hand. "My name's JoBeth Bellinger." Her voice had the softness of a chocolate bar left too long in the sun, and she said the word "name" as if it had two syllables. "You're the new girl in town, ain't cha?" She took a sip of soda. "We've been wondering what the new girl was like and when we were going to meet her." JoBeth giggled, looped her arm through Sarah's, and guided her toward the other students on the beach. "What church you belong to?"

Sarah withdrew from JoBeth's grasp and struggled for the right words. "We don't really go to church."

"Well, that's just fine." she beamed, as though nothing Sarah said could be wrong. "You can come along with me to the First Baptist. Most of the kids go there. Next Sunday we'll carry you to the nine o' clock meeting. My step-daddy can drive. You be ready, okay?"

She stuffed a few potato chips in her mouth then held out the bag, gesturing for Sarah to take some. Crunching filled the silence between them. Sarah felt like a bug in a Petri dish. Silence wasn't going to solve anything. Sooner or later, everyone would know. This was a small town, and in small towns, news travels fast.

"My family is Jewish," she said, then turned and walked rapidly toward the lake's edge. She could hear JoBeth bouncing along in small running steps, trying to keep pace with her. She looked back and saw her tuck the bag of potato chips under her chin and, with her free hand, wipe off the soda that had splashed down her arm. Sarah waited for her to catch up.

"Well, I'll be. Jewish," JoBeth said, falling into step with Sarah. "Reckon you can come with us to youth fellowship on Wednesday night. The actual fact is that we hardly ever pray at those meetings. And you'll love the youth minister. Let me tell you, my momma says that he's just one of us kids."

"We'll see," Sarah said.

The sound of the last of the luggage bumping its way into the belly of the bus startled Sarah and brought her into the present. The driver slid into his seat and began the trip that took almost as long as the flight from Chicago to Columbia. As they progressed westward, Loblolly Pines closed in on the highway from both sides, giving the illusion that the bus was standing still while someone hidden backstage rolled a picture of trees round and round a large drum. The only hint that anything existed beyond the repetitive scenery were the mile markers that ticked off the distance to Greenville in ten-mile increments, and an occasional sign identifying nearby towns: Scotts Corners 4 mi., Beauville 10 mi, Powder's Creek 12 mi. For all anyone knew, these places were the invention of some creative sign maker who meant to trick the passers-by into believing that a world existed outside the long, concrete path the bus was following.

Lulled into a comfortable place, Sarah dozed on and off, waking only when the bus left the highway and entered one or another of the small towns hiding behind the forested roadside. Each displayed a remarkable similarity: brick store fronts, some plastered with stucco; a large bank, always The First National; an impressive Baptist church, also always the first; an even larger courthouse fronted by a grand staircase and an imposing portico; a mill, more than likely long closed; and small shops, none bearing the names of the big chains. With few exceptions, the bus passed a large clock with Roman numerals standing prominently on the main street, its sole function to inform everyone that time was not really standing still. To Sarah, the sameness from town-to-town spoke eloquently of the fabric of rural southern life, honoring the past, resisting change, and providing a surface gentility as suffocating as the kudzu vines that rampaged over the southern landscape.

Once Sarah had asked JoBeth to visit her in Chicago but her friend scorned the idea. "Mercy, Sarah. Why ever would I want to go north? Folks up there don't think the way we do in the South. We take good care of each other here."

"But Chicago has theaters and museums and great parks and a lake as big as an ocean!"

"I belong to this country," JoBeth replied. "It's my home and when I have children, it'll be their home, too. If this town is good enough for my momma and my step-daddy, it's good enough for me."

"Don't you ever dream of another kind of life? To travel? Maybe even see the world. Anything but live your whole life in this boring place."

"Sarah, honey, folks around here say that we're born with this here red clay under our fingernails, and it never washes off. No matter how far we go, when we look down at our hands we know where we belong."

JoBeth's devotion to her life's goals wasn't any less uncompromising than Sarah's; it was just that hers were different. Sarah planned to leave; JoBeth to stay. A few weeks after they started their junior year, JoBeth had pointed out Phillip Ruland.

"See that boy over there? That's Phillip Ruland. Don't you think he's cute?" JoBeth reached into her turquoise blouse and hitched up her bra strap. "These damn things don't ever want to stay up," she muttered.

Phillip was a dark and thin, always a neatly dressed young man. He was one of the good boys at school, not a winner, just a good boy who hung around the edges of his classmates wherever they gathered, wanting to be part of the group but unwilling to call attention to himself. He was a fair student, a miler on the track team, remembered for ending each race toward the back, his long thin legs working furiously and his arms outstretched, hoping they would save him from being last to cross the finish line. She didn't think he was good looking but, to be agreeable, Sarah told her friend he was the cutest ever.

Before coming to Eight Mile Junction, Sarah hadn't thought much about boyfriends because studies, not marriage, were the primary concern of her classmates at the Academy, and graduate school the main topic of conversation. The day she and her father had gone for the admissions interview, Dean Horowitz made the school's priorities clear, stating them in a low, well-modulated voice. Sarah sat at the edge of her chair, back straight, ankles crossed, hands folded on her lap. Dean Horowitz's piercing, gray-green eyes settled on Sarah when she asked about Sarah's future plans.

"She's going to law school," her father said. Sarah was accustomed to having her father answer for her, so she wasn't surprised when he spoke up.

The Dean opened Sarah's application, picked up her reading glasses, slid them up her long narrow nose, and flipped through the pages. She tapped her forefinger on the desk as she read. A thin spindle that perforated a stack of messages caught Sarah's eye as she awaited her fate. In a way, sitting without fidgeting was like being one of the messages, spindled.

Her father took his glasses on and off and wiped his face with his handkerchief. He was unaccustomed to having someone else in charge. The clock on the wall counted off the minutes with clicks of the second hand and Sarah's father shifted in his seat, trying to find the right position for his long legs. Finally, the dean turned to Sarah.

"I see you mentioned law school in your application."

"We want her to be accepted into one of the top colleges," Sam answered. "That's why her mother and I are looking at Prescott as a prep school for her."

A soft "A-hem" hung in the air between the Dean and Sarah's father. "Mr. Wasser," the Dean said after she cleared her throat and returned her reading glasses to the desk, "All our young ladies come here with well-furnished minds. We expect the most from them, and they, in turn, reach their highest potential. I can assure you, if she is accepted, Sarah will not disappoint you or Prescott." She turned to Sarah. "Now, can you speak for yourself? What are your goals, my dear?"

"To be at the top of the class. My father expects it."

As a coed at Eight Mile Junction High School, Sarah had been able to observe boys closely, watching as they strutted and leered when girls were present, teasing some, baiting others, scorning the rest. During free time, the girls hung about in clutches, very much like guinea fowl, guided by the group's wisdom, traveling everywhere together, first in one direction, then another, without plan, remaining close to the earth, unmindful of their ability to fly.

They played the game of see and be seen, but Sarah didn't know how to play. She was out of place and longed to return to Prescott where she understood the rules. For the entire three years she spent at Eight Mile Junction High School, Sarah kept her head down, excelled in her classes, focused on going north to college, and relied on JoBeth to guide her through the confusing maze of teen social life.

Despite JoBeth's daily report on her relationship with Phillip, Sarah was taken by surprise when her friend announced mid-way through their senior year that they were going to marry right after graduation. When she blurted out the news, her face reminded Sarah of the sun's rays reflecting off the copper roof of the United Methodist Church, blindingly bright. She was happy for her friend but wondered about her rush to marry.

She and JoBeth achieved their high school goals. Sarah went to the

University of Chicago, the place her parents met, and JoBeth married Phillip the week after they graduated. She was seventeen, Phillip, eighteen. She wore a white dress with a train long enough to reach the Georgia border. Eight bridesmaids, each wearing a different color of summer, preceded her to the altar. Sarah suffered the long ceremony in pink.

The wedding was held at the First Baptist. It was a humid day. Rivulets of perspiration made a zig-zag pattern on JoBeth's powdered back, and Sarah kept pushing her glasses upward as they slid down her nose. The bridesmaids bouquets wilted, and the ushers fingered the inside of their starched collars while The Right Reverend Stuart Waldfield's deep voice, magnified by the public address system, filled the sanctuary and buried the wedding party in an outpouring of warnings and admonishments.

"The Lord has a plan for your life," he promised JoBeth and Phillip. He stopped and gazed at the young couple.

"Amen," the congregation responded in unison.

Looking back at the wedding, Sarah wondered if the Lord's plan for JoBeth and Phillip included divorce and murder. A sad ending to such a hopeful beginning.

Chapter Three

The driver pulled into the parking lot of the train station at Eight Mile Junction early that evening. The opening doors hissed a sigh of relief as the bus came to a stop. The station had closed permanently after the textile mills discontinued producing cotton cloth a decade or so before. Other than the twice-weekly freight on its way north to Charlotte, the tracks were idle. Sun-bleached and ragged advertisements for Leady's Real Estate, the Rotary Club, and the First Baptist Vacation Bible School covered the now defunct passenger train schedule. A feral cat leapt onto the station's window sill and squeezed through the broken glass.

Sarah grabbed her roller board and began the short walk home. Everything about the town looked as it did when she last visited. The hands on the town clock's round face were at 6:30. The fading sunlight, the aged patina on the buildings, and the dome formed by the cobalt sky turned the town into a movie-set, masking the horror of the recent murders with a smooth and tranquil hand, preserving the town's veneer of untarnished civility.

Her heart warmed as she approached the corner of Hampton and Second and her home came into view. A Georgian Colonial, it was a two-story box of a house dignified by twelve-pane windows and two great ground-to-sky chimneys, one at each end of the building. A dogwood tree, some twenty feet tall and in bloom, graced the corner of the lot. Azalea bushes hugged the steps leading up to the front door on which hung an enormous, brass knocker, the kind on which you might expect to see Jacob Marley's face appear.

The old Volvo was in the driveway, but her father's Mercedes was absent. As she opened the screen door, it made the same twingey sound she remembered. Chewie, her black Lab, was waiting inside the kitchen door. She wagged her body with happiness, hitting Sarah legs with her rump and long tail. Some white hairs rimmed her nose and she had put on considerable weight.

"Good dog," Sarah crooned. Chewie pressed against her and extended a paw. She bent on one knee and took the Lab in her arms. "You never forget me, do you?"

The dog flopped onto her side, exposing her stomach. Sarah gave her a good scratch, then rose clicking her tongue softly. Chewie followed her into the kitchen. The light over the stove made a small circle of light in the darkening room; the scent of lilacs in a vase on the table greeted her sweetly. The Post-it on the refrigerator door said that her mother and father were in Charlotte and wouldn't return until late. "Pizza in the freezer, feed dog. Love you, Mom." Her mother still finished off her notes with X's and O's just as she did when Sarah was a little girl.

Everything in her bedroom remained exactly as she had left it. Raggedy Ann and Andy rested hand-in-hand on the bed, Grandmother Solonsky's wedding picture stood on the dresser in its silver frame with lilies trumpeting from its four corners, her high school graduation honor ribbons hung from the curtain valance, and the sheepskin rug her uncle had sent from New Zealand waited to caress her feet as it had each morning. The room, like her mother, continually awaited her return.

Chewie's eyes followed Sarah as she inspected the closet, opened the dresser drawers, and straightened the framed certificate for the half marathon she had run in high school. She opened the blinds. Through the branches of the maple tree she could see St. Agnes Catholic Church crouched on the corner, diagonally across the street. It was a small wood-framed building with an afterthought of a room protruding from the rear of the sanctuary. The size of the property on which the church stood suggested that the diocese hierarchy at one time had believed the congregation would prosper but, despite their early optimism, the congregation languished and the building, now surrounded by a brown untended lawn, had fallen into disrepair. The sign board advertised "*St. Agnes Roman Catholic Church, Sunday 8:00 A.M.*"

Sarah believed it to be the smallest Catholic church in existence, and that the discreet clicking of the congregation's rosary beads was never able to compete with the choruses of amen and hallelujahs emanating from the Baptist church and resounding throughout the town on Sunday mornings. Despite St. Agnes' unpretentious assemblage, she admired the way the building clung to its place on the corner. It was a visible reminder she wasn't the only one in this town who didn't quite fit in.

Downstairs, she pulled the pizza from the freezer, popped it into the toaster oven, and searched the drawers for the telephone directory. She'd tell JoBeth's parents that she was home for the summer and that she hoped she'd find some way to help their daughter. But the answering machine at the Maitlins' told her to leave a message. She decided to try again the next day.

But what if JoBeth wasn't the same person she remembered? Could she still defend her? And what if the defense team refused to hire her? She ground her teeth, temporarily paralyzed by the prospect of having made a horrendous mistake. Chewie pawed her leg begging for attention.

"What do you think? Did I do a dumb thing?"

The dog wagged her tail and panted heavily, her brown eyes adoring Sarah.

"Anything I do is all right with you. Could you put in a good word to Dad for me?"

Sarah knelt. Chewie leaned into her, placed a paw on her shoulder, and with a sloppy lick, gave Sarah her vote of confidence.

What was done was done. She took the pizza, went up to her bedroom, and turned on the radio. The dial was still on her favorite station, WCAR, soft rock. She gathered Raggedy Ann and Andy in her arms, gave them a hug, and sat them on the chair. Their beady eyes sparkled as they stared blankly at Sarah as she lay munching the pizza and drifting to the music. Chewie settled on the sheepskin rug. The old house creaked with familiar sounds.

It was a stroke of good fortune that she didn't have to face her father that night. She finished the pizza, tossed the last bite to Chewie, and crumbled the paper napkin. She went to the window and watched St. Agnes fade in the evening twilight. Tired, she returned to her bed and slept soundly.

The next morning, Sarah turned away from the light entering through the half-shut blinds, tucked a pillow under her head and tried to guess the time. The water running in her parents' bathroom signaled that her father hadn't left for work, and the quick opening and closing of the front door meant that Ellen was taking in the newspaper. The morning routine had begun. She rose on one elbow, reached for her glasses, and looked at the clock radio on her bedside table. Not yet seven; too early to get up. She pulled the covers to her chin and snuggled.

It was the end of May, the best time to be in the South, and the perfect time to hike in the mountains. The rhododendrons, tucked away in the shadowy protection of the trees, would soon burst into bloom, and the softly rounded mountains would be colored by the early spring-burst of tiny green leaves. An engine started and her father's car backed down the driveway. She wouldn't have to face him until evening but, by then, she'd better have something planned other than a hike into the mountains. He might insist that she work in his office at the factory. Imagine what that would be like. He'd assign her to some menial job but overpay her for doing it, reminding her of his generosity and threatening her with his expectations. That's the way he was—his munificence overshadowed by his demands for perfection.

Her mother was at the table, lingering over a cooling cup of coffee and polishing her nails when Sarah entered the breakfast room. As Sarah bent to kiss her, she held out her arms, spreading her fingers to avoid smearing the polish.

"Good morning, dear." Ellen withdrew her arms from around Sarah's neck, held her bent fingers before her lips and blew on her nails. "Sleep well?"

"Great to be back in my old bed." Sarah surveyed her mother's blue duster, now faded and a bit ragged around the neckline. "Mother, are you going to be buried in that old thing?"

"I suppose I will, but at least you'll know I'll be comfortable in the cold, cold ground." They both laughed. Ellen looked at her daughter fondly and reached over to touch her cheek. Her eyes softened by love, searched her daughter's face for things a mother wants to know but is wary of asking. "So good to have you home."

As Sarah poured coffee, she noticed a bottle of Tums next to the toaster. Dad's indigestion. What was he getting himself all worked up over now? The kitchen walls had been painted a shade lighter than her mother's blue duster.

"Kitchen looks good. Did Dad paint it?" She filled the dog's water dish.

"No, we hired Gil Spracker. Do you want bacon and eggs?"

"Not really. I usually skip breakfast."

Chewie padded over to the water dish. Sarah bent to pet her. "Want to go for a hike at Ramsfield Rock?" The dog looked up at Sarah, water dripping from her jaws.

"You should really eat something. You're looking awfully thin to me," Ellen observed.

"Mmmmm, I'm fine, Mom. Don't worry."

Sarah reached for the newspaper her father had scattered about the table, found the front page, and read the headline, Ruland Jailed for Murder of her Children. The last paragraph of the article reported that Margaret Bellinger Standcroft was spokesperson for the family, and that Vera and Howard Maitlin, JoBeth's parents, were in seclusion.

She pointed to the headline. "So tell me, what happened since we talked last." She spread jam on a piece of toast.

Ellen's eyes moistened; she pulled a tissue from her sleeve and began to finger the neckline of her duster. "Oh, Sarah, I just don't know how she could drown her own children." Ellen wiped her eyes with the tissue.

"Please, Mother tell me what you know."

"I don't know much more than I've already told you. Just that JoBeth drove out to the lake near Star's Crossing and let the car roll down the boat ramp with Daniel and Casey still strapped in their car seats. She must have stood and watched those two little children drown."

Images of the children gasping for air invaded Sarah's thoughts. Her hands trembled. She held her coffee cup against her cheek, soaking in its warmth. "Has she said anything about why she did it?"

"Everyone says she must have been bitter when Phillip left and asked for a divorce."

"Bitter enough to kill her children?"

Ellen shook her head, then stood and stared out the kitchen window, clutching the duster tightly about her waist as if she needed to hold herself together. "How can anyone explain a thing like that?"

"What has Phillip got to say?"

"That he hopes JoBeth will go to prison and never get out."

"Wonderful."

"What can you expect, Sarah? His children." Ellen's voice trailed off. She left the breakfast room and returned with a newspaper from several days past. She smoothed the wrinkles and handed it to her daughter. "Here, you can read what he said."

"Who did they get for an attorney?" Sarah folded the paper and laid it beside her cup.

"Williams, Williams, and Standcroft. They're here in town."

"Is that the same Standcroft as the spokesperson for the family?"

"Yes. I think Margaret is JoBeth's mother's cousin on her father's side or something like that. Anyway, Margaret and Vera are related, and

Margaret is married to the partner."

"Sounds about right," Sarah said, rolling her eyes. "Everyone is related to everyone else around here. Is the law firm any good?"

"Your father says it doesn't matter. He thinks JoBeth will be put to death for what she did. According to him, the sooner the better so the town can get back to business. As far as he's concerned, the whole matter is taking up too much of everyone's time and energy." Ellen cleared the table. The dishes clattered as she rinsed and put them in the dishwasher.

"Hope Dad's wrong," Sarah mumbled. She raised her voice so her mother could hear her above the running water. "I'm going up to dress."

Sarah sat on her bed and turned to the article featuring the interview with Phillip. In the accompanying picture, he wore a white shirt and tie and looked pretty much as she remembered, neat and clean-cut but with thinning hair. The newspaper reported that he was the assistant manager at Selkirk's Shoe Store, and engaged to marry Miss Jaynelle Hollenbeck. In the picture, Miss Hollenbeck stood at his side, holding his arm in her two hands and looking at him as though she was trying to memorize his face. Sarah couldn't find much sympathy for him, not with Miss Hollenbeck hanging onto him like a leech. She turned her attention to the article.

"When I believed the children were taken away by someone, I supported JoBeth a hundred percent," Phillip had told the reporter. "Not anymore. I hope she goes to hell."

When the reporter asked him why his former wife murdered their children, Phillip said, "I told my wife when I left that I was doing it for her. Things weren't going so good between us and, in my mind, neither of us was happy. I guess she went off when I left. Just took them away for spite. She figured if she couldn't have me, I couldn't have them."

Yeah right, Sarah thought. Left your wife and two little children for their own good. You wimp! Hang your wife out to dry so you won't feel guilty. That way, you can live happily ever after with that Jaynelle Hollenbeck.

Sarah put the paper aside and thought back to when Phillip deserted his wife and family. JoBeth had telephoned to tell her that he wanted a divorce.

"How awful," Sarah said. She had found it difficult to give JoBeth her full attention during that call. The winter term had started and she was trying to get on top of her new study schedule. As JoBeth spoke, Sarah tore off a piece of her note pad and marked her place in the book she had been reading.

"At least he waited until after Christmas to leave," JoBeth choked. "He did that much for the kids. You have to give him that."

"Good of him." Sarah grunted. She leafed through pages of another book looking for a citation. Her finger slid down the index. Ethical implications in durable contracts. Page 242. She turned down the corner of the page. "What are you going to do now?" she asked.

"I'm going to begin all over." JoBeth sniffled. "My step-daddy's been a real comfort to me, Sarah. He comes over so I'm not so lonely. He likes helping out with the kids. You'd think they was his."

"That's nice."

"I'm going to get a job. I talked to your daddy about it, and he said he'd hire me." JoBeth's voice brightened. "He said I needed something to improve myself. What do you think, Sarah?"

"Sounds like you're on the right track. Call me anytime if you need to talk."

Great, another woman to manage. Just what Dad needs. Anxious to return to her studies, Sarah excused herself, hung up, and cleared her mind of her friend's marital problems.

After she finished her coffee, Sarah dialed the Maitlins' again. As she waited, she watched the Ruby-throated humming birds fight over the sugared syrup in the feeder hanging outside the window. Surprised at their unexpected savagery, she wondered if any creature, pushed far enough, could become vicious. Was there something JoBeth wanted so much that she could kill her babies for it?

The recording machine invited her to leave a message but cut her off before she finished giving her phone number. She turned and bumped into her mother who was standing behind her. Ellen's shortness surprised her. Sarah didn't remember being that much taller. Had her mother shrunk during the past year, or was it a memory thing?

"No luck?" Ellen asked.

"No luck."

Ellen picked up the watering can and tended to the coleus in the greenhouse window over the sink. "From what I hear, Margaret never returns calls." She wiped up the excess water and squeezed the sponge into the sink.

"I'll keep calling. Anyway, sooner or later JoBeth will be allowed visitors at the jail."

"Did you come home just to see JoBeth?" Ellen looked at her daughter expectantly.

"I really can't tell you why, but I had a strong urge to come home," Sarah answered. "I guess I wanted to find out if there is an explanation for what JoBeth did." Lying to her mother made her guilt weigh heavier.

"You were never one to make such a big decision so suddenly."

Sarah knew that her mother wanted to say that she had never known her daughter to make such a dramatic shift in her plans without her father's approval, especially one that was contrary to his wishes. Sarah watched her mother empty the watering can and place it under the sink. The water pushed its way through the grouchy drain.

"I keep telling your dad we need to get these pipes fixed. Patience, he tells me. One thing at a time."

"I know I have to come up with some plan that'll satisfy him and that I better have it ready tonight."

"I think having you home for the summer may be enough for him. We miss having you around."

"You don't really believe that's enough to satisfy him, do you? And he won't sit still for some idealistic talk about helping out an old friend. Be real, Mother."

"Well, whatever you decide, make it sound like something important. You know how he is."

"I've been toying with the idea of asking the defense team for a job," Sarah confided. "It's been in the back of my mind ever since I decided to come home, but I'm not sure they'll take me on."

"I think that's a great idea, Sarah." Ellen clapped her hands. "You can tell those lawyers that you had a position in Evanston this summer but, instead of taking it, you came home to see if you could help your friend."

"It might work. But criminal law isn't my main interest and I'm still a student. This is a big case, maybe too big for them to take me on."

"What if you offer to help around the office? Tell them you don't expect a salary. Who can refuse free help these days?"

"You have a wonderfully devious mind. It might be a long shot, but it's worth trying." She touched her mother's arm. Ellen gave her daughter a shy smile.

For the second time that morning, Sarah opened the telephone book; this time she dialed the Williams' law firm. When the receptionist answered, she tried her best to sound professional but spoke faster than she intended.

"Could you hold, Hon?" The receptionist didn't wait for an answer.

It wasn't long before a man's voice blasted in her ear. "Ms. Wasser?"

"Yes, this is Sarah Wasser."

"This is John Williams, John, the Second. Everyone around here calls me John-Two."

He paused. Living up north, she had become unaccustomed to the little silences that punctuated southerners' speech. The delay made her jump in to keep the conversation going. She filled the silence with, "How are you?"

"To tell you the truth, young lady, I might be better now that you called. We're kind of busy around here, what with two murders and all. Janet said you're interested in working with us and we can use some help, that is, if the little lady don't mind working hard and late."

"Can't be worse than my schedule at law school."

He got right to the point. "We have time around four this afternoon. If things work out, maybe we can give you a job. When you come in, ask for John-Two. John-One's dead."

Sarah's heart flipped. "Four it is," she said sedately.

She did a little whirl-around and hung up. Her mother was in the living room watching a morning talk show from New York City. She turned the sound down when Sarah entered.

"Thanks for the push, Mom. I have an interview at four."

"Oh good," Ellen smiled broadly. "I knew they couldn't turn down free help. Four you say? How about doing something with me until then?"

"What's that?"

"Mrs. Weeber is giving a luncheon today. When she heard you were coming home for the summer, she invited you to come along."

"Oh, Mom."

"You don't have anything to do until four. Why not go with me? We haven't done anything together for a long time."

A luncheon at Mrs. Weeber's house sounded deadly. But, she had no excuse. She owed her mother this one. "Just this once," she conceded. "I'll do this just for you. You know how I hate those things."

Mrs. Weeber escorted Sarah and her mother into a living room crowded with women wearing an assortment of floral dresses, looking like a summer garden set in a forest of burgundy and green furniture. The blinds, drawn against the sun, kept the darkened interior cool. A vase of artificial roses and pictures of children and grandchildren rested on the fringed shawl covering the piano. Stairs, leading to the second floor, were stacked along one side of the room. The women's faces turned expectantly when Mrs. Weeber and her guests entered the room.

"Why, Sarah, so nice to see you home after so long." The woman speaking, Mrs. Ellston, had been her eleventh grade history teacher. Older and heavier, she wore the same black smock over her dress as she did when Sarah was in high school. Her ankles swelled generously over the tops of her sensible shoes, and she sat back, fanning herself with a copy of *Southern Living.* "You home for good now? Your momma must be sick with worry what with you living up north among Yankees all this time."

A woman, someone Sarah didn't recognize, moved over on the sofa and patted the cushion next to her, motioning for Sarah to come and sit. Before Sarah could answer Mrs. Ellston, Virginia Kellings broke in.

"That new siding Charles put on your house looks good, Ceily. I never did see a man work that hard. My husband says he would've hired some of those coloreds over on Millside to do a job as big as that."

Mrs. Weeber interrupted with an invitation to eat. A buffet was set on a table over which a wooden plaque read, *"A woman who fears the Lord, she shall be praised."* The "L" in the word Lord was scripted so that it looked as though it was wearing a crown of thorns. By the time Sarah helped herself to the Jell-O salad and finger sandwiches and returned to the living room, the women were discussing JoBeth and the murders.

"My Justin says she must be crazy," Elmira said. She looked around to see if the other women agreed. Seeing no objection, she continued. "I reckon anybody'd have to be crazy to kill her own children."

"Law, I'd say so," Mrs. Weeber said. "No mother can bear the thought of her children being hurt, let alone do the harm herself." She passed a dish of pecans to Ellen. "Mr. Weeber bought these up from Macon when he was there last week. Says nobody in the South grows pecans like the folks over there."

"Well, I hope those lawyers of hers don't say she's crazy," Ceily said. "If they do, they'll send her off to one of those mental hospitals downstate and she'll never be punished for what she did to those young'uns."

"Right," Betty said. "She needs to be punished, not sent to some mental health resort until everyone around here gets to forgetting what she did."

Mrs. Weeber asked for everyone's attention, and introduced the young woman standing beside a card table filled with plastic handbags. "Y'all know my daughter Kaylan. She's here today to provide some afternoon entertainment. And those two sweet little things are my grandchildren." Mrs. Weeber said the word things as though she had plucked the strings on a banjo, and pointed to the two little girls perched on the stairs, their faces pressed tightly between the wooden rails, their blond, frizzy hair puffed out like freshly spun cotton candy.

"I'm here today for your pleasure," Kaylan began. She completed the sentence as though it was a question, lifting the word pleasure up, and spreading its syllables slowly over the group. She pulled her knit shirt down, covering the slight bulges above the waist band on her jeans.

The women settled agreeably in their seats, adjusted their hair, stretched their dresses over their knees, smiled, and murmured a return greeting. Oh God, thought Sarah. I'm stuck. Mrs. Weeber collected the dirty dishes and hurried them into the kitchen.

"I represent *Company 47,*" Kaylan began. "Like that verse in Psalms that says by organizing your lives, y'all can best serve your Lord and your husbands. It gives me the distinct pleasure to bring organization into the lives of Christian women by introducing my company's product." She held up one of the handbags and gave the group a toothy smile.

The women nodded. Sarah looked at the clock. Almost two hours before her appointment with Williams. She could be doomed to afternoons like this if she didn't get the job. That would be worse than working as her father's flunky every day.

Promptly at three, Sarah thanked her hostess and, carefully avoiding the order blanks piled discreetly on the table beside the sofa, left. She walked slowly, giving herself time to think. If the women's opinions were a measure to the town's attitude toward JoBeth, the legal system could just as well go straight to the sentencing phase. She was already convicted. Assembling an unbiased jury would be nearly impossible. She cleared her mind and hastened her step.

Chapter Four

*Al*though Sarah arrived early, the receptionist immediately escorted her into John-Two's office. Two men were present. An older, robust man, obviously the senior partner, sat behind the desk. A younger man sat rigidly upright in a chair across from him.

"John-Two," the man behind the desk said as he stood and held out his hand. "John-One is dead."

He wasn't the unkempt, tobacco-chewing, balding man with a sizable paunch Sarah had expected. Except for reading glasses and graying hair, he could have passed as much younger. If the senior partner wasn't the person she imagined, his office was more like one she would have anticipated in a small town like Eight Mile Junction. The room was crowded with over-sized oak furniture and piles of folders covered every flat surface. There were no personal pictures, no trophies, no photographs, no memorabilia, not even a brass spittoon. Either John-Two was a no-nonsense kind of guy or the firm was on the verge of bankruptcy and he was getting ready to move out. Sarah had her preferences.

He came out from behind the desk and removed some folders from a chair and, with a courtly gesture, invited her to sit. "This here's Albert Westfall." He pointed to the younger man sitting in the chair next to hers. "He's up from Columbia helping with the trial."

Westfall nodded, hardly glancing at Sarah before leaning over and closely examining the papers on his lap, impatiently brushing back the shock of black hair that fell across his brow. His feet were tucked under his chair and he was bent forward, as though he might spring forward at any moment. Lean and tightly stretched, he looked too young to be taking on a case as high profile as this. Good looking, in a rugged sort of way. With his spare frame, black hair and off-putting demeanor, he brought Bronte's Heathcliff to mind.

"Now young lady, tell us something about your lawyering experience," John-Two began. He leaned back and crossed his arms over his chest. His up-and-down gaze made her uncomfortable. She steadied and reassured herself his demeanor was one of style rather than outright chauvinism, a combination of traditional southern gentleman and cunning mischief.

"I completed my second year at Northwestern this spring." She check to make sure all the buttons on her blouse were closed. "My program combines a law degree with a master's in business administration. Last summer I interned for a law firm that specializes in poverty law and have worked with the Cook County Housing Agency and the county council on rent control issues."

John-Two continued looking at her from above the reading glasses perched on the end of his nose. He rubbed his chin reflectively. She wasn't sure if he was thinking or inspecting it to see if he needed a shave. The smile he wore when he greeted her hadn't faded.

"I gave up an internship with a patent law firm to come back to Eight Mile Junction this summer," she lied. It sounded good, and she was certain that they wouldn't be able to discover the truth about Molitor. Even so, her stomach churned. "You see, I'm interested in the Ruland case because JoBeth and I were good friends in high school."

Al interrupted. "Patent law?" He wasn't rude, but close. A sharp lump appeared on his jaw, as if he was clenching his teeth. He had permanent frown lines, but there was something charming about his perfectly shaped black eyebrows and the way he kept pushing his hair off his forehead. His fingers, thin and long like a piano player's, fiddled with a Conway Stewart. She recognized the pen because her father had one just like it. Tastefully expensive. If someone had asked, she would have described him as good looking but very intense. Perhaps not as savage as Heathcliff, but a complex man. She pushed her glasses higher so he wouldn't notice the bushy eyebrows she refused to pluck. She spoke to him directly.

"I plan to write and defend patents for pharmaceutical firms after I pass the bar. I have an undergraduate and master's degree in the biological sciences."

"Then why do you think you can help us?" Al asked. "This is a murder trial."

It wasn't the question. It was his attitude that ruffled her. Clearly, if he had his way, the job wouldn't be hers. She felt opportunity slipping away. Perspiration moistened her forehead. Did he notice? She wildly searched for words that might, if not impress him, at least win him over.

"I'm—an experienced—legal researcher," she stammered. She slid her hand under her purse, clenched her fist, and took hold of herself. "Last summer I searched for precedents to support cases involving discrimination in housing, worked with clients on filing complaints, and appeared before the arbitration unit on their behalf. I can get a recommendation from that firm if you'd like. I have completed classes in criminal law, and I'm at the top of my class. I believe you'll find that I learn quickly and can carry out assignments with minimal supervision. I can assist by doing interviews, and I'd be willing to be a go-fer during the trail." Breathless, she paused.

"Does that mean you'll go-fer coffee?" John-Two asked. He raised his eyebrows quizzically.

Sarah laughed, certain that he wasn't serious. The tension had eased, but Al didn't relax. Was he having a bad day or was there something about her that he instantly disliked?

John-Two sat upright in his chair, his body language indicating that he had made a decision. "This is how it is, young lady. The defendant's bound for the death penalty if folks around this county have their say. I can assure you there's not a sympathetic person between Atlanta and Richmond. I do taxes and business law; Standcroft, the other partner in the firm, does estates and family stuff. That's all we have in this town, taxes, partnerships, wills, estate settlements, and divorces. Murders are rare and, if one does occur, it isn't something we take on. This case is an exception because the Maitlins believe they have a connection with the firm and can rely on us to put together the best defense."

"However, Standcroft has excused himself because his wife's related to JoBeth, and I have my own workload. Westfall's criminal law background and his courtroom experience are why we brought him up from Columbia. He was raised over in Perkins County so he knows his way around these parts. But this is a big case and we need help with the day-to-day details. That's why we'd like to bring someone else in, someone who can pick up some of the detail work. You called at just the right time, right Al? "

Al's head was down and he was stuffing papers into a folder, indicating that he was finished with the meeting. He didn't answer. Maybe something between him and John-Two. If there was, Al was making her feel responsible. She'd have to live with that. Anyway, even with John-Two's little lady stuff and Al's hostility, it was better than going to work with her father every day or accompanying her mother to luncheons. She smiled at Westfall, showing him she had no hard feelings. He acknowledged her smile with a nod. Sarah sensed victory.

"When do I start?" she asked, deciding to take the initiative. If Al didn't want her to have the job, she'd force him to come right out and say so.

"How much you want?" John-Two stood up.

Taken by surprise, she couldn't come up with a number. She had concentrated on getting hired, not on bargaining for a paycheck.

John-Two took advantage of her hesitation. "Okay, young lady, I'll tell you what. How's four-fifty an hour? That's what we pay for unskilled labor in these parts." He thumped his hand on the desk, signifying that the deal was closed.

She wasn't exactly unskilled labor, but she had a job for the summer, not an internship, a real job, and the first law-related one for which she was being paid. Her father might approve of that. She'd sell it to him as a big deal.

"And no overtime pay." John-Two looked at her sternly, making sure she understood. Emboldened, she asked him when she would have a chance to see JoBeth.

"You'll see plenty of her during the trial," John-Two answered.

"I'd like to see her soon. I want to talk to her alone, if that's possible."

"Let's see how it goes. Westfall's in charge of that." He nodded toward Al as he spoke.

Sarah glanced at Al, but he was ignoring her question. It was clear that her eagerness to see her friend wasn't something he was going to consider right then. She decided not to push it. She'd to wait for the right time to take on that battle.

John-Two called Janet over the intercom. She walked into the room, smiled at Sarah, and handed John-Two some papers which he quickly signed. His signature looked like a long line with the Roman numeral two at the end.

"Fax them right away. And Janet," he added, "fix up a corner of the library as an office for the young lady. Get her a desk lamp. You know, everything she needs to work in there. And oh yes, I don't think she knows how to make coffee." He winked at Sarah.

Despite the young lady stuff, she was going to like this guy. He was a tease, but not mean-spirited. Al was going to be her problem. She followed Janet into the reception area. After she completed the employment papers, she asked, "What time does John-Two want me in tomorrow?"

"After ten. One or the other will have time to sit down with you."

Sarah noticed a picture of a young woman about her own age on Janet's desk. It was signed, "Love, Laura." She wanted to ask if she was Janet's daughter, but the receptionist's quick movements gave notice that she didn't have time to waste.

"And Sarah, don't mind John-Two," Janet said. "He has a good heart, but sometimes he thinks he's funny when he's really annoying. The more he gets under your skin, the more he'll tease you." She turned to her computer. "See you tomorrow."

When Sarah arrived home, her mother was in the kitchen defrosting a chicken. "Thank goodness you're home. I stayed a little too long at Mrs. Weeber's. Here," she directed Sarah with her head, "grab this other leg so I can get some hot water down into the cavity. Your dad will be home soon and he'll want his dinner on time."

Sarah pulled on a pair of vinyl gloves, took hold of one leg and pulled. The chicken was still frozen so some of the skin on the thigh tore. "Careful Sarah, you know how your Dad insists on a crispy skin. How did your meeting with Williams go?"

"I got the job. I start tomorrow."

"That's such good news. Your father will be happy." To show her approval, she bumped Sarah's hip with hers.

"Damn, this bird is hard as a rock. Don't you have anything in the refrigerator that's already thawed?"

The smell of raw chicken assaulted Sarah's nose and nasty, yellowish foam stuck to the sides of the sink. Raw chicken always made her queasy.

"I promised your dad chicken tonight so he'll be expecting chicken. You know how he is. Everything is planned and everything as planned." She dried her hands on her apron and kissed her daughter's cheek.

"Do you want me to run to Bi-Lo's and get one of those already-roasted ones?"

"He'd never hold still for one of those. You know better than that. Here, hold the chicken under water while I warm up the oven."

"Mom, let Dad think I had this job planned before I came home for the summer."

"Of course, dear. What he doesn't know won't hurt him. Now go set the table. I'll get this chicken cut apart and cooked up in no time."

My mother isn't so clueless after all, Sarah thought as she set the table. She saved my bacon and the chicken dinner all in one day, and she did it without chipping her fingernail polish. This summer might turn out all right after all.

By the time her father's car entered the driveway, dinner was ready and a bottle of white wine, chilled and uncorked, was resting on ice in the silver wine bucket. Her mother had taken off her apron, combed her hair, and renewed her lipstick. She looked fresh, not at all like someone who had been wrestling with a frozen chicken not much more than an hour ago. Sarah could smell the sweetness of her perfume. Shalimar.

They met Sam at the back door. He thrust himself into the room as though he was being chased by a raging bull, gave Ellen a brief kiss, barely grazing her with his lips, and handed her his briefcase. He gave Sarah a hug. "How are my two girls tonight?" he asked, leading the way toward the dining room. The two women followed.

Sarah was relieved that her father hadn't said something wilting about her coming home against his wishes. She had expected him to pummel her with his criticisms or at least punish her with silence. Instead, he was behaving as if nothing had changed. He was still in charge and she was still one of his troops awaiting inspection.

The dining room table was covered with a white damask cloth and set with Ellen's best china and silver. Candles and soft light from the overhead chandelier added a certain elegance to the room, quite different than the school cafeteria at Northwestern. When she was at school, Sarah didn't miss her mother's devotion to tradition, but tonight, she was happy to be home, to feel the warmth of the room, and see her mother's pleasure of having the family together again.

"How does it feel to be home?" Sam asked Sarah. Not waiting for an answer, he turned to Ellen. "What's for dinner?" He unfolded his napkin.

Although anxious to tell her father the news about the job, her father controlled the conversation at the dinner table just as a conductor directs an orchestra. As usual, she was the bassoonist, patiently waiting for her rare turn to play. She waited. Ellen asked her husband to fill the wine glasses; he poured into his wife's glass first.

"Just half," Ellen cautioned.

Ellen brought out the soup tureen and ladled cream of tomato into each bowl. Sarah sipped her wine. Her father tasted the soup and nodded his approval before he began to speak.

"Coach Acheson sent a picture of this year's Little League team to the office today. The kids look great in their new shirts. I'm having it framed down at Kwan's and adding it to the others on the office wall."

"Your dad's company bought the Cardinals their baseball shirts and equipment again this spring," Ellen explained. "As an added treat for the kids, he gave each boy an athletic bag with the team's name printed on it, didn't you, dear?"

"That's my Dad. A one-man Chamber of Commerce." She raised her glass to her father, and finished off the last bit. Her father refilled it.

It wasn't until dessert was served that he turned his attention to his daughter. By then, Sarah had had too much wine and, rather than talk to her father, wanted to go upstairs and lie down.

"So, how did your day go, Sarah?"

He took off his glasses, polished them with his napkin, and laid them on the table next to his plate. Without them, his eyes looked different. They were smaller than she remembered, and there were slight indentations on each of his temples where the stems hugged his face. He rubbed his forehead as though he was tired. She rubbed her eyes so she could focus.

"Did you get out of the house at all?" he asked when she didn't answer.

She fumbled her fork and it fell to the floor. As she bent to retrieve it, her mother came to her rescue.

"Sarah went with me to Mrs. Weeber's luncheon. I bought a cosmetic bag as a Hanukah gift for your sister, Bekkah."

"And how did you like the luncheon, Sarah?" Sarcasm was embedded in his voice. It was all right for his wife to lunch with a bunch of ladies, but not an approved pastime for his daughter. Sarah tried to concentrate, but the flickering candle kept drawing her attention.

"It was …" she faltered.

She wanted to say it was boring, but she didn't want to hurt her mother's feelings. An acidic taste lodged in her throat. Her stomach churned; she put the napkin to her lips, and gagged. Her mother gave a soft, sympathetic sound, and then spoke brightly.

"Sarah has some big news for you, Sam. Tell him, dear."

"I got a job today." Damn. That wasn't how she wanted to tell him. She wanted to make it sound planned and important. Instead, she blurted it out like a school kid.

"Job? Who hired you?"

He sipped his wine, not taking his eyes from her face. The damn candle flame kept leaping around in front of her eyes. She squinted and forced herself to concentrate.

"I was hired as a legal assistant by JoBeth's defense team." She made up the title, hoping it impressed her father.

"Williams hired you? He must really be desperate."

Ellen's breath caught, but she said nothing. A thread of rebellion stitched itself to the edge of Sarah's tongue, but she was unable to gather it into a flip response. A fever rose to her cheeks and a faint ache pulsed behind her eyes.

"Yes, Mr. Williams said the firm was swamped." Another dumb thing to say. It sounded as though Williams was so desperate he was ready to hire any bum off the street.

"I heard he brought in a hot-shot lawyer from the capital."

"Al Westfall. He's from around Columbia and evidently has made quite a name for himself. John-Two said he's an expert in criminal law."

"He'd better be. Is Williams paying you?"

"Yes."

"How much?"

"Four-fifty an hour," Sarah whispered.

"Minimum wage. Figures." He finished his wine, picked up his glasses and pushed his chair back. "Well, I brought work from the office. I'd better get started." He left the table and walked toward the den.

"Oh, Sarah. I'm so sorry," Ellen whispered. She put her arm around her daughter's shoulders and gave her a squeeze. "He's like that. We've been married over thirty years and he still gets to me sometimes. He doesn't mean anything by it."

Sarah pulled away. She wanted to escape, wanted to be alone in her darkened room. Most of all, she wanted to go to sleep and forget the entire evening.

"It's okay," she assured her mother as she headed for the stairs. "I just need to lie down."

"He's really proud of you, dear. He'll come around."

Sarah clutched the stair rail. She felt as though she'd been in one of those karate movies and just had the crap kicked out of her. And by her father. The one who had always been her mentor. She threw herself on the bed, holding back her tears and gritting her teeth. She'd make her father proud of her. She had a whole summer to work on it. And that Westfall. She'd show him what she was made of. Unbidden tears slid down her cheek. Damn that Molitor. This could have been such an easy summer.

Chapter Five

*S*arah woke with a headache. It wasn't one of those sick-to-your-stomach headaches that makes you want to stay in bed all day. It was just a dull throb accompanied by a dry mouth, the kind a shower and a glass of orange juice fixes. Not bad considering the foul ending to last night's dinner. She had been foolish to drink too much wine. But her father's behavior was worse; he'd been a prick. A few minutes more in bed and she'd go for the cure. She stretched, wondering how her mother put up with her father for so many years.

The Solonskys, her mother's family, were New Yorkers: Upper East Side. Her father was a diamond merchant, well connected in the business world and respected in the Jewish community. Ellen, the youngest of four children, was his only daughter. Her father spoiled her, but Sarah's mother absorbed the Solonsky's lavish lifestyle the way a sponge soaks up water, keeping its shape no matter how full, no matter how hard it's squeezed. Sarah's grandfather treasured his only daughter as he treasured his rare gems.

When Sarah's father met the Solonskys, there must have been a clash of wills. Sam wasn't from New York, and he didn't come from a privileged family. His self-assurance and determination would have irritated the old man who would have preferred a son-in-law willing to take his place at the bottom of the family business and work up in the ranks of management alongside his brothers-in-law.

Anyone who met Sam Wasser could tell right off that he wasn't that kind of man. He wasn't put off by the old man's lack of enthusiasm, and he didn't waste much time trying to win him over. He managed the situation by playing to Ellen's mother, complimenting her on her home and cooking, noticing when she had her hair done, admiring a new dress or shoes. Ellen may have chosen Sam as a husband to escape her father's over-protectiveness, but she had gone from being dominated by a benevolent dictator to one not quite so considerate. Sam was generous with his wife. Sarah gave him that. But as far as she was concerned, her mother had been bought and installed somewhere between the refrigerator in the kitchen and the Mercedes in the driveway.

Downstairs, a note on the refrigerator reminded Sarah that this was her mother's day to volunteer at the hospital. Sarah gathered up the newspaper, but the telephone rang before she had a chance to look for news about the trial.

"Is Sarah there?"

She recognized Janet's voice. "Yes, this is Sarah."

"The boys won't be in this morning, but John-Two wants you to come in anyway. He has some background material for you to read."

"Is ten still okay?"

"Sure. I'm always here."

When Sarah entered the office, Janet picked up a pencil and pointed toward the library. "The stuff's on your desk. If you want, you can take everything home to read." The telephone rang.

"What time will they be back?"

Janet covered the mouthpiece with her hand. "John-Two wants you back tomorrow at ten. "No," she spoke into the phone. "Can I take a message?"

Sarah hid her disappointment. She had hoped that John-Two would begin by filling her in on the case, telling her something about the strategy for the defense, and showing how she fit into the workload. Instead, he assigned her to a bunch of newspaper clippings. Important as the reading probably was, she could have done that at night. Her father would have something belittling to say if she told him she had spent the entire day reading newspaper clippings. Oh God, that could lead to another one of those dinners.

The library was a windowless room and dark except where the lamp cast light on the folders Janet had placed on the desk. The size of the pile hardly corresponded to the magnitude of the case. It wouldn't take long to go through the stack. In law school she'd learned to read fast, memorize details, focus on the obscure. Law books were full of cases won on small points remembered, or lost because of those forgotten. She settled into the task easily, and was soon engrossed.

The first clipping contained JoBeth's report that she had left the sleeping children in the car while she went into the Bi-Lo to pick up milk and a few groceries. The reporter observed that, when he arrived on the scene, she seemed confused and told the police that she only remembered coming out of the market to find the children gone.

The police notified the Maitlins. They arrived accompanied by Phillip, JoBeth's estranged husband. The couple held and comforted each other in one picture. In another, JoBeth was surrounded by a phalanx of policemen, several of the Bi-Lo staff and a few bystanders holding onto their grocery carts faded into the darkness on the outer edges of the picture.

Subsequent articles detailed law enforcement's search for the children. At first, it had been assumed that it was a car theft, and that the perpetrator didn't realize that children were sleeping in the back seat. A nationwide alert had been immediately implemented, and the sheriff assured the public that every effort to recover the children was underway.

The next folder contained JoBeth's confession that she remembered taking the children to the boat ramp on Fenton Lake but had no memory of what happened there. Their bodies were subsequently found in the submerged car. The sheriff, Thorsten Grimes, made the announcement at a press conference held on the steps of the courthouse. A photo of the sheriff showed a trim man, about her father's age, wearing a western style hat with a deep crease in the crown. He was accompanied by several deputies and the mayor. JoBeth wasn't present.

"Information gained from repeated interrogation of Mrs. Phillip Ruland," the sheriff was quoted as saying, "led the police to the missing car and the bodies of Daniel Phillip and Casey Ann. The car was found resting at the bottom of Fenton Lake near Star's Crossing. After the discovery of the bodies, Mrs. Ruland was formally charged with the murder of her two children. No further details will be forthcoming from this office at this time as the investigation is still in progress." No questions were taken from the reporters.

A discreet cough drew Sarah's attention. An older man stood in the library doorway; his vest buttons and gold watch chain straining across an ample midsection. One hand rested on the door jamb, and Sarah could see the diamonds in his Masonic ring glittering against the black onyx stone like tiny stars in outer space. A generous graying mustache hugged his upper lip. The banner of *Time Magazine* peeked from his jacket pocket.

"So, you're the firm's latest asset?" He grinned widely. "I'm Clayton Standcroft, the other partner."

"Sarah," she said as she walked toward him with her hand extended. "Pleased to meet you. John-Two told me the firm had another partner. You're not working on the murder trial, right?"

Clayton took her hand and warmly, covering it with both of his. "Right. Wills and divorces—that's what I do. Pays well and the pain of the contest passes quickly. The dead are buried and the divorced don't waste any time finding new lovers. Besides," he continued, "I'm JoBeth's relative. What if the defense loses? I may not be invited to any more family reunions. Now wouldn't that be a shame?"

He gave a funny little laugh, like he was sucking in gasps of air, and motioned toward two leather club chairs on the opposite side of the room. "So what are you up to?" he asked, turning on the reading lamp between the chairs. Sarah settled in one of them.

"I'm not quite sure. John-Two gave me some clippings to read. Wants me to familiarize myself with the case." Sarah waved her hand toward the folders on her desk.

"Had a chance to form an opinion?"

Sarah tilted the lamp shade that obstructed her view of Clayton, leaned forward, and eagerly responded to the question. "Nothing much. I'm impressed with the way the sheriff is handling the case. It seems he's trying to keep tight control of the details. Given the negative attitude toward JoBeth around here and the potential for a media frenzy, it's probably the best thing to do."

"You know JoBeth?"

"We were classmates, best friends until Phillip came into her life. She was the first person I met when I moved to Eight Mile Junction."

"That's JoBeth. My wife says she's the kind of person who is always casting about for a new fish to hook."

"I know what you mean. I never knew her to be anything other than a genuinely kind person, so I can't understand what happened to her. Do you have a clue?"

"I'm afraid that's something you'll to have to find out. And when you do, you can tell me." He smiled and rose to go. "Come talk to me anytime. I'll always be in for you. And Sarah, be kind to John-Two. He's a gas-bag, but he's all right."

Sarah smiled as she returned to her desk. So far, she'd lied to her parents and wilted under her father's criticism. At work, things were not much better. She was held at arm's length by Janet's strictly business façade, put down by John-Two's chauvinism, targeted by Al's intemperate disposition, and sent to the library to read newspaper clippings. Not much ego-building going on. Then, good old Clayton walks in and puts it all together by asking her opinion and offering his friendship. She opened the next folder.

A photo in one clipping showed JoBeth at her first court appearance. Dressed in the baggy jail coveralls, she was dwarfed between two beefy guards that looked as though they had been sent to the courtroom by central casting. JoBeth's hands were bound and her hair was pulled back in a ponytail. No more sculptured curls and ringlets; no longer an innocent cherub in a painting of mother and child. The fullness of the tragedy was etched on her face, and she looked older than her twenty-five years. The outcome of the trial notwithstanding, JoBeth's life as it once was, was now over.

At the hearing, bail had been denied and JoBeth remanded to jail until the outcome of the trial. The case dawdled in the nether-land between judge-attorney conferences and pre-trial motions. The remaining clippings reiterated the false lead that JoBeth had given the police and the grisly details surrounding the discovery of the children' bodies, reprinting the most prurient facts of the case. Her assignment completed, Sarah walked back to the reception area.

"How did it go?" Janet asked without looking up.

"I finished reading the clippings. Want them back?"

"No, keep them. They're your copies."

Janet stopped typing, smiled patiently, and waited for Sarah to speak or leave. Her fingers remained on the keyboard.

Gesturing toward John-Two's closed office door, Sarah asked, "Will they be in the office later?"

"No, they'll be off the course around one, then lunch."

"Off the course? As in golf course?"

"Dunning asked John-Two and Al to meet him for golf this morning. He's prosecuting the case and he had some procedural details he wanted to discuss."

"Golf with the DA's office? What is this, a good old boys get together?"

"I guess you could call it that," Janet laughed. "But that's the way things are done around here."

"Really?"

Janet turned toward Sarah. "The two families go way back. Dunning's grandfather and John-Two's father started this law practice. The elder Dunning retired, his son never took up the law, and his grandson, Ian, pursued criminal law and ran for public office. Technically, John-Two and Dunning are on opposite sides, but outside the courtroom they're friends."

Was this how JoBeth's future was to be decided, on the golf course? Was her fate to be determined as casually as friends planning charity benefits over lunch? Sarah's resentment pasted a wry smile on her lips, but stopped there. She couldn't make a scene her first day. Maybe it was fate that brought her home to be part of the defense team, perhaps to be the only one curious enough to try to understand JoBeth's side of the story. She made one more effort to hang around.

"Is there anything else I can do?" she asked Janet.

"Yes, you can take care of this court order. It has to be filed today and I don't know when the boys will be back. Clayton is gone and I need to cover the office."

Another menial task. Well, she had volunteered to be a go-fer, hadn't she? Sarah mustered up as cheerful a response as she could, took the package, and left.

Her mother was still at the hospital when she got home, but she could hear the housekeeper upstairs, vacuuming. She hadn't met Orda Mae, but her mother once told her that the housekeeper was obsessed when it came to cleaning and became surly if someone interfered. "On cleaning day," Ellen had told Sarah, "Orda Mae rules the house."

"Come on, Chewie. Let's go for a walk." The dog ran for her leash and stood waiting patiently while Sarah changed her shoes.

Main Street was only five blocks long, anchored on one end by the railroad station and on the other by the courthouse and jail. The Burger Spot, next to the railroad tracks, was the last business on the road that wound into the countryside, passing the entrance to Fenton Lake five miles away. Millside, the neighborhood for the former workers of the closed textile mill, lay at the opposite end, just beyond the courthouse and jail. More elegant homes nestled in the rolling hills to the east of the main drag.

On her way to the courthouse, Sarah passed Gladys's Beauty Shop where she and JoBeth had their hair done for their high school graduation. Sarah was giving the valedictorian address, and JoBeth was getting gussied up for the dance held in the school gym afterward. Sarah slowed and looked in the window. The interior was exactly as it had been that day. The hair dryers were hunched over the same chairs that sprouted spidery arms and legs. Dozens of hair-do magazines lay scattered about the tables, and the floor was littered with bunches of hair. The chairs where she and JoBeth had sat side-by-side were still in place, facing the mirrored walls stenciled with now fading lilies and ferns. Gladys, her henna-dyed hair tied up in a bright orange scarf, was still doing her best to create beauty.

Next door, Bernie Graves leaned against the barber pole outside his shop. He was wearing the same cowboy boots with exaggerated pointy toes that Sarah remembered, but now his hair was completely white. His face was lifted toward the sun; he seemed to be dozing. Sarah passed without disturbing him and continued on toward the courthouse.

An antique store, Another Life to Live, had opened between Third Street and Fourth Streets since Sarah was last home. In the window, a teddy bear dressed in a middy blouse and sailor's cap sat in a saddle mounted on a saw horse. A vintage baby carriage filled with artificial daisies was parked outside the shop; a welcome sign hung from its handle inviting customers to enter.

She tied Chewie to the carriage and stepped inside. The odor of undisturbed dust and mildew greeted her, and the shelves were cluttered with trinkets, most from the 1930s. She moved to the rear of the store where quilts, arranged on wooden racks, looked as though they had been laundered and left to dry. One caught her eye. It was a small piece with ABCs tumbling around a scalloped edge in colors surprisingly bright. Piles of blocks in pastel colors numbered one through ten formed a frame within which the quilter had neatly stitched the words, *Now I Lay Me Down to Sleep.*

The clerk, who had followed her, noticed Sarah's interest. She took the quilt off the rack and spread it over a chest of drawers, giving it a pat it as she would an old friend's shoulder. She searched Sarah's face for signs of appreciation. "We call this the children's quilt," the clerk told her. "It probably dates back to the Civil War." The clerk's anxious fingers fluttered over the piece.

"Some mother must have made it for her child's bed."

"No," the clerk corrected. "It was put together by a little girl. In those days, girls weren't excused from their household duties to go to school so quilting projects taught them to count, read, and recognize shapes and colors."

"How much is it?"

"$250."

"Do you take lay-away? I can give you $25 to hold it"

"You just give me that $25, and take it right home." She took the quilt off the rack and folded it.

"I couldn't do that," Sarah protested as she followed the clerk to the front of the shop. "You don't even know me."

"My Lord, deary, that's how we do things here in Eight Mile Junction. You go on now, take that quilt with you. It's been looking for a good home for a long time and it's about time it found one."

"How can I…?"

"Go on. Just come around with the money when you see fit." She slid the quilt into a used plastic bag and pressed it into Sarah's hands. "Keep it out of the sun," she advised. "And wash it by hand with mild soap."

"Will do." Sarah hung the plastic bag over her arm and headed for the door. She turned before she left and waved to the smiling clerk. Maybe the place didn't smell so bad after all.

Sarah and Chewie walked over to the courthouse. The square, two-story building was grandly fronted by a rounded portico supported by eight columns topped with Doric capitals. The walls returned the heat they had absorbed from the afternoon sun. The American and South Carolina flags hung limply from the poles placed at the foremost edge of the portico.

The quiet stateliness of the building reminded Sarah of law school, restoring her confidence in achieving justice for JoBeth. Maybe the golf course business was nothing to worry about. She hoped so, because once the trial started, Eight Mile Junction would be turned into a stage for a grand media event. The memory of JoBeth as a young girl and her love for her children would be pushed aside, leaving only the image of the monster who killed them.

After she filed the court order, Sarah walked the short distance between the courthouse and the county jail. Several wrappers from Burger Spot littered the empty parking lot, and a sign hanging on the back wall of the jail warned the public against parking in unoccupied spaces. The brick building was surrounded by an iron picket fence and a large pine tree shaded the colonnaded walkway to the front door.

Sarah stared at the building while Chewie investigated the empty food wrappers. JoBeth was somewhere inside that building. Because she was charged with an offense against children, she would be housed alone, a horrible situation for someone named Miss Social Secretary in the high school yearbook. The sun dropped behind the pine tree and a breeze cooled the perspiration on Sarah's arms. She checked her watch. It was after four. Last night she had left a mess for her mother. Perhaps she could make it up to her by being more helpful tonight.

On her way back, John-Two and Al were coming out of the Agusta Hotel, walking directly toward her. How embarrassing, having them see her idling around downtown with her dog. Not the image she wanted to project. She ducked into the pharmacy to wait until they were out of sight.

"Can I help you, miss?" The young man speaking had been a classmate in high school. "You're Sarah Wasser, right?"

He came out from around the counter. His white pharmacist coat hung open; a silver clip held a black tie to his shirt. His shoulders, bent forward from continually leaning over the counter toward his customers, made him look older. She could smell a mixture of lotions, creams, and powders as he bent to pet the dog.

"Is it okay for Chewie to be in here?" She picked up a bottle of shampoo and examined the label.

"I heard you came back to work for the Williams?"

"Ummm, yes. Just for the summer." Not two full days had passed since she had been offered the job and everyone in town knew she was back.

"Are you working in the pharmacy for the summer?" She asked to be polite, but she really didn't care. Even in high school she thought his heavy red-blonde eyebrows and lazy eye made him appear vague and slow. Time had not improved his appearance.

"No, Daddy owns this place. I'm here all the time."

"Yes, I remember now. How's your father, Jameson?"

"He's doing all right. I might go on to pharmacy school in the fall, but I haven't made up my mind. Daddy says it's cheaper to hire a pharmacist than to educate one. I guess he's knows best."

"I guess so," Sarah agreed, mentally sympathizing with him about the strong influence fathers have. "Here, I'll take this." She pushed the shampoo toward him.

"How'd you like to come over to Momma's for dinner one night?"

"Uhhh, thanks, but I can't say." She paused, scrambled for an excuse. "John-Two warned me that we'd be working late almost every night. I'll call you if I have some free time."

She purchased the shampoo and hurried out, but hadn't walked very far before she heard him calling her name. She turned to see him running toward her, waving the plastic bag containing the quilt.

"You left this." He was panting hard from the short run. His lazy eye slid involuntarily to the side while the other eye begged her to reconsider his invitation.

"Thank you." She smiled and walked away, fearful that a prolonged conversation might force her into a dinner a momma's house.

Her mother was preparing meatloaf when she got home. "I'd hug you, but my hands are a mess." In place of a hug, she leaned against her daughter, and raised her face for a kiss.

"Mmmm, meat loaf. My favorite." Sarah pinched a piece of raw round steak, shook some salt on it, popped it into her mouth and then snatched a piece for Chewie.

"It's your dad's favorite, too. My mother's recipe. He always made a fuss over it when he came to our house for dinner. He sure knew how to get on her good side." She gave a little laugh and ceased kneading the bread crumbs into the meat, a dreamy look overtaking her eyes.

"I was thinking about you and Dad this morning, about how you two met," Sarah said, rinsing her fingers.

"At Chicago. My father didn't want me to go to college that far away, but I insisted. I wanted to get out of New York. Fell for your father right away. He was quite the guy, big and handsome, full of himself, known as a catch among the Jewish girls on campus." She took two eggs and broke them into the mix. "Here, take these shells and put them in the container for your father's compost pile."

"Did you set your heart on him right from the beginning?"

Ellen smiled mischievously. "You bet. I was the envy of all the girls in my sorority. They were gaga over him. Made such a fuss when he came to call on me."

"Did that make you jealous?"

Her mother closed her eyes and smiled. "Your dad always made me feel as though I was the only one for him."

"Does he still make you feel that way?" Sarah had intended that as an idle question, but her mother's response was testy.

"Every marriage is a compromise." Her dreamy happiness disappeared. "Without that, relationships degenerate. Compromise keeps things right side up."

"Does Dad ever compromise?"

"Yes, he does," she said firmly, slapping the meatloaf into an oblong shape.

"But you're the one who compromises most of the time."

"Yes, dear. That's the way it is for women like me. Your dad was looking for someone who would support him no matter what. I bought into that and I've never regretted it."

She rinsed her hands, retrieved her engagement and wedding rings from the window sill, and slipped them onto her finger. She held her hand toward the light, turning the rings so that the diamonds sparkled.

"I always loved them," she said, her good mood returning. "Your dad wouldn't accept it at a discount from my father. He insisted on paying full price."

Sarah tried to understand the meaning that the rings held for her mother. Was it the beauty of the stones or was it that her father paid full price? In some ways, her mother and JoBeth shared the same priorities. Meeting her future husband and taking a back seat to his achievements shaped both their lives. Sarah shrugged. She'd never understand, but she knew she could never live the life her mother had settled for, not even for a big showy ring.

"Get ready for dinner. Your father will be home soon, and you know he wants to eat on time."

It wasn't until she got to the top of the stairs that Sarah realized she had forgotten to show her mother the quilt. She'd wait until later, sometime when her father wasn't around. He'd have something to say about buying it before she received her first paycheck. Might as well avoid that conversation.

She spread the quilt across her bed and thought about the little seamstress who made it. Did she see her life as making a series of compromises, or did she know right from the beginning that she was the one who had to give up her dreams and make do with scraps. Sarah's growing-up life had been very different. Her father had taught her to think of herself first and never settle for less than she wanted.

But the little quilter was sure of her place in life. She learned to create something meaningful out of the scraps given to her. Sarah's life had no such certainty. Hers was full of temporary way stations: a student, a soon-to-be-lawyer, an apartment that wasn't a home, and classmates, most of whom she'd never see after graduation. Everything permanent was put off until the future, and that future was full of unknown challenges.

She picked up the quilt and held it against her face inhaling its dry sweet smell. She folded and put it in her suitcase. The quilt now had another life to live, perhaps as a lodestar that would keep her on a more balanced course.

At dinner, everyone behaved as though nothing had happened the night before. As her father leaned forward to pour the wine. Sarah covered the top of her glass, grateful that he didn't comment.

"Mom made your favorite tonight. Meatloaf."

"Yes, but she'll never be able to make it the way her mother did," he said picking up his soup spoon.

Sarah stiffened. Her face flushed with anger, signaling an impulse to defend her mother. Ellen caught Sarah's eye, warning her that it wasn't worth an argument, silently begging her not to repeat the unhappy ending they had endured the night before. Sarah turned her attention to the soup.

Chapter Six

*A*neon coffee cup hung in the window of the Pinker Dot Restaurant, its phosphorescence cast a glossy stain on the steam-streaked glass. As Sarah entered, a waitress behind the counter motioned to an empty table near the window and called out, "Seat yourself."

The restaurant was crowded with men sitting in small groups, talking and smoking, looking as though they had nothing to do for the rest of the day. The waitresses, dressed in pink and white polka-dot uniforms, moved about making small talk with the customers and keeping their coffee cups filled. At the counter, one man was reading a newspaper while another talked to the cook, discussing the prospects for the Atlanta Braves getting into the World Series that fall. The waitress working the counter walked over to the reader and pointed toward the donuts on a pedestal tucked under a scratched plastic cover.

"Which one?"

"You know my wife says I gotta watch my weight. Stop tempting me."

"You go on now," she drawled plopping a plate with a chocolate donut in front of him. "Your wife knows you're safe with me." They both laughed.

Sarah put the menu down and looked out onto the street. Bernie Graves was sweeping the sidewalk outside his barber shop. The handyman at Gladys's was rolling the awning down over the front window and the street sweeper churned by, cleaning gutters before cars filled the parking places along Main. As was its habit, Eight Mile Junction was getting a slow start on the business day.

"Well now, if it isn't Sarah Wasser," the waitress said, spooling out words in the way some Southerners had, like squeezing the last bit of juice from a lemon. "We haven't seen you in, Lord have mercy, I don't know how long."

"I'm here for the summer," Sarah replied. The waitress was one of the girls in high school, a class or two behind her, but Sarah couldn't remember her name.

"Ready to order? How about ham and eggs? We got some of that fresh ham from Einar Taubert's place—came in just this morning." She threw her hip out to the side and rested her hand on it while she waited for Sarah to respond. Two buttons on her uniform had been left open, and when she twisted her body, one breast bulged roundly.

"A cup of coffee and one slice of dry toast."

"That all? You need to put some flesh on those bones of yours." She laughed and poked Sarah's shoulder with the eraser on her pencil. "Can't find a man looking like that." She winked and called the order to the kitchen.

Al Westfall entered and sat at a table close to Sarah's. If he noticed her, he didn't acknowledge her presence. As he studied the menu, Sarah kept glancing his way, careful not to be caught watching. But she needn't have worried; he was buried in the menu as if he was memorizing the fare.

A waitress approached his table. "The same, Al?"

He nodded and handed her the menu. "Two over easy on toast," she called to the cook.

Al withdrew a pad and began writing, taking an occasional sip of coffee. Unafraid of being discovered, Sarah stared with impunity. He was a good looking man, not much older than she. Maybe early thirties. His closely shaven face was darker where his beard grew and his square chin had a faint cleft. When his hair fell forward, he pushed it back with a quick gesture that somehow transformed the severity of his demeanor into one that was quite boyish.

He ate mechanically, reminding Sarah of Chewie when she was a puppy, gulping down her food without tasting it. After he pushed back his plate, the waitress refilled his cup and left the check. Perhaps this was a good time to make a fresh start. On neutral ground. Sarah walked to his table, bringing her coffee cup and expecting an invitation to sit.

"Good morning."

"Sarah, isn't it?" The wrinkles in his forehead cut deeper, as though he was trying to remember where he'd seen her last. Before she could answer, he mumbled. "I'm late for the office," stuffing the pad in his brief case. He placed several bills on the table, leaving Sarah to watch as he exited the restaurant.

It took a few seconds for her to recover and a few more to walk back to her table, focusing her eyes on the speckled linoleum and hoping no one had noticed the humiliating brush off. She paid her bill and left. She could see Al ahead. Maybe he's shy. No, she amended her thoughts. Don't make excuses for him. He's a shit. She suppressed the urge to catch up with him and tell him so. He may be a shit but she'd show him. Give it time.

"John-Two's not in yet," Janet said when Sarah entered the office. "I'll call you when the boys are ready."

While she waited, Sarah scanned the newspaper clippings again, staring at the pictures, trying to wrest from them some hidden piece of information. But, as in most newspaper photos, the figures were wooden and the pictures grainy. Everyone looked as though a great Ice Age had descended, leaving them frozen and lifeless.

Sarah heard Janet greet John-Two warmly. "This morning you're looking at a happy man," he said.

Janet said something in a tone that made Sarah's ears perk up. Sounded personal and conspiring, but the words were unclear.

"Right," his voice modified, less exuberant.

"Hmm," Sarah hummed suspiciously. Sounds very cozy. She continued to look though the clippings and improve her notes until she was called to the meeting.

"Good morning, young lady. Been keeping busy?"

"Trying to."

John-Two sat back in his chair and gave her the same once-over as he had when she first entered his office. His direct gaze was disconcerting. She straightened her belt, pulled her skirt down, and slipped into her seat. Al was already seated and, as he had been the day before, bent over some papers.

"Saw you downtown yesterday," John-Two commented.

"Getting reacquainted." Strange. They had seen her but intentionally ignored her. Not on the team, that's for sure. She wanted to counterpunch by asking him how his golf game went but thought better of it.

"Let's get started," John-Two said leaning toward her. "What do you think now that you've read the clippings?"

"Everything points toward JoBeth taking the children to the lake to drown them. Somehow, I don't think that's the entire story."

"How so?" John-Two asked. "What's missing?"

"JoBeth loved those children. If you asked a hundred people who knew her, I'm sure every one of them would vouch for that. Why would a mother who loved her children drive them out to a lake and intentionally drown them?"

"Quite right," John-Two said. "That's why the defense has to take the wind out of the prosecution's charge that she took the children to the lake intending to murder them. Right, Al?"

Al nodded, then turned to Sarah. "Any ideas?"

"Not yet. After I see JoBeth ..."

"Al's already set discovery into motion to see what the DA's got," John-Two interrupted. "Might find something. But right now, they have JoBeth's confession that she was at the lake, and forensics haven't come up with anything that suggests someone other than she and the children were there. The DA is pretty sure of his case."

"I'd still like to know why she did it," Sarah said.

"You and everybody else in this town. It's possible that we may never know. The sad part is that she may not know herself. Anyway, the DA presents the prosecution's theory and it's up to us to punch holes in it."

"I'm concerned that this case has been already decided," Sarah said.

"Whoa, you're getting ahead of us, young lady. The defendant has been charged with murder but the verdict is still out. The outcome depends on what we come up with."

"I haven't been in town long, but I can see that public opinion is unfavorable. How do you plan to change that?"

"The only ones we have to influence are the jurors. Al's working on jury selection and you can help us with the defense strategy."

"And what is that?"

Al leaned forward so he could look directly at Sarah. His eyes were almost as black as his hair. "Before we discuss strategy, I want to warn you that once we enter a plea, this town will be filled with reporters wanting something, anything to print. It's best you understand that you are not to speak to any of them."

Sarah seethed. Of course she knew that. John-Two watched the interaction between them, his eyes wreathed in amusement antagonized her further. Is that why he hired me? For his entertainment?

"As for the plea and the defense, there aren't very many choices, so we're pretty sure of the direction it will take. But until the plea is entered, we're not giving any statements to the press." Al held her gaze, forcing her to answer.

"Of course," she said tightly.

"Good. Just so you understand. John-Two and I have something we want you to do," Al continued. "We're asking the court for a change of venue. That's where you come in. You've already noticed that everyone around here has an opinion about this trial and that the majority of opinions are negative. We want you to help us make a case for moving the trial out of Eight Mile Junction by collecting evidence that will show that, in the majority of minds, JoBeth's guilt has already been decided."

"I have something I need to finish before I leave for court this afternoon," John-Two said. "Go with Al and he'll give you instructions. On your way out, please tell Janet to come in."

Al led the way into John-One's office, the workplace he had been given for the duration of the trial. Unlike John-Two's office, the deceased senior partner's memorabilia hung on the walls, his wife's picture remained on the desk, and his umbrella and galoshes were in their place near the coat rack. It was as though everyone expected him to return momentarily. The only clue to his long absence were the pages on the calendar that hadn't kept up with the passing years. In this office, it was still 1985.

"How long has John-One been gone?" She shriveled under Al's pained look. Stick to business when you're with this jerk, she warned herself. He's not interested in chit-chat.

"As I said, we want to enter a motion to move the trial to a county where the residents are less familiar with the case," Al began. "So, we need to convince the judge that a jury selected from this area will very likely be prejudiced against the defendant. To obtain the necessary evidence, we want you to conduct a survey. Ever done that?"

Sarah shook her head. "Not since my undergraduate days in a research methods class."

"This will help." He brushed his hair back and handed her a statistics book. After he went over the details of sample selection, he gave her a draft questionnaire. "I've written some questions so you can see where I'm going with this. If you think of any more, show them to me. I'll have to approve of them. When you're finished, give it to Janet and she'll format it into a survey instrument."

Sarah looked at the list of questions but was unable to make sense of it. Everything was happening so fast. First she was irritated by the simple tasks given to her, and now she was inundated with responsibility for something she had never done before.

"Then start making the phone calls. You'll find that evenings and weekends are best. You don't mind working those hours, do you?" He didn't wait for her reply. "To increase validity, be sure to keep calling until you reach someone in the household for every number on the list. The person must be an adult, old enough to serve on a jury."

"When do you want this completed?"

"Let's see, this is Thursday. How about a week from tomorrow? John-Two can ask for a hearing by the end of the following week. That will give you time to write the report and prepare to testify at the hearing."

"What're the chances of the motion being granted?"

"Not good."

"Then why do it?"

"Change of venue is just one of the tricks in the bag," he said. "Get started tonight."

Sarah waited for some word of encouragement, but Al picked up the phone and began dialing. She hesitated, hoping to ask him about seeing JoBeth. Then thought better of it. He'd give her one of his penetrating looks of disapproval. There'd been too many of those already. He didn't look up as she left the room.

Seated at her desk in the library, she reviewed the questions. After she finished, she took them to Janet to format, but she was still in with John-Two. Sarah wrote out Al's instructions and returned to the library.

She spent the rest of the morning developing a sample of respondents, then tip-toed down the hall toward Al's office. She wasn't sure if she should walk in or if Janet had to announce her. She was in limbo, somewhere between kid-intern and paid attorney, not sure how she was expected to behave. The door to Al's office was open; he wasn't behind his desk. In the reception area, Janet was back at her desk.

"Al around?"

"They went to lunch and probably won't be back for the rest of the day. Can I do anything for you?"

"I just wanted to tell him that the list of respondents is completed."

"Did you change any of the questions?" she asked, scanning the draft.

"No."

"Then don't wait for him. He'll expect you to go ahead. I'll run off the questionnaire so you can get started after lunch. He'll like that."

Janet took out a lunch bag and placed it on her desk. It looked like one of those handbags Kaylan sold at Mrs. Weeber's luncheon. Janet didn't seem like the type that would spend her time with a bunch of women, eating lunch, and purchasing plastic handbags. But, this was a small town.

"Bring your lunch every day?" Sarah asked.

"It's cheaper, and faster than eating out. Besides, I'm not overly fond of the food at the Pinker Dot."

Sarah didn't want to go to the Pinker Dot either. She was afraid John-

Two and Al might be there and see her eating alone. Damn. Afraid to be seen on the street, afraid to walk into Al's office unasked; afraid to be seen alone at the restaurant. Next, she'd be afraid of her shadow. She'd been a star in law school. Now she was back to being a jumpy teen. Next thing she knew, she'd be breaking out in pimples. What was this job doing to her?

Janet took a bite out of her sandwich and turned to her computer. "Have a good one."

Dismissed again, Sarah walked home for lunch. "Anything for lunch?" she called out as she entered the kitchen. Ellen was polishing the chrome on the oven door. "Why are you doing Orda Mae's work?" Sarah asked. "Wasn't your life supposed to be easier when we moved here?"

Her mother stopped and leaned against the stove, still holding the can of chrome polish in one hand, smiling a sideways grin. "Orda Mae can't do everything. Besides, using a little elbow grease makes me feel as though I am earning my keep around here."

Sarah opened the refrigerator. A pan holding a large cut of beef filled the top shelf. "This for dinner?"

"It's for some company executive visiting from up north. They're opening a plant in Alabama and want your father's advice."

"I'll bet he's got himself all worked up over that." Sarah winked at her mother. "You know how he likes giving advice."

"Oh, he's happy enough."

Sarah put on the tea kettle. "Have lunch and leave that work for the housekeeper or I'll tell Dad what you're doing."

Ellen wrinkled her nose playfully and sat down. "How's the job going?" She tossed her vinyl gloves onto the counter.

"Fine. John-Two will ask for a change of venue and file a motion to move the trial. It'll be in tonight's paper, and the town will be a-buzz over that news. Folks here won't like moving the trial. It's like taking a juicy bone away from a dog—if they take the trail away, they'll have nothing to gnaw on."

"Why do they want to move the trial? JoBeth's friends are here. They should be on the jury." Ellen dropped two sugar cubes into her tea; the spoon scraped the side of the cup as she stirred.

"Not really. John-Two will suggest that jurors selected from this area will have already formed their opinions about the crime. My job is to conduct a telephone survey and collect enough information to support a change of venue."

"Sounds important."

"Will Dad get huffy if I don't make it home for dinner tonight? He's been a little distant."

"Where are you going?"

"Nowhere. I'm working late—weekends and nights are the best time to reach folks by telephone."

"If your Dad thinks you're working, he'll understand. What should I tell him?"

"Just say I have a deadline so that I can meet a court date by the end of next week. He'll like that."

"Oh, yes he will." Ellen reached across the table, squeezed her daughter's hand, and said, "I'm so proud of you."

It wasn't so long ago that she would have criticized her mother for that same gesture, accusing her of pandering. But the warmth contained in her mother's small squeeze made Sarah feel as though she was doing everything right. She liked the feeling.

"Love you, Mom," she said, giving Ellen a peck on the cheek. "Got to go. Have fun with the guys tonight." The screen door squealed closed behind her.

By 8:30, the respondents to her telephone calls began to voice their annoyance at being disturbed. Sarah stopped calling and entered the results onto a spread sheet. Twelve calls had been completed. All had heard of the trial, all knew JoBeth, and the majority had met the children. Almost all had first heard about the murders from friends or relatives and all were following the aftermath of that night at the lake in the local newspaper. Everyone was sure JoBeth had committed the crime. The majority believed that the death penalty was a suitable form of punishment.

The light coming from Clayton's office gave her a reason to linger and not get caught up in her father's business meeting. She rapped on his open door. "Busy?" she asked.

"Not for you, Sarah. Come in and sit."

"I'm not interrupting anything important, am I?"

"Nothing that can't wait until tomorrow."

She eased herself into one of two matching Queen Anne chairs facing the desk. The contrast between his and John-Two's office was startling. Clayton sat behind a flat desk with a photo of a woman and three children positioned so visitors could see it. A gilded ink well held two feathered pens and a curly-headed brass cherub presided over a shell-shaped paperclip tray. Several fine oil paintings hung on the wall, the largest a still life with cheese, fruit, a vase of flowers, and a dead pheasant with his head hanging off the edge of the table. Flemish, Sarah guessed.

"Working late?" she asked as Clayton capped his pen.

"Tonight's the wife's bridge night so I usually make myself scarce."

Sarah noticed that he'd been working a crossword puzzle, using a fountain pen to fill the squares. Must be pretty sure of himself.

"Is that your wife and kids?"

"Yup. It's about five years old now but I like the picture. It makes me think that things are standing still and we're not getting any older."

Sarah sat quietly for a moment, warming herself in the pleasantness that was a part of Clayton's presence.

"How long have you been with this firm?"

"Forever," he smiled. "Actually, since I graduated from law school. John-One knew my father. Offered me a job. I came back home and got right to work. Slipped back into my old life with the promise of becoming the managing partner. That was before John-Two settled down and decided to attend college. His graduation from law school changed everything. Naturally, he took over the firm when John-One died."

"Ever think of going off on your own after that?"

"No. I promised John-One I'd look after the boy."

"Did he need looking after?"

"Well, some might say so. At least at first. He calmed down after his wife died."

Clayton took a picture off the shelf behind him and handed it to Sarah. "That's him with his wife, Allison. Just after they married."

John-Two had his arm around a pretty woman, much shorter, a red band holding back the long brown hair that almost reached to her waist. She wore a pale green summer dress, low-heeled shoes and ankle socks.

"She died? When was that?"

"Seven years ago. She was a beautiful woman. You can see that in the picture." He reached over and took the picture back from Sarah, staring at it a few minutes before he returned it to the shelf. "Everyone had a crush on her."

"How did she die?"

"She was epileptic, had a seizure, and fell down the stairs. Broke her neck in the fall. When John-Two came home from work, she'd been dead several hours."

"Children?"

"They never had any."

"And he never married again?"

"I guess you could say not married."

Clayton's mouth formed a let's-leave-it-there smile. He looked away. Sarah figured if there was anything worth finding out, she'd probably hear it sooner or later.

"Was it hard to sit back and watch John-Two take over?"

The pendulum on the gold anniversary clock quietly spun way the minutes. Clayton turned his pen end-on-end as he thought. "I was never cut out to be a manager of anything and, for many years, John-Two was unmanageable. I was better off in the back seat."

"So, is this partnership a Mexican standoff?"

"The firm suffered for some time after John-One's death. We didn't fight each other but we didn't offer each other any help, either. But when Allison died, John-Two changed. And maybe I changed, too. We shared the grief, you might say. One of the few things we had in common. Something Allison couldn't get us to do during her life, she was able to accomplish in her death."

"What was that?"

"To talk decently to each other."

They sat in silence. Clayton apparently lost in his fond thoughts of Allison, Sarah trying to imagine blustery John-Two with a gentle loving wife.

"It's all over now, the disappointments, the arguments, the grief, and life is good." He reached into his desk drawer, took out a cigar, and rolled it between his thumb and forefinger. "When all else fails, one of these takes care of everything." He lit a match and pulled heavily. Pungent smoke filled the air.

Sarah nodded and rose to go. "I'd better get home. My mother thinks I'm still in high school and worries if I'm not in at a decent hour."

"Mothers, God love them. Mine was a saint."

When she passed Al's office, he called her to her. She wanted to ask if the half-eaten candy bar and the bottle of water on his desk was dinner, but didn't. She could be familiar with Clayton, but not him. He looked up from the pile of papers before him.

"How's the survey coming?" he asked. His eyes were blood shot and his cheeks and chin were darkened by a day's growth of beard. She suppressed the urge to say something sympathetic and reported the survey results from memory. She wasn't sure, but she thought she received a look of approval.

"Keep going on that," he said as he searched for something lost in the jumble of papers on his desk. "Starting Monday, we want you to interview prospective witnesses for the defense. Start with this one." He handed her a name and address. "Interview in the morning and work on the survey in the afternoon and evening. Can you handle it?"

"Of course I can," she said. There was a slight edge to her voice.

"I gave Janet a list of other prospective witnesses. She'll set up the appointments and give you any help you need. Some live out of town so you'll need a car. Do we need to rent one for you?"

He finished the candy bar and crumpled the wrapper. Instead of pitching it into the waste basket, he held it in his tightly clenched fist. He'd probably still be holding it when he brushed his teeth that night. She covered her mouth to hide her grin. "I'll see if I can use my mother's car."

He grunted. She rose to go. "Nice job, Sarah," he said. "Better than I expected." He lowered his head and began writing. She didn't get raves, but he hadn't given her one of his looks.

John-Two's office was dark when she passed and Janet was gone for the day. She remembered their intimate whispers that morning and Clayton's sly hint. She wondered if they were somewhere together. Not that it was any of her business.

On her way home, she detoured so she could pass the high school, just to see if things had changed. She and JoBeth had walked this way every school day. That was a long time ago, but Sarah clearly remembered their intimate chatter and how JoBeth had possessively held her arm.

"Is your daddy rich?" JoBeth had asked during the September of Sarah's first year at Eight Mile Junction High School. An autumnal crispness had filled the air to which the just- released students added an end-of-the-school-day joyful chatter. The green lawns were retreating into winter brown and the leaves, shed by trees preparing for the cold weather, were waiting at curbside to be collected. A boy passing on a skate board popped JoBeth's back with his notebook.

"You got no call to act like that, John David," she'd yelled after him. The boy executed a perfect heel flip and, rolling backwards, placed his hand across his waist and bowed. "Show off," JoBeth muttered.

"I never think of us as rich," Sarah answered. "Why do you ask?"

"Everybody in town says your daddy's rich. They say that Jewish people have lots of money because they help each other."

Sarah had heard that tiresome stuff about Jews helping each other before, but JoBeth's question had been so candid that it didn't seem objectionable. She had learned to take these things into account and let them rest. "My mother says we're comfortable."

"My momma was poor until my step-daddy carried us right from

Millside over to where the well-to-do folks get to live. In those days Momma had such an agreeable nature, and I recollect that all that newness in my life made me happy, too. 'Lord', my momma kept saying, 'ain't we lucky, Little Darling'? Now she says I'm too old, and doesn't call me that any more. But I do like the sound of Little Darling, don't you?"

Sarah tried to imagine her mother calling her that. Her mother loved her, but the language of northerners didn't include as many words of endearment as southerners commonly used. "Sarah, dear" was about as flowery as it got.

"Your stepfather must be very good to you and your mother," Sarah observed.

JoBeth had fallen silent and bit the inside of her cheek. "All I know is that my step-daddy says he loves me better than anyone else."

"That's nice," Sarah had replied.

She walked around the track. The crunch of the cinders underfoot reminded her of how, in the absence of a girl's track team, her father had bullied Coach Emmons until he eventually gave in, agreeing that Sarah could work out with the boys as long as she didn't expect to compete against teams from other schools. He was quite a guy, that father of hers. Always knew how to get what he wanted.

She breathed in, enjoying the cool night air. It was heading into the middle of June and the cloying mugginess of the deep summer would end these lovely evenings. She looked to the sky, searching for the moon. Now a small sliver, it seemed to be hanging precariously from the branch of a nearby tree, like an ornament, belonging more to the tree than the sky. Then, after taking a few steps, Sarah watched the moon fall off the branch and return to its proper place among the evening stars. Funny thing about perspective, how a small change in one direction can dramatically affect everything else.

Things with Al seemed to have changed that night, also. She certainly felt better about him after their short meeting than she had after the Pinker Dot episode. Only a small nod of approval and a few words of praise but his attitude was more positive. Despite its convolutions, it had been a pretty good day and she felt pleased with herself. Maybe tomorrow she'd ask again if she could visit JoBeth.

Chapter Seven

Sarah backed her mother's 1989 Volvo station wagon out of the driveway. Although more than ten years old, the engine ran smoothly and the seats had the satiny glow of new leather. A Star of David hung from the key chain and, after all those years, the speedometer registered only 42,000 miles.

Janet had scheduled the first interview with Dora Channing, JoBeth's supervisor at the manufacturing company managed by Sarah's father. Now retired, Dora lived in Channing Hollow, one of the small valleys etched into the foothills where generations of Channings lived out their lives. According to family lore, the only way out of the Hollow was through the cemetery.

It felt good to be out of the office and away from the change of venue survey. Sarah had labored over it the entire weekend but progress was slow. Her court date was only a week away and forty of the 100 calls remained unanswered. Al wouldn't be pleased. A better introduction might speed things up. She rehearsed several new approaches as she drove.

At the turnoff to the Hollow, Sarah entered a dirt road that was hardly more than a wagon track crossing an abandoned hayfield gone to weed. In less than a mile, the road descended into a thickly wooded valley where bits of filtered light struggled to brighten the landscape. Occasionally, sunlight flashed off a metal roof or a faint curl of smoke rose from a house hidden among the trees. A feeling of loneliness clutched at Sarah's chest. She grasped the steering wheel tighter and focused on avoiding the deepest ruts.

Dora's place wasn't visible from the road, but the mailbox displayed

HENSON CHANNING in bold, black letters. The empty mailbox door dangled on its hinges like a large protruding tongue. One of the support beams held an abandoned jay's nest, apparently as unused as the mailbox.

A long driveway led to a mobile home with a wooden deck stretched across its front. Several chipped enamel cooking pots planted with red and pink geraniums decorated the entrance and a 50-gallon drum, fashioned into a meat smoker, stood next to a card table with four metal chairs. Nearby, a tire swing hung from a maple tree and two bicycles lay in the dirt. Beyond the edge of the woods, mattress springs topped the smoldering burn pile.

Three barking dogs rushed toward the car when Sarah opened the door, their tails and long loose jowls wagging. One was a puppy, the other two much larger. She believed a dog doesn't bite if its tail is wagging but, for insurance, she crooned to them in the sweet voice she used with Chewie.

"Nice doggies." She held out her hand for them to sniff.

"Chelsea and Max, you get right back here. Get now." The woman at the door waved and called to Sarah. "No need to worry. The worst thing them dogs can do is slobber you to death." She walked toward the car, grabbed one of the dogs with one hand and beckoned Sarah to come forward with the other. "Dora Channing," she said. "You must be Miss Wasser from that lawyer's office. Sam Wasser's daughter, right? That receptionist over there at Williams place said y'all would be wantin' to talk to me."

Dora, a tall big-boned woman, wore a stained white apron over her denim overalls and a print blouse with ruffles around her neck. A pair of purple and green dream-catcher earrings brushed her shoulders. Her large chin and the bangs that edged her eyebrows made her face look perfectly square. Dora grasped Sarah's extended hand, holding onto it as they climbed the stairs. "Come on in," she said. Dora entered first.

"Excuse the mess," Dora said. "Lordy, I thought when I retired from that job over at the plant that I'd have plenty of time, but look at me. Just don't know where the day goes."

Sarah stared at the leftover food on the breakfast dishes, the coffee stains on the table covering, and the flies cleaning up the last bit of bacon grease on the plates. Dora was right; the place was a mess.

"Sweet tea?" asked Dora. "Getting to be that time of year, ain't it?" She poured the tea over ice and sat across from Sarah. "Are you wanting some corn bread to go with that? Fresh made last night."

Sarah shook her head and gingerly sipped the tea. The sugar substitute left a metallic taste in her mouth. "Perfect," she said, tapping the side of the glass with her finger. "Have you always lived here?"

"I was born in the house that stood on this very spot. My Daddy built it before he married my Momma. After the shivaree, they settled in and after momma died and Daddy got old, my husband and me took over the big bedroom. By then, the old house was dry rot all over and still had an outside privy. We bought this here modular after Daddy died. Would've broke his heart to see the old place tore down."

"And children?"

"Lord, yes. Five of 'em. All growed now. My oldest daughter's closest. She works at the plant in shipping." As she spoke, Dora pointed her chin in the direction of town. "I watch her young'uns after school now that I'm retired. Helps her out some, what with her husband down with multiple sclerosis and her working all the time."

"No wonder you're so busy. Watching children's a full-time job."

"More sweet tea?"

Sarah glanced at her empty glass, then at her watch. "That would be nice, but we'd better get started." She moved a dish and coffee cup to the side and placed her tape recorder on the empty spot. "This isn't about the murders," she assured Dora. "It's more about JoBeth and anything you might know that can help with her defense."

"Seems like that lawyer of hers shouldn't be fretting about something done and gone. Nothing a body can do about it now."

Sarah nodded slightly. "You supervised her work so you might give us some insights into her character."

"Character?" Dora pursed her lips and blew air through them. Her bangs lifted slightly. "Didn't know she had one. Especially after what she done to those little ones." Dora picked up a knife and scratched jam off the table top, then wiped the knife on her apron.

"Can you tell me what she was like when she first came to work for you?" .

"Her youngest was born, oh, about six months before she came to the plant but in my mind that girl was still not growed up herself."

"I'm not sure what you mean."

"Lived in a fairy tale, she did. But she was smart enough. Can't take that away from her. She took to the work like she'd been doing data entry all her life. But her head was always full of silliness."

"Silliness?" Sarah cocked her head quizzically.

"That girl thought that some man was going to discover that she was Cinderella. Everyone at the plant said she was headed for trouble."

Cinderella described that last year in high school when JoBeth was planning her wedding, that's for sure. Phillip was Prince Charming and JoBeth imagined herself the princess, about to be carried off. But that was high school. Was JoBeth still living that dream?

"What made everyone think she was headed for trouble?"

"The way she talked. Putting on airs, like that boyfriend of hers was gonna carry her to someplace where she'd live like a queen."

"Boyfriend?"

"Kenny Bendhurst. She took up with him right after Phillip left. You should've heard her. Kenny's wants to buy me this and Kenny's got plans for that. Why you'd a thought he was some kind of a millionaire instead of a mechanic down at Harvey's Fix-It Shop."

"Was she seeing him at the time of the murders?"

"Heavens, no. That ended when he went away to some mechanic's school up around Charlotte or thereabouts."

"How long was that before the murders?"

"Don't rightly remember. But she didn't miss him none, I can tell you that. She was looking for someone else the day Bendhurst left town."

"Where does Mr. Bendhurst live?"

"Around Charlotte last I heard. But he comes from around here, over yonder in Traveler's Corners. There's so many Bendhursts in that town you can't walk down the street without falling over one of them." Dora gave a short laugh. "More sweet tea?"

"No thank you. It's very good, though." More tea and she'd need a bathroom. She had no desire to see what the one here looked like. "How long did JoBeth work for you?"

"A couple of months."

"Is that all?"

"Huh," Dora grunted. "She was promoted right on up to human relations." Dora replaced the cover on the butter dish and put it in the refrigerator. She seemed too restless to sit still.

"What did she do there?"

"Lord knows. She was only there a month or two before she was promoted to the front office." Dora returned to the table, leaned heavily on it and sat.

"Front office?" That was a surprise. Her father never mentioned that JoBeth had worked in the executive suite. She'd have to ask him about it.

"Yes ma'am. I worked in that plant for fifteen years before I got promoted from data entry to supervisor."

"Why do you think she was promoted so quickly?"

"Guess I'll get me some sweet tea. Sure you're not wanting some?"

"No, thanks. Maybe later. About the promotions," Sarah asked, trying to get Dora back on track.

"Look at the clock," Dora said. "Almost noon. It'll be dinner time before I get these breakfast dishes done." She took a ham hock out of the refrigerator, placed it in a pot of water and put it on the stove. She fussed around the sink, rinsing the silverware and wiping the counter.

"What were you saying about JoBeth's promotions?"

"Let's say there was plenty of talk." Dora scraped the leftovers from the plates into the dog dishes, put them out on the deck, and whistled. The dishes grated across the wooden floor as the dogs lapped up the food. Cicadas whistled their dizzying call, reminding everyone that the day's heat was about to increase. "Going to get hot today," Dora said as she reentered the kitchen.

"Can you remember what the talk was about?"

"Sometimes folks around here don't know enough to mind their own business." She lifted her apron and fanned herself. "Sure glad we got that air conditioner put in last year."

A car engine revved, then died. The dogs ran off the deck, barking. A man's voice greeted them.

"Well looky here, my husband's home." Dora held the screen door open. A smile crinkled her broad face. "I was beginning to think you got lost," she called.

Henson Channing's large frame filled the doorway. He patted his wife's shoulder as he entered.

"That your car sitting out there?" he asked Sarah. "Wasn't expecting company mid-day."

"This here's Sam Wasser's daughter, Sarah. Williams, that lawyer JoBeth got, sent her on over to ask me about when she worked with me."

"Morning, Ma'am." He nodded at Sarah and sat at the table, his baseball cap pushed back so that the bill stood almost straight up. "Got coffee?" he asked his wife.

"What took you so long this morning? By now, I would've thought you'd be all used up and ready to get some sleep before dinner."

"We got in a little overtime." He turned to Sarah. "What's Williams want you to find out?"

"About her growing up; about how she could have committed such a crime."

"Tell her about you and Orrin," Dora urged her husband. "They more than likely want to know something about JoBeth's real daddy,"

"Him and me was best friends. Why, it was Orrin's daddy's mule that kicked these out." His crimson lips, framed by a black- tinged-with-grey moustache and beard, smiled at Sarah. She could see the gap left by his missing front teeth. "We was just boys then. That old mule was a smart one, laying there, worrying and waiting until he got a good angle on me."

Sarah tried not to stare at the hole in Henson's mouth, but her eyes were drawn to the way his tongue caught on his teeth, making him lisp. How could someone live almost their entire life without two front teeth?

"What was Jo Beth's father like?"

"Orrin Bellinger? One of the best hereabouts. He worked his daddy's farm 'til the day he died. Never made no money but he was too stubborn to come into the plant. Said indoors was no fit place for a man to work."

"I understand he died young," Sarah commented.

"He did," Dora cut in. "He wore himself out. JoBeth was just a youngster." She placed a cup of coffee in front of her husband.

"What happened to the farm?" Sarah asked.

"Sold," Henson replied. "Vera moved into a rented flat in one of them old houses over on Millside."

Dora brought out a colander of crowder peas and began to shell them. The peas pinged off the sides of the aluminum bowl.

"Got some ham to go with them peas?" Henson asked.

"You go on now, you know I do," Dora answered gruffly.

Sarah found the interplay between the two charming. There was an easiness between them that she never saw in her parents. "How did Vera meet her present husband?"

"I don't rightly know," Dora answered. "But she didn't waste no time getting hitched up again. That woman knew what she wanted."

"To get out of Millside?"

"Yes'um. Latched onto Howard. He'd never been married and always made good money at that used car lot of his. Still does."

Henson lowered his lips to the cup on the table and sucked in the coffee through the hole left by his missing teeth. The odor of burnt coffee hinted that the pot had been sitting on the back of the stove for some time.

"My wife cooks up the best coffee," he said to Sarah, blowing into the cup. "Strong and hot. Makes my gums ache." He smiled widely at Sarah. "Everybody says, Henny, all you got left in front is them eye-teeth. Can't bite so good no more but you probably can see pretty darn near everything."

Sarah tried to smile but her face felt stiff. Missing front teeth held little humor for her and there wasn't anything she studied in the law school that had prepared her for this.

"JoBeth once told me that her stepfather treated her very well," Sarah said.

"Yes, Ma'am, he did. She was always down at the car lot. Saw her there myself, always sitting on Howard's lap and fiddling with his bolo tie, making that cowboy boot slider go up and down like it was riding on an elevator. Would've drove me crazy. But Howard never paid no mind to anything she did. He spoilt her like she was his own kin."

He took another gulp of coffee. "What time's dinner ready?" he asked his wife.

"One, one-thirty, same as every day." Dora turned to Sarah. "He asks me that every time he comes home from work. Makes me crazy." She smiled at her husband. "If he didn't ask me I guess I'd miss it." She took the peas over to the stove and poured them into the pot.

"Guess I'll nap before dinner." Henson walked into the living room, turned on the television, and settled comfortably into the indentation in the couch. "Nice meeting you," he said as he lay back.

Sarah looked at the clock on the kitchen wall. "Dora, I need to get back for a meeting this afternoon. Can I call you if I think of any more questions?"

"Sit a spell. No need to hurry off. We got plenty enough dinner for three."

"Thanks for the invitation but I really can't."

Sarah walked to the door and stepped out onto the deck. When she reached the bottom of the stairs, she looked back at Dora standing in the doorway.

"Just one more thing. Why do you think JoBeth murdered her kids?"

Dora stood, one hand on her hip, and swept her bangs back with her other, letting that hand come to rest on her forehead. Her eyes seemed to be searching for something beyond the burn pile. Just when Sarah thought she wasn't going to answer, Dora broke her silence.

"How'd anyone know why a mother kills her children? I heard some say she was looking to start over again, looking for a new life and that them kids was in her way."

"Do you really believe that?" Sarah asked.

"Never know what goes on in a person's mind until they do something, do you?" Dora turned to go, then stopped. "If you ask me, that girl was all pulled apart and couldn't find no way to put herself back together. My granddaddy used to say that if you kick a dog long enough it's gonna turn round and bite somebody." She gave Sarah a nod, and closed the screen door.

Sarah turned to go, puzzling over what Dora had just said. Did she mean that JoBeth had been abused and that she murdered her children to take revenge on those who ill-treated her?" Odd thing to say. Sarah had never thought of her friend as having a troubled life. A few ups and downs with Phillip, but... Sarah started the car. JoBeth was just a sweet southern girl who wanted to be friends with everyone.

Sarah was back on the main road when she remembered that Henson's arrival had interrupted the interview and that she hadn't pursued the topic of JoBeth's promotions. Maybe she'd call Dora when she back to the office, even though it seemed unlikely that she'd reveal anything more. At first she'd been forthcoming, but later, she seemed tired of the questions. Her father might help. Since JoBeth had worked in the front office, he would be able to explain the promotions. On the way back, Sarah stopped at the Burger Spot and ordered one to go.

"How'd it go?" Janet asked when Sarah arrived at the office. Salad in a Tupperware dish sat next to her computer.

"Pretty well. You were right, that road to Channing Hollow is a bitch. Mind if I join you?" Sarah held out the bag holding her burger.

"Folks up there in the hollow like the roads that way. Keeps strangers out. What's that? From the Burger Spot?"

"Yep, and there goes my diet."

Janet clicked her tongue. "You young people, always on a diet. And look at you, so trim."

Janet turned from her computer and attended to her lunch. When she bent her head, Sarah noticed some gray hairs along the part in her hair.

"Janet, Dora said that JoBeth did well at her job but hinted that her promotions came unusually fast. Did you ever hear any gossip about that?"

"No. Not about that. But there was talk for a while about JoBeth hanging around Dora's nephew, Chase."

"Dora didn't mention him."

"She'd be tight lipped about that. Folks up in the Hollow don't mix with outsiders, marry each other more often than not. Usually, they're reluctant to discuss family with strangers."

"Do you know JoBeth?"

"When my niece visits, she always looks up JoBeth and brings her over to the house." They met over at Gladys's one summer." As she spoke, she motioned toward the photograph on her desk.

"So that's your niece," Sarah said. "Very pretty."

"Laura's the best thing that ever happened to me. Like having a daughter." Janet pushed back the sleeves on her blouse, signaling she was ready to get back to work.

"I'd like to meet her sometime."

"I expect you will. She spends time with me every summer, even if it's only a few days. I know she'll be interested in the trial." Janet covered the empty Tupperware dish and shoved it in the bottom drawer of her desk.

"Dora mentioned a Kenny Bendhurst. Ever hear anything about him?"

"The one JoBeth went with after she and Philip separated?"

"What's he like?"

"Kind of a wild guy. Rode a motorcycle and got into trouble here and there. Nothing serious. Just rowdy stuff."

"Dora said he went to Charlotte. Do you know why?"

"Not really." Janet began typing, her pale pink finger nail polish looking like stray rose petals floating across the keyboard.

"One more thing. Am I going to interview Bendhurst? If not, I think I should."

Janet pulled a paper from under the desk blotter. "No, not on the list John-Two gave me."

"I'll mention it to him," Sarah said. "It might be worth having a talk with this Bendhurst character."

When Sarah left the office that night Janet was still at her desk, her hair and blouse as tidy as when Sarah saw her at noon. She had a message from John-Two.

"He wants you in court tomorrow morning. Meet him here at 7:30. He'll go over the procedure before you head out."

Just what Sarah wanted, to be right where things were happening. "What's tomorrow?"

"They're entering the plea."

Sarah hadn't heard anything about it and was a little miffed they hadn't asked her to sit in on the discussions. "How are they pleading?"

"He'll go over that with you in the morning." Janet rose and walked from behind her desk to the file. She unlocked the cabinet with the key she wore on an elastic band around her wrist and began filing documents. Her gray skirt fell gracefully from her hips and her two-inch heels brought her chin to the exact height of the top file drawer. What a tiny, compact person, Sarah thought. Looks as though someone fashioned her expressly for this office.

On the walk home that night, she planned how she would construct her report of the Channing interview. She wanted to earn her way into the loop. An exceptionally good product might do it. When she rounded the corner on Hampton, she was surprised to see a car parked in front of the house. Her mother hadn't mentioned company. Couldn't be business. None of her father's associates would drive an old Chevy station wagon that looked as though it had been stored in some grandmother's garage for the past twenty years.

The kitchen had been scoured clean. The small lamp over the stove was the only light in the room. Sarah could hear the television. Her mother must be in there, most likely knitting. She made a sandwich and took it into the living room.

"Did Chewie finish her dinner?" her mother asked. "She's been off her feed."

"She's not sick, is she?"

"Don't know. I'll take her to the vet if she doesn't do better tomorrow."

"If I'm not busy, I'll go with you. She's getting old. Could be just cutting back."

"How was your day?"

"Pretty good. Thanks for the car. Someone said it looks in great shape for its age. I told him if he thought the car was in great shape, he should see its owner."

Ellen blushed and looked at Sarah over her reading glasses. "Speaking of the car, your father wants to talk to you."

"About what?"

"Just go in and see him." Ellen pointed her knitting needle toward the den.

"Can't you tell me?"

Ellen shook her head. "Just go on in."

The click of her mother's knitting needles followed Sarah to the den door, reminding her of the metronome that had ticked away while she practiced her piano lessons. What was all the secrecy was about?

Her father's den was a duplicate of his office at the factory with its leather furniture, memorabilia, books, and a glass paperweight with a picture of her as a small child. Unlike John-Two's office, the walls documented the history of her father's accomplishments: letters of congratulations from the company president, thanks from politicians, and photographs of him smiling with the mayor of Chicago, his arm around the Secretary of Labor, shaking hands with union dignitaries, and standing among all the Little

League teams he had ever supported.

He was going over a list of numbers and adding them on the desk calculator. Except for the desk lamp, the room was dark. He looked up when she entered. "You're never at dinner. I have to get all my news from your mother."

Sarah drew up a chair, sitting just outside the circle of lamp light. She was still stinging from her father's reaction to her news about the job. Neither had ever mentioned that night but it lay heavily between them, like yesterday's potatoes, cold and unwanted. Not wanting any more of his criticisms, she'd vowed not to volunteer anything about work. "It's going all right," she said.

"I hear you're doing interviews for Williams."

"Yes, I am."

"Your mother said you borrowed her car. How did that work out?"

"Fine."

"Did you see that station wagon outside the house?"

"Mmmm."

"It's yours. Howard Maitlin arranged it."

"You spoke to Howard Maitlin? How did that happen?"

"I called Margaret, that relative of theirs, and told her I needed to talk to Howard about a car for you. He arranged for one of his salesmen to help out. Good of Howard to do this, what with all this going on right now in his life."

How did her father get through to Margaret when she couldn't? He's amazing. Not willing to give him credit, she looked away and kept her hands folded on her lap.

Sam reached into his pocket and took out a set of keys. He jangled them in front of her, like he was enticing a baby with a colorful toy. "Take it down to Maitlin's place for maintenance; they'll give you a discount. The salesman says Howard wants to thank you for helping JoBeth."

He laid the keys on the desk and punched a few numbers into the calculator. "You can repay me from the money you earn this summer." He tore off the tape and looked over the numbers. "Twenty-five dollars a week and you'll have the car paid for by the time you return to law school in the fall. If you take care of it, Jake says Maitlin will buy it back at the end of the summer for the price I paid. You can either sell it back to him or take it to Evanston."

"Don't I have any say?" Sarah asked.

"I'll take care of the insurance. Doesn't cost me that much." He pushed the keys toward her.

"Mom and I were going to work out a schedule between us."

"Well, I worked it out," he said firmly. "Now here, take the keys."

Accepting the car was giving in to her father again. She wanted to tell him to keep the god-damned car, but the pattern of their relationship had been established and she hadn't found a way to break out. And he was right. It was unfair of her to use her mother's car. Bitter and feeling helpless, she took the keys. Her father had her where he wanted and he meant to keep her there.

Ellen was smiling when Sarah returned to the living room. "Wasn't that generous of your father? I told you, he always has your best interests at heart." She rested her knitting on her lap.

"He went out of his way to make sure you wouldn't be inconvenienced," Sara said, thinking that words like "generous" and someone else's "best interests" didn't fit her father.

"Now you can take off without asking anyone for anything. Your Dad's taken care of everything."

"He certainly has." She bent and kissed her mother lightly on the cheek. "It's been a long day and I have to be at the office by 7:30. Think I'll get to bed."

As she climbed the stairs, Sarah passed the photographs her mother had hung on the wall. It was a gallery of Sarah's life from birth to her graduation from college, the first picture showing a round-faced baby with a red birth mark on her cheek and her hair molded into a kewpie-doll curl. Embedded in the frame was a string of pink and white beads spelling out her name and year of birth, "Sarah Katerina Wasser, 9/10/1980." She stared at the picture. Had her father looked upon her on that day and decided that she would become an attorney? She searched the picture but could only see a baby with no goals, no ambitions, just a little creature needing to be fed and loved.

She scrutinized each picture, trying to discover the exact moment when her father had begun to shape her into the person he was determined she'd become but could find no visible signs of any transformation in the photographs. They simply chronicled her life. But Sarah knew that somewhere between the first and last picture, her father had written on that clean slate the vision that he had for her. She continued up the stairs, holding the car keys tightly. Their uneven edges bit into the palm of her hand.

Chapter Eight

John-Two was silent as he and Sarah walked to the courthouse. His head was bent forward, as though his thoughts were trying to stay ahead of his long strides. Sarah struggled to keep pace. The overcast sky, darkened by the promise of rain, sent long white tendrils of fog down the cuts and gulches of the nearby mountains. A small patch of blue unexpectedly appeared as the black turbulent clouds boiled eastward. "Just enough blue to make a Dutchman's pair of pants," her grandmother had always said when she saw a sky such as this. Sarah wondered if she might need her umbrella and if she'd have enough time to slip into the women's room to comb her wind-mussed hair before the court session began.

Earlier that morning, Sarah had met with John-Two. Janet hadn't arrived yet, and Al had gone directly to the jail to prep JoBeth for her courtroom appearance. Coffee was ready when she arrived. John-Two filled two cups and handed one to Sarah. "JoBeth's been charged with two counts of murder in the first degree," he said. The DA will argue that JoBeth went to the lake intending to murder her children. He's already notified us that he'll ask for the death penalty."

"Black," Sarah said when John-Two held up the Cremora.

"We'll enter a plea today and get this show on the road. Dunning's anxious to move the trial along. JoBeth has already been tried and found guilty by the public. Delays might give folks time to reflect on the circumstances surrounding the murders and JoBeth could evolve into a sympathetic figure. Dunning wants to avoid that."

"Was there ever a possibility of having the charges reduced to involuntary manslaughter?"

"As far as the DA is concerned, the case is a done deal. Dunning's certain he has enough evidence to show that the murders were premeditated."

"Looks grim," Sarah mused. Although she was certain the murders were not premeditated, the evidence suggested a strong probability. The prospect of seeing JoBeth for the first time filled Sarah with trepidation. Her friend might not be the same person she remembered. She rubbed the loose cuticle on her left thumb with her forefinger.

Janet's arrival was announced by the opening chimes on the computer and her quick steps approaching John-Two's office. She placed a packet of mail on his desk.

"Clayton in?" he asked.

"His office is dark." She gave Sarah a nod as she left.

"In this state, the law permits *'the defendant did it, but'* defense. Even if the prosecution shows beyond doubt that the defendant committed the crime, the chance remains that, given extenuating circumstances, the defendant can be shown leniency. If we get a reasonable judge and a favorable jury," John-Two continued, "we might be able to cast doubt on intent."

"All we have to do is figure out the 'but,' right?"

"Al's working on it. We have a few things in our favor. Death penalties have declined steadily in this state over the past 15 years. And, she's white and she's a woman. Fair or not, all that's in our favor."

John-Two pointed to the clock, grabbed his coat and briefcase. Before heading out the door, he stopped at Janet's desk.

"Tell Clayton that Benning called to discuss his estate planning. Ask him to fill in for me, schmooze Benning, take him to lunch."

"So, we're going with not guilty?" Sarah asked as they left the office.

"You got it."

John-Two paused at the security check when they reached the courthouse, giving Sarah time to catch her breath. "Still keeping us safe, Harry?" John-Two said, his eyebrows rising in that quizzical way he had when he was teasing.

"Right you are, sir."

John-Two rested his hand on Sarah's shoulder. "This is Sarah Wasser, she's working with us on the Ruland trial. Get used to seeing her, she'll be a regular."

"Welcome to the zoo, Miss."

In Department 10, Al was already sitting behind the defense table. The DA sat opposite, discussing something with his assistant; two newspaper reporters sprawled in the front row of the jury box, their legs hung over the rail. The court reporter and the bailiff were in place and a few of the curious were straggling into the courtroom.

After John-Two escorted Sarah to the first row behind the defense table, he walked over and shook hands with Dunning. She couldn't hear what they were saying but both were smiling. After a brief exchange, they shook hands, appearing as if they settled on their next golf date. She understood this part of the courtroom dance, the few moments of civility before the opposing attorneys tore into each other. This preliminary politeness was routine but, with JoBeth's life in their trust, it seemed callous. While justice would be served, she could only hope that mercy was forthcoming.

"That's Sarah Wasser," someone behind her whispered.

She turned and saw Howard and Vera Maitlin, JoBeth's mother and stepfather sitting behind her. Howard was much heavier than when Sarah had last seen him, his chin having multiplied several times. Loose skin sagged under his eyes, and his nose and cheeks were reddened by thousands of exploded capillaries. He sat with his eyes cast downward and head sunk toward his chest, revealing a comb-over held in place by glistening pomade. His right arm circled his wife's shoulders and his fingers trembled as he fidgeted with her scarf.

Sarah might not have recognized JoBeth's mother if she hadn't been sitting next to her husband. Vera's hair had been dyed red-brown and the steel framed glasses, the ones she had always worn, had been replaced with plastic ones embedded with rhinestones. A bright pink scarf was gracefully draped over a plum-colored suit. The pink stones in her earrings matched the scarf. Vera's head drooped toward Howard's shoulder as if she hadn't the strength to hold it upright. Sarah nodded. Vera smiled and listlessly fluttered a hand on which a large lapis ring covered her middle finger from first joint to mid-knuckle.

Back in high school, Mrs. Maitlin had always puzzled Sarah. She wasn't a cookies-and-milk kind of mother and Sarah had been rarely invited to the Maitlin's house. JoBeth said her mother was too busy helping out at the car agency and couldn't have kids hanging around. When they did go to the Mailtlin's, they studied downstairs because JoBeth said her bedroom was too messy and she didn't want anyone to see it.

A stir accompanied JoBeth's entrance into the courtroom; she was overshadowed by three deputies. She wore an orange regulation jumpsuit and her hands and feet were shackled. The wooden floor boards creaked under the footsteps of the small group as they walked to the defense table.

Sarah's eyes burned; she pressed her fingers against them. What would Al say if he caught her crying in court? He wouldn't say anything. He'd give her that look. Cherry pie. Cherry pie, she repeated, trying to distract herself with a silly mantra. Don't cry. Cherry pie.

John-Two stood as JoBeth approached, pointed to the empty chair between his and Al's, and watched as one of the deputies guided her into place. When she was seated, the deputies retreated. Vera Maitlin blew her nose.

Unable to see JoBeth's face, Sarah concentrated on her friend's hair. It was tightly drawn back and held by one of those stretchy things purchased in a dime store. Like JoBeth's life, the hair band was frayed. Al leaned over and whispered. JoBeth nodded but didn't turn toward him. Sarah hoped that Al was being gentle.

"All rise," the bailiff called out.

The judge entered, face impassive, his eyes fixed on the seat behind the bench. The muffled sound of the court reporter's fingers tapping on the keyboard deepened the silence in the room. Once seated, the judge browsed through a folder, quickly turning the pages. Satisfied that everything was in order, he shifted his reading glasses to his forehead and turned his attention to the defense table.

"The State vs. JoBeth Bellinger Ruland. Who is representing the defendant?"

John-Two spoke. "The law firm of Williams, Williams, and Standcroft, Your Honor, specifically John Williams, the Second, and co-counsel, Albert Westfall.

"Is the prosecution ready?"

"Yes, Your Honor."

The judged fixed his eyes on JoBeth. Sarah couldn't see if her friend was returning his gaze but Al had placed his hand on her arm, as if to reassure her. The judge began.

"JoBeth Bellinger Ruland, you are charged with two counts of murder in the first degree with the special circumstances, the murder of a child or children under the age of eleven. This is the time set for you to enter your plea to the charges. How do you plead?"

"Not guilty, Your Honor." Her voice was low and hoarse, as though it had been a long time since she had spoken aloud.

"You'll have to speak up so the court reporter can hear you." Without waiting for a response, the judge continued. "Have there been any promises made to you in exchange for your plea and admission to what's already been discussed here in court or what appears on your plea form?"

"No, Your Honor."

"Does the defendant waive time?" the judge asked.

"No, Your Honor," Al answered.

"Set the time of the next appearance." The judge gaveled, indicating that he was ready to go on to the next case. Sarah watched the deputies lead JoBeth away.

Back at the office, John-Two asked Al and Sarah to join him. She entered his office with a broad grin, hoping she didn't look too giddy. She was finally on the team.

"Well Al, how did it go?" John-Two began.

"Routine. Nothing unexpected."

"The court date has been set for the change of venue motion. It'll be next Thursday. Also next week," John-Two ruminated, "discovery, a review of the schedules of the presiding judges, and jury selection. Anything else?"

"The psychiatrist's report came last night," Al said.

"And he found?" John-Two asked.

"Dependent personality disorder. We might be able to mitigate intent by arguing she suffered from severe depression."

"Depression?" Sarah asked. "I never saw JoBeth depressed."

"Perhaps some of those you are interviewing can offer some insights. Be sure to cover depression in your questions."

"Sounds weak," she said.

"Right," John-Two said. "But we will argue that it was her state-of-mind that explains her unstable behavior as well as the underlying cause of her final act of desperation. Somehow, we can weave depression into that."

"What could have made her desperate enough to murder her children?" Sarah asked.

"We'll show that she was so ill-used as a child that, as an adult, she became the victim of several destructive sexual relationships."

"Victim?" Sarah asked.

"To begin with, she had an unhealthy relationship with her stepfather," Al said.

"What are you talking about?" Sarah asked. "I know her stepfather. He treated her as if she was his own daughter."

John-Two slid his watch off and scratched the underside of his wrist. The indentation of the watch band was etched onto his skin. He leaned into his desk.

"We have reason to believe she was molested by her stepfather."

Sarah looked past John-Two and stared at the bookshelves. Howard? Couldn't be. She and JoBeth had been best friends, hadn't they? If something like that had happened, Sarah was pretty sure she would have known about it. "There must be some mistake," she said.

"It been the town gossip for years," John-Two said. "Al asked her about it. She didn't deny that Maitlin had molested her as a child, but she wouldn't talk about it either."

"Has Howard ever been accused?"

"Rumor has it that JoBeth made a complaint at school, but when we requested evidence of the alleged meeting we were told that there was nothing in the files. The school's administrative staff at the time the complaint that was made has either retired or left service. The only thing the present staff knows is what I told you."

"And what was that?"

"That a complaint was made but nothing ever came of it," John-Two explained.

Al interrupted. "Even if there is a record of the meeting, the prosecution could argue that Maitlin was never formally charged with a crime, and that he isn't on trial. Somehow, we have to connect the early molestations with their adult relationship."

"What adult relationship are you talking about?" Sarah asked.

Al touched Sarah's hand to get her attention, then handed her a folder. It was thick and stamped confidential. "We got an anonymous tip that Maitlin and JoBeth were in a sexual relationship at the time of the murders. Our informant suggested they were meeting at motels."

"You mean they were at it while we were in high school?"

"It would appear so."

JoBeth's words about her step-daddy loving her more than anyone else came to Sarah's mind. They seemed innocent at the time. But now, the words took on a totally sinister meaning.

"What if JoBeth testifies?" Sarah asked. "I know it's an outside chance but, if we get a change of venue, her testimony could work in our favor."

"We're thinking about putting her on the stand, but we're not sure," Al said. John-Two nodded in agreement. "Right now, it's up for grabs. JoBeth is unstable, fluctuating from worrying about how she looks in the newspaper to hysteria when reminded of the night at the lake. Even if she agrees to testify, there's a strong possibility that the jury might not see her as a reliable witness. Then there's the DA. In cross, he'll try to destroy our allegation that she's an abused woman by portraying her as sexually deviant."

"What a mess. Howard and JoBeth." Sarah shook her head. What's wrong with me? How could I have been so blind and not seen what was happening? "Anything I can do?"

"Talk to her," Al said. "See if she'll confide in you. Verify her complaint to the school authorities and that, as adults, she and Maitlin were seeing each other. As soon as we're sure that Maitlin was taking her to motels, a detective can ferret out and document the details. Get as many names, places and approximate dates as you can."

"By then, she will have been a consenting adult. How will tracking down their meetings help the case?" Sarah asked.

"You might uncover something confirming that the incident reported at school wasn't imagined. It will support the argument that the early abuse initiated a life time of sexual victimization," Al explained. "By the time she got to Fenton Lake, her notions about sex and love had become so confused that taking the lives of her kids seemed the right thing to do." He surprised Sarah by reaching over and touching her arm. "I know you can do this," he said.

"Obviously," Sarah said, "you're going to do more than argue that murdering her children was just a poor decision because of an unhealthy relationship. That might be difficult for a jury to swallow."

"Not if we show how the relationship with her stepfather distorted her perception of the world," John-Two explained. "And if we're lucky, we might be able to show that Vera knew about it all along. Knowing that, the jury could take a different perspective on what happened. It might give us the 'but' we are looking for."

"Okay," Sarah nodded. "Get me started."

After the meeting, they walked into Janet's office. John-Two signed several letters and Al picked up a list of calls to return. Clayton entered and handed Janet some signed invoices.

"You want these mailed today?" Janet asked.

Clayton nodded. "Went well with Benning at lunch," he told John-Two. "He wants to proceed."

"I'll get at his stuff tomorrow. Thanks for filling in." John-Two turned to Sarah. "How did yesterday's interview with Channing go?"

"Well, but I ..."

The telephone rang. Janet held the speaker close to her cheek and spoke in a low voice. "It's for you, Sarah. Want to take it in the library?"

"Probably my mother." She took the phone.

"Sarah, this is Jameson."

Sarah blanked. Why's he calling?

"Jameson," he repeated. "Remember me?"

Sarah nodded as if he could see her positive response. Oh, that. Momma's house again. Sarah glanced around to see if anyone was listening. She turned her back to the group.

"You remember me, right? Jameson, from over at the drug store?"

"Of course I remember. I'm just surprised to hear from you."

"Can you come over for dinner tonight? Momma's having barbequed chicken."

Sarah glanced over her shoulder. John-Two was thumbing through papers and Al was talking to Clayton. Janet had returned to her computer. Why hadn't she taken the call in the library? She wanted to yank the telephone cord from the wall.

"We're working late tonight," she lowered her voice. "I told you I rarely have a free evening, especially during the week."

"Just a minute," Jameson said. When he returned, he said, "That's all right with Momma. How about Saturday?"

"We're having company from Illinois and I'm expected for dinner. So sorry." She congratulated herself for her quick thinking.

Without consulting his mother, Jamieson asked, "How about Saturday night?"

"We'll see."

"Great, Sarah. We'll leave it for Saturday night unless I hear otherwise from you."

When she hung up, John-Two winked at her. She tried not to blush.

"I'm leaving," John-Two said. "Close up, will you Al?"

Janet shut down her computer, picked up her purse and followed John-Two out of the office. "Have a nice evening," she said.

Damn that Jameson. This personal stuff could erase the small gains she had made with Al. She took a deep breath. Enough entertainment for one night. Get back to business.

"Al," she called after him as he turned toward his office, "do you want to see the change of venue report tonight or wait until morning?"

"Let's go over it tonight. The court date is at the end of next week. We have to give Janet time to finalize it."

When she returned with the report, Al was on the phone. She waited, sitting at Janet's desk, admiring the yellow-gold Citrine ring set in elaborate silver curlicues. Her father had given it to her for her graduation from Chicago. Really, he had given her so much—a comfortable life, the confidence to go on to law school, and introductions to anyone who might further her career. Perhaps she was too judgmental. It wasn't his fault she'd flubbed the interview with Molitor. The whole thing came down to that one night when she had too much to drink. The summer had just started. Plenty of time to make it up to him.

The cleaning lady came in. One hand pushing a cart with furniture waxes, spot removers, and cleaning cloths, the other hand dragging a vacuum. She nodded as she passed by.

"Good evening," Sarah greeted her as the cleaning lady rolled the cart into the restroom, leaving the door open. The toilet flushed. Al appeared at his office door with his briefcase in hand, his jacket over his arm.

"The change of venue report, didn't you want to go over it?" Sarah asked, trying not to sound disappointed.

"Let's do it over dinner."

She followed him into the hall. Was Williams going to buy dinner? John-Two had never discussed an expense account. She wondered if she had enough money with her to eat out.

"The cleaning lady will lock up," Al walked ahead. It was like being in trouble, trotting after some stiff-necked reform school matron to some undisclosed place for punishment. Was the rest of the summer going to be like this, running after these two guys? And dinner. It all happened so quickly, there was no time call her mother. What would Al think if he had to wait? "Call your mommy?" he would ask. She couldn't bear the thought. Shouldn't give a damn what he thought but, the trouble was, she did.

Al strode past the Pinker Dot and headed toward the courthouse.

"Where are we going?"

"My place."

His place? She guessed it was all right. Just business. She couldn't imagine it as anything else. But his place?

The sky was dark except for the evening star. It hovered close to the surrounding mountain tops, bright enough to pierce the darkness but not enough to cast a shadow. The business day had ended. Only the Pinker Dot and the Agusta Hotel were open. Other than Al and Sarah, there were no pedestrians; traffic was reduced to one patrol car. It slid by, the officer's hand, appearing above the roof on the driver's side, waved to them.

Al lived on the edge of Millside in a Mount Vernon style house that had been divided into four apartments. It was in an advanced state of disrepair. Ivy, probably rooted in the gutters, hung between the columns, stretching downward and reaching for the earth. The carpet on the stairs was worn and some of the rails on the banister were missing. The bulb in the hall had gone dead. They climbed the stairs in the dark.

The walls in Al's apartment were pock-marked with nail holes and painted a wretched hospital green. A rack constructed of plastic irrigation pipe held his suits and shirts. The futon, stretched into a bed, was unmade and covered with rumpled sheets and a blanket, and a large bean bag chair rested lopsidedly in front of a television that sprouted rabbit ears. Unopened mail was piled on a small round table placed near the windows. Behind a beaded curtain, a stove, sink, refrigerator and cabinets were lined up against the opposite wall as if they were felons, waiting to be photographed.

Al tossed his jacket and briefcase on the futon and headed toward the kitchenette. "I'll cook," he said, passing through the curtain. The beads rattled, reminding her of the *Charlie Chan* movies in which a beautiful dragon lady in a *chi-pao* stood sideways in the doorway, the strings of beads dripping down a long leg pushed forward through the hip-to-floor slit in her dress.

"What's for dinner?" she asked.

"Mac and cheese."

She suppressed a laugh. "That your specialty?"

Beneath the curtain, Al's legs moved rapidly between sink, refrigerator and stove. Water ran. Dishes rattled. His head appeared, the beads falling around his shoulders like long, multi-colored tresses.

"They had ten boxes for a dollar at the market. I bought thirty boxes. Getting pretty good at making it."

"Can I help?" It seemed the right thing to say.

"Make yourself comfortable. This won't take long."

She looked for a place to sit. Not the futon, that might be taken the wrong way. Not the bean bag chair either. Getting up and out of that thing with her tight skirt might be embarrassing. Her eye fell on four metal folding chairs leaning against the wall. She unfolded one and looked for something to do. "Can I set the table?"

He passed plates and silverware through the curtain. She busied herself, clearing away the mail and setting their places.

"Specialty of the house," he announced, emerging from the kitchen with the bowl of mac and cheese in one hand, two glasses in the other and a bottle of wine tucked under one arm. He smiled. It didn't transform his face as smiles usually do. Instead, it produced a series of lines that ran from his mouth to his stark cheek bones, creating what looked something like a grimace. He opened the wine, sat, helped himself, and began to eat.

"Could you pass the mac and cheese?" Sarah asked.

"Oh, yeah, yeah." He passed the bowl without putting down his fork, then rose, and went into the kitchen and brought back a roll of paper towels. "Napkins," he said. He tore off a piece and handed it to her. They ate in silence, Al concentrating on his food just as he did when she watched him that day at the Pinker Dot.

"Are we going to have that wine with dinner or after?"

He grinned and poured. The wine glasses were water streaked; they wouldn't meet Ellen's standards. A bit of cheese clung to his lower lip. She wanted to reach over and wipe it off and, while she was at it, push his hair off his forehead. She wondered what he'd do if she actually touched him. Probably slap her hand.

She ate slowly, careful not to drink too much wine. What would her father say if she brought Al home? Wouldn't that be a kick? Talk about immovable objects and irresistible forces. As soon as he finished eating, Al brought his briefcase to the table.

"Let me clear the table and wash up," Sarah offered. "That's the least I can do."

"No. I only do dishes on Saturday."

Al gathered up everything but the wine glasses from the table in one swoop. Dishes clattered onto the counter. The refrigerator door slammed. He returned, wiped the table with a paper towel, crumpled it and threw it toward the curtain.

"Let's get started. Where's the report?"

Sarah sat quietly, watching his eyes scan the pages, holding her hands on her lap so she didn't fidget. His concentration was fierce; his left hand was zipped up as though he was trying to keep the unruly thing in check. He wrote notes in the margins in several places and once crossed out a line. She didn't have to wait long.

"Here," he handed her the report. "Make the changes and have Janet type it. When you testify, start with the conclusion. Emphasize the respondents' predisposition toward the death penalty. That's important."

"Nothing else?" She had expected a long discussion.

"Oh, yeah. Good job."

"No, I meant any other corrections. Suggestions?"

He shook his head, rose from the table, and began looking through the CDs stacked above the TV. Sarah smoothed her hair and watched him sort them, tossing the ones that didn't interest him onto the carpet. Who was going to clean that up? No one probably. They would be in the exact place the next time she visited. What made her think she would be visiting again? Someone in the hallway laughed, and footsteps passed. A door to the other apartment slammed.

"I really should be getting home," she said.

"Have another glass of wine." He pushed the play button and Mahler's Ninth music, pulsating like an irregular heartbeat, filled the room. She hadn't anticipated any particular kind of music, but Mahler was a complete surprise. Mahler was one of her favorites.

"More wine?" he repeated.

"Just a touch. Remember, I have to walk home," she joked.

He didn't laugh. Not much of a sense of humor. Sarah watched as he poured. The wine swirled slowly around the bowl of her glass, almost in slow motion. Its color matched the tempo of the music, deep and magical. The wine and the music pushed aside the room's squalor.

Al broke the magic. "Why did you go to law school?" he asked.

She didn't want to leave that moment when wine and music and his presence came together. She looked into her glass, tipped it from side to side, and tried to come up with some startling incident that had guided her decision.

"Don't tell me you wanted to go to law school ever since you were a little girl."

"I can't remember when I wanted to be anything other than an attorney. My father talked about it a lot. It was never a question of *if* I'd study the law, it was always a question of *where*."

Al watched her closely as she talked. His eyes looked as though he used make-up. Why do men get the long lashes and darkly shaded eyes? Conscious of her glasses, her hand moved across her cheek. She curled her fingers around the glass stem, sipped, and tried to appear poised.

"My father believes that corporate law is a good place for female attorneys. He doesn't want me to end up a government clerk."

"Do you always listen to your father?"

"I'm afraid so." She frowned and looked away. His questions made her uncomfortable.

"Now that you're working on a criminal case, is he still your chief mentor?"

Good god, he was like her father. Abrupt to the point of being rude. But, he wasn't her father, and she didn't have to answer any more questions.

"I don't discuss this case with him."

Al nodded his approval. "That's good. So, what made you come to Williams for a job?"

She didn't have the courage to tell him that she was motivated by her failure to get the position with Molitor. Easier to say that she came home to help an old friend. "But now that I know about Howard," she said, "I wonder if I really knew JoBeth."

"It doesn't matter."

"It does to me."

"It shouldn't. You're her attorney now, not her friend." Al rose and walked to the window. "The courts pressure attorneys to get cases off the calendar. That means we have a lot of work to do in a short time." He turned toward Sarah. "You understand that, don't you?"

She nodded. Crossed and uncrossed her ankles.

"Our work must be precise and our arguments clean. If your efforts are encumbered by remorse and sentiment, you won't be able to keep up with the work I give you."

"But I keep thinking back to when we were young."

"Let that go. I expect the best from you, Sarah." He leaned toward her before he spoke. "No matter how this case turns out, I want this team to give JoBeth the best defense possible. That's the only way attorneys can live with cases that go against them. Can you do that?"

He poured himself another glass of wine and tilted the bottle toward her. She waved it away.

"I believe I can."

"Good. I'm beginning to believe I can rely on you." They fell into an awkward silence.

"It's getting late." She placed her glass on the table and retrieved her brief case.

Al didn't object. He drained his glass and walked her to the door. "Don't lock the door downstairs when you go out. We leave it open in case someone forgets his key."

She stepped into the dark hall. Al was framed in the lighted doorway, his elbow leaning on the jam, the other hand holding the door. She groped her way to the top of the stairs.

"Hey, can you give me a ride to the lake Saturday afternoon? The jury will be taken to the scene of the crime, so we'd better be familiar with it. Pick me up at one." The door slammed.

Dammit. He did it again. Asked her a question and assumed he knew the answer. Of course she'd have said yes, but he could at least have given her the chance to say so. She felt her way down the stairs.

Outside, the night had cooled. The moon, three-quarter now, was outshining the evening star and full enough to send a soft powdery light cascading to earth. It gave the evening a magical transcendence, casting whimsical shadows on the sidewalk and lawn. She picked her way carefully along the broken cement to the street.

What a strange guy, she thought. Quick and smart. He wants the best from her. She could live with that. But he's self-absorbed, overly focused on what he is doing. The Pinker Dot episode came to her mind; she could feel her face flush at the remembered embarrassment. And his questions about law school. She should have asked him how he decided to study law. Maybe he had a father story hidden somewhere in his past.

As she passed the jail, she thought about JoBeth and how she'd looked earlier, all used up, not old, but at the end of her life. No wonder. That damned stepfather of hers. JoBeth's words echoed in her mind, "My step-daddy loves me more than anybody else." Sarah gritted her teeth. The thought of Howard Maitlin disgusted her.

And Vera. What kind of mother was she? If she had suppressed JoBeth's complaint, she'd murdered her daughter, at least ruined her childhood. Sitting in the courtroom with that gaudy lapis ring, looking all sad and weepy-eyed. I could smack her, Sarah thought. The two of them. Howard and Vera. A perfect pair.

A horn tooted lightly. It was the same patrol car. This time the officer was on Sarah's side of the street. He leaned toward the window. His face, like the moon, was suspended in an expanse of darkness.

"Nice evening, Sarah."

She was surprised he knew her name. "Very nice, officer." Probably knows my father.

"Need a ride home?"

"No, I'm okay. I'm enjoying the walk."

As the policeman drove off, the car's powerful engine throbbed pleadingly, showing its resentment at being held to a modest speed. Sarah watched the rear lights disappear as it turned onto Fourth. Sweet silence returned to Main Street.

When Sarah entered the house, her mother called from the living room. "Is that you?"

"Sure is." She joined her mother. The brass weight on the grandfather clock clicked off a notch and the clock chimed the quarter hour. Nine-fifteen.

"Sorry I didn't call. We decided to work over dinner. Didn't wait, did you?"

"Dad and I figured you were at work. Where'd you go for dinner? Here," she said to Sarah, handing her the remote, "pick something you want to watch."

"Where's Dad?"

Ellen pointed her chin toward the den. Sarah took the remote and idly surfed the channels. The mac and cheese wasn't something she wanted to discuss with her mother. Especially dinner at the apartment of a young man. Her mother would jump to the conclusion that a son-in-law might be hovering in the near future.

"I found out something awful today," Sarah said. "Rumor has it that JoBeth's stepfather molested her. Did you know that?"

Her mother spoke in a low voice, as though there was someone else in the room and she didn't want them to overhear what she was saying. "It was mentioned at Mrs. Weeber's handbag party. Something about a complaint JoBeth made to the school nurse before we moved here. Emily knows the inside story. This murder case has dredged all that messy stuff up again."

"Exactly what did they say?"

"Just what I told you. It happened when JoBeth was in junior high. Nothing ever came of it. The nurse who reported the complaint quit at the end of that school year and left town."

"The women at the luncheon didn't have much sympathy for JoBeth. Did that change when they talked about the complaint against Howard?"

"Most felt a good man's reputation shouldn't be ruined without proof. Since nothing came of it; everyone pretty much thinks Howard must be innocent.

"Mother. She was just a child when she made that complaint. How can anyone believe that the fault lies with her? Doesn't make sense, does it?"

"You asked me, and I'm just telling you what I heard" Ellen's voice was breathy and defensive. "I don't know what to think, and I don't like thinking about it."

"Why didn't you mention this before?" Sarah asked.

"I thought you already knew. Everyone in town seems to know. Anyway, I'd rather not talk about it."

Sarah wanted to ask her mother what she would have done if her daughter had been molested, but that was unfair. It's easy to be righteous in a hypothetical discussion, easy to say you would have shot the bastard.

But when faced with such a situation, what a person would do is anyone's guess.

But if the allegations were true, Vera must have sold out her daughter. Who can understand something like that? And what about her? Was she any different than Vera? The car her father had given her had caused inner conflict, but she succumbed because it was easier than fighting against his persistent posture that everything he did or believed was right. Perhaps she was like Vera, not challenging the things that made her life easier. Would she ever come to the place where she would stand up for herself? Luckily, her father was no Howard Maitlin. Oh God, that was a depressing thought.

"I'm too tired to watch television." She laid the remote on the table and went upstairs.

Chapter Nine

*B*efore going to the boat ramp, Sarah and Al drove into the main entrance to Lake Fenton and stopped where Sarah had met JoBeth that first day. A small, impromptu memorial to Daniel and Casey had been assembled at the edge of the parking lot. Two men sitting in canvas chairs were smoking, casting their lines into the water, willing the fish to take the lure. Their radio was tuned into The Reverend Hollingsworth Billings' Holy Hour of the Resurrection of the Mind and Soul, his voice demanding repentance while The Women of the Word gospel choir, singing in the background, pleaded with the listeners to come to the Lord.

At the concession stand, paddle boats huddled together as they waited for customers. A woman standing on the dock pulled her straw hat lower over her eyes and watched a small boy cast stones into the water. The intermittent plopping exploded into small circles that quickly dissipated as the stones sank. The lake took little notice of the human intrusions and, except for the gentle push of the water against the dam, the surface remained undisturbed.

Bird song and insect talk accompanied Sarah and Al as they walked toward the memorials. Al pointed to the far end of the lake at a fast moving storm and brushed a mosquito off Sarah's arm, leaving a thin trail of blood. Sarah's skin prickled where his fingers held her forearm and rubbed the spot with his handkerchief. Warmed by the sun, they stood watching as the distant storm, blown into a furious black mass by an unseen wind, released torrents of rain and shrouded the distant landscape with cloud-clogged air before moving on to its business elsewhere.

Sarah was left breathless by the speed at which the storm came and went. Had JoBeth's decision to let the car roll into the water happened as quickly as the storm passing over the lake? Had she watched, horrified and unable to stop what she'd set in motion? Or like the clouds, had JoBeth been so bunched up that there was nothing else to do than release her fury and change her life forever?

Al nudged Sarah's arm and led the way across the rocky beach toward the granite monument. The inscription promised that the children, carried heavenward by angels, were now resting safely in the hands of God. Sarah and Al stood frozen, like deer at an unexpected sound, starring at the polished surface. She tried to connect the words with the lives lost, but was unable to make sense of what she was reading. It was difficult enough for her to believe that they were dead, without trying to visualize an actual ascension into heaven flanked by angels.

"Do you believe that?" she asked, pointing to the words inscribed on the memorial.

"Believe what?"

"That Daniel and Casey were carried to heaven by angels; that they're now resting in the hands of God."

"I guess," he said.

His off-hand remark diminished their deaths. She wanted to shake him, make him seriously consider what she was saying, that the image of the children in the hands of angels somehow took away the horror of what happened to them. "You guess what?" she asked.

"I suppose you don't."

"I don't," she answered firmly. "That requires a suspension of reason that isn't possible for me. Why do so many buy into such nonsense?"

"It gives them comfort."

She'd expect such platitudes from her mother. But Al? Shouldn't he be more rational? He started back to the car but Sarah remained behind, staring at the memorials.

Nietzsche was right. Words, once written, become an immutable part of how we understand the world. Write down angels and heaven on enough memorials and they become an unquestioned part of the community's belief system. And if someone questions the veracity of the words, the challenged fall back on "comforting." For Sarah, there was little consolation in such words. She looked about. Everything was far from comforting, the grass growing up untidily between the stones in the parking lot, the cigarette butts thrown carelessly about, the bits of paper blown against the flowers, teddy bears, and candles left as remembrances.

Sarah continued to think of the children as she last saw them, alive and growing, living in a building that looked more like a motel than an apartment house, its front doors facing a covered parking lot. Dying geraniums interspersed with milk weed and dandelions filled the window boxes. The parking lot was empty except for an old Ford parked near the fence, a sign on its windshield advertised "parts—for sale." As a cheerful afterthought, the Ruland's door had been painted fire-engine red.

During that visit Casey had been sitting on JoBeth's lap, nested against her mother, fingering a blanket, sucking her thumb, and eyeing Sarah shyly. She was barefoot and her toes were pudgy lumps of clay. Daniel was crawling about on his bedroom floor, noisily imitating a siren as he played with his Lego police car, calling his mother to come look, interrupting with requests for juice and cookies. He wore blue jeans rolled at the ankles and dirty white tennis shoes, the laces tied in bulky double knots.

"Get some right away, Little Treasure." That's what JoBeth called Daniel. She said she found that name in a novel about China she was reading when she was pregnant. "You know, I wish I'd been more like you when we were in high school," JoBeth had told Sarah. "More serious about my studies. I should have waited to get married."

"But look at what you have," Sarah had reminded her. "These two small ones. Sometimes I envy you. I think I might be like my namesake. It took her 80 years and an intervention by God before she could have a child."

JoBeth looked down at Casey, patting her head, kissing her fat cheek, nuzzling her sparse, blonde hair. Casey closed her eyes, pulled the blanket up to her chin, and snuggled more deeply against her mother.

"I adore them, but I'm in a restless state all the time. Phillip is never home and I'm lonely. I need to be out among people. My step-daddy spends more time with these children than their own daddy. The fact is, he's with them so much of the time anyone'd think they was his instead of Phillip's."

The thought of Howard around the children made Sarah's skin crawl. What if they were his? Or what if he thought they were his? Sarah searched her memory of Casey's face to see if there was any resemblance to Howard.

"Let's go over to the boat ramp," Al called from the car. She turned from the monument and joined him.

Sarah was lost in thought on the long drive to Star's Crossing. How does a mother decide to kill her kids? Does she plan it carefully, as one does a long vacation, or is it a spur of the moment thing, like a good idea? Was she filled with remorse at the thought of what she had done, or did she feel a sense of relief? But relief from what?

At the Star's Crossing turnoff, she carefully navigated the car onto the heavily shaded dirt road that led to the boat ramp and worried that Al might think she was driving like an old woman. Spots of sunlight danced on and off the hood as they passed from shade to sun and insects smacked against the windshield leaving hundreds of miniature Rorschach figures.

At the boat ramp Al walked toward the lake, scribbling notes on a small pad. Sarah followed slowly, wondering if she should have been so blunt about her opinions earlier. She joined him at the point where the ramp began to descend into the lake.

"JoBeth must have stopped the car here," he said, pointing to the lip of the boat ramp. "The back wheels were probably at the edge where the incline begins. She must have stepped out, released the brake, and let the car roll into the water." His finger followed the path the car must have taken.

"Did she tell you that?" Sarah asked.

"No, she insists she has a kind of amnesia. Even when I tell her that it will be difficult to use loss of memory as a defense, she sticks to it. Right now, I'm guessing."

"Then how do you know she stepped out and released the brake?" He was too smug for his own good. But things had gone well the last two days. No reason to upset things any more than she already had by her strident discussion back at the memorials. And then, there was Al's advice from the night before. She was JoBeth's attorney now, not her friend.

But still, she couldn't believe JoBeth had intentionally come to this place to murder her children. The scene was so bucolic. Surely, if murder had been committed here there would be some tell-tale sign. She tried to conjure up a mental picture of JoBeth standing, watching the car roll into the water, knowing that her children were going to drown, but her mind rebelled. It seemed more like a bad plot in a detective novel than something that had actually happened.

"Maybe the car got went of control and she jumped out, thinking she could save herself and the children," Sarah countered. "Maybe she stepped out for a breath of air and the car got away from her and she tried, but couldn't stop it. Maybe the whole thing was a terrible accident."

"The fifty or so yards the car traveled before it reached the bottom of the lake indicates that the car rolled into the water very slowly," Al said, ignoring her suppositions. "Forensics has that all figured out."

"Then you don't think it could have been an accident?"

"Could have been, but I don't think so."

"What makes you so sure?"

"Because she hasn't said it was an accident. Wouldn't she have told the sheriff right away?"

He was right, of course. If it had been an accident, JoBeth would have said something. "But still—watching the children drown might have left her so traumatized that she was unable to explain or even remember how it all happened."

"Nice thought," Al mused. He searched Sarah's face, then wrote on his pad.

"If you're so sure it was intentional, then why do you think she did it?"

"Deep depression. Maybe even crazy."

"Crazy. That's a meaningless answer," Sarah protested. "Whenever a horrific crime is committed, everyone assumes the perpetrator is crazy. It's the only way we seem to be able to deal with such an irrational act."

"What other reason is there?"

"Revenge?" She didn't think JoBeth did it for revenge, but that was the only idea that immediately came to mind.

"Isn't killing your children for revenge a form of craziness?"

"Can't a person be so damaged that whatever it is inside her that normally prevents deviant behavior no longer works?"

"Interesting, the word damaged," Al said. "But I ask again, isn't that another way of saying crazy? And if she is defined as damaged, does that make the crime any less reprehensible or her any less responsible? The DA will find someone who will say that, despite her emotional circumstances, she knew right from wrong."

"No use talking about this," Sarah grumped.

She was being prissy. But Al was unwilling to consider anything other than his own point of view. She wanted him to at least acknowledge that her idea had possibilities. He really was like her father. So damn sure of himself. Silently, she followed him to the car.

"Home or the office?" Sarah asked shortly as they drove away from the boat ramp.

"Home. Want to do dinner?"

"Mac and cheese again?"

He shook his head and looked away.

"Sorry, but I have plans for this evening," she said. "Thanks though. Let's do it again sometime. I might develop a taste for your cooking."

Sarah dropped him at his apartment, left the car at her house, and walked to the office. She had to complete the Channing report so Janet would have it first thing on Monday. The light was on in Clayton's office. She walked down the hall and poked her head in.

"Hey, Clayton, what are you doing in the office on Saturday?"

"Just trying to get away from my wife's honey-do list." He reached into his desk drawer, pulled out a cigar and lit it. "You got here just in time for my afternoon break."

"I think you like me to come down here just so you can smoke," Sarah teased. She eased herself into one of the Queen Anne's chairs. "Al and I went to the lake today to look around."

"Heard you were at his place Friday night."

Sarah flushed. How did he know? She searched for some sassy reply but none came.

"Discover anything at the lake? About the murder I mean." Clayton looked at her over his cigar and gave her a sly wink. He was teasing but he touched a soft nerve. Her hand swept over her arm where Al's fingers had tightened when he wiped away the blood from the mosquito bite.

"Al took notes, I supplied the ride. It was sad being at the place where it happened. I thought JoBeth loved those kids."

"People kill for love, don't they?"

Clayton inhaled and blew smoke at the ceiling. He was playing Socrates, and she liked it. She wanted to examine all the possible reasons, tear them apart, and piece them together into something that, if not exonerating JoBeth, at least made sense so that everyone would understand why it happened. It was a game Al had refused to play.

"I don't know," she replied. "JoBeth killed those she loved, but killing for love? I'm not so sure. Perhaps it is the pain of love that drove her into irrational behavior."

"Is there a difference?" Clayton asked.

"Intuitively, I'd have to say it doesn't seem to be the same thing. I guess if you kill someone you love, the act could be an accident."

"Yes, I suppose so."

"But if you kill for love or for the pain of loving, it might involve vengeance, even premeditation. The first could be unintentional. Not the second."

"You might have something there." Clayton rolled the cigar in the ash tray. "Maybe we'll find out by the end of the trial."

"I'd like to think so. Got to go. A dinner date. And not with Al so don't get excited."

Sarah returned to her office doubting that, even by the end of the trial, anyone would know how JoBeth came to murder her kids because everyone was so certain JoBeth was crazy. She completed the final edits, ran off the Channing report, and placed it on Janet's desk.

"I'm leaving," she called down the hall to Clayton. "Better get home and get at that honey-do list. Remember, happy wife, happy life." The chuckle she heard from Clayton's office made her smile.

At home, she changed for her dinner date with the Hillyard family. She'd let Jameson's invitation ride, so now she was obligated to go. This was not occasion she wanted to over dress for; it might send the wrong message. She chose a dress she had set aside for the Goodwill box. When she came downstairs, Chewie was waiting with her leash in mouth.

"Sorry. In the morning, I promise." The dog's dish was full. "Not hungry, girl?" She licked her lips at the treat Sarah held out but turned away. She touched Chewie's nose to see if it was warm. "What's the matter girl?" The dog circled, sighed, and dropped heavily onto her bed.

Sarah picked up the morning newspaper. News about the murders had moved from the front page to the end of the second section. The only item related to the trial in the first section was an interview with the DA. It portrayed Dunning as a formidable opponent. He'd earned his degree at Yale, served on the *Law Review*, interned at the appeals court level. Did Al's biography stand up to Dunning's? What if JoBeth's defense team was inadequate? She glanced at the clock. Better leave for the Hillyards. She'd make up for her lack of enthusiasm by being on time and scrupulously polite. She gave Chewie a quick pat and left.

The Hillyards lived a few blocks from Sarah's home in a white, two-story farm house set in a thicket of beech and oak trees. The door was opened by a freckled boy about seven with a cast on his leg and braces on his teeth. Leaning on his crutches, he lisped, "Jameson's girlfriend's here," and disappeared into the interior.

"That's my cousin, Arnold," Jameson explained. "My aunt sends him down from Baltimore every summer. Come in." Jameson, looking not-quite-right without his pharmacy coat, stood back as Sarah entered the darkened hallway. He took her purse and hung it over his arm. It made him look less appealing than usual.

"What happened to his leg?" Sarah asked.

"Broke it climbing the oak out back. He's getting to be a handful but my folks enjoy having him, especially Momma. She says he keeps her young."

A man reading the paper looked up when they entered the living room. Before Jameson could introduce his father, Mrs. Hillyard bustled in, wiping her hands on her apron. Sarah winced under the intense look mothers give someone they suspect might be interested in their sons. Hanna, Jameson's younger sister, glided languidly after her mother, tucked herself under her brother's arm, and whispered a greeting to Sarah. She didn't catch it all. Something about how nice of you. Arnold's crutches thumped as he moved about the house.

Mr. Hillyard folded his newspaper. "Dinner ready?" he asked.

"We expected you earlier," Mrs. Hillyard said to Sarah calling attention to the clock, its hand a few minutes past the half hour. "Everything's ready to be put out on the table. We don't want it to be getting cold now, do we?" Sarah followed her hostess into the dining room. "You sit there, next to Jameson," Mrs. Hillyard directed. "Hanna, you're next to Arnold." She pointed to each chair as she spoke.

Mr. Hillyard took his seat at the head of a massive mahogany table that dwarfed the room. His hair, like Jameson's, was red and his shaggy eyebrows made him look as though he was viewing the world from behind a tangle of barbed wire. He shook his napkin and turned to Sarah.

"How's your father? Still busy at the plant?"

"Always," Sarah answered.

"Bring that roast in here before it gets cold," he shouted after his wife who had gone into the kitchen. "Hanna, tell that youngster to sit still," he added irritably.

Arnold, sitting across from Sarah, ogled her from behind his glasses and flashed her with his braces. Mrs. Hillyard returned with the roast beef, placed it before her husband, and took the seat opposite him. The band on her gold watch cut deeply into the fatty roll hiding her wrist, making her hand look as though it was attached directly to her arm. Sarah was reminded of a baby doll she had as a child. Rubbery, with no wrists, and able to wet her pants when fed water from a tiny bottle.

Mrs. Hillyard's voice jolted her back to the table. "Jameson tells me you're going to be a lawyer." She drew her chair closer to the table, and pressed her lips together.

"I just finished my second year."

"Will you work at Williams place when you finish?"

"They don't practice the kind of law I'm interested in. I may have to look for a job elsewhere."

Mr. Hillyard stood to carve the roast. The blood ran down the grooves in the carving board and pooled in the depression at one end. Arnold stuck the round end of his fork into his ear, let it dangle, and rocked his head side-to-side so that the fork swayed. Sure that Sarah was watching, he crossed his eyes, and let his hands waggle over his plate.

"Arnold, you stop that now. Lord Amighty, you'll puncture your ear and go deaf." She grabbed his fork and set it on the table, letting out a hefty gust of air.

"Boys will be boys," Sarah mumbled.

Mrs. Hillyard nodded. "Chicago," she said, "That's too big a place for a single lady to be living by herself, isn't it?"

"Now Momma," Jameson said, "she's been living in Chicago for a long time. How long Sarah?"

"Six years."

"I'd never live in Chicago," Hanna said, returning from the kitchen and handing a plate of hot rolls to her mother. She wriggled a bit, settled her butt into the chair, and gave one of those self-satisfied looks that made Sarah's want to gag.

I'll bet you wouldn't, Sarah thought. She glanced at Mr. Hillyard. He was the only one at the table who didn't give a damn whether she was there or not. As if on cue, Arnold rolled his napkin into a spiral and stuck one end up his nose. He grunted to attract Sarah's attention. Mrs. Hillyard slapped his hand.

"You can't trust strangers up there," Mrs. Hillyard persisted. "And a body knows, it's not a place to find a husband."

"I haven't had time to think about that."

"You better, my dear. You're not getting any younger. Just the other day, I was telling Jameson ..."

"Now, Momma, she has plenty of time," Jameson stopped her. "Don't you Sarah?"

One thing about Jameson. He didn't let her hang out to dry. She should have been pleased by his defense, but couldn't warm up to him. Too bad. Her mother would love it if she worked with Williams, married an established business man, and brought the family for dinner every Friday night. She would be so happy, she wouldn't even comment on Jameson's lazy eye. And her father, he'd enjoy spending every Friday night chewing up his son-in-law and spitting him out.

"All I can say is that I want to marry while I'm still young, as soon as I finish college," Hanna said. "Have kids right away so my husband and I can grow up with them. Just like Momma did. Right, Momma?"

"Hanna's only in high school but she she's smart enough to know what she wants." Mrs. Hillyard looked to Sarah for approval.

The carving completed, Mr. Hillyard asked each person which they preferred, medium or rare and filled each plate with great slices of beef.

"Hanna," Mrs. Hillyard said to her daughter, "don't just sit there. Pass those sweet potatoes along to our guest."

"How's the trial going?" Jameson asked.

"Slowly."

"It's a frightful thing when someone like Williams thinks he can actually save that woman," Mrs. Hillyard said. A forkful of string beans hung midway between her plate and her mouth.

"The law guarantees that everyone deserves a defense, no matter how horrible the crime, even the crime of murdering one's own children." Legalese, but safe.

"I'd say save the taxpayers' money and put her right to death," Mrs. Hillyard said. "My word, the gravy is going cold already. Hanna, go heat this up."

To defend JoBeth was useless, but it was difficult listening to Mrs. Hillyard pass judgment. Her voice droned on like a fly caught between the window pane and screen. Sarah ate in silence, nodding occasionally. Hanna watched her like a cat waiting outside a mouse hole, and Mr. Hillyard concentrated his food.

"Now, Momma," Jameson kept whispering every so often, but Mrs. Hillyard prattled on.

After he finished his dessert, Mr. Hillyard rose. "Tell your father hello," he said, and escaped to the living room. Mrs. Hillyard took another piece of pie. "This is too good to be going to waste," she said as she topped it with whipped cream. Hanna went upstairs and Arnold tried to wink but couldn't quite get it. Sarah stared at a lump of sweet potatoes hardening on the tablecloth and wondered how she could gracefully leave.

"Maybe we could go to a movie," Jameson said.

"Nothing but killing in the movies these days," Mrs. Hillyard observed. "Why would anyone want to see that kind of thing?"

"Some other time, maybe," Sarah answered. "We were at the lake all day and it was awful, seeing the spot, well, you know ..." She looked away from Jameson's pleading eyes. "I really need to get going."

"Can I walk you home?"

He was always so damned agreeable. "Thanks, but I have to stop by the office to pick up some work. It'll take me awhile to get it together."

"We'll have to do this again," he said as Sarah headed toward the front door.

"Perhaps. But we're really swamped. Don't take it personally if I can't make it."

She hurried down the steps.

Jameson called after her. "Momma says you're welcome anytime."

She looked back and gave him a noncommittal smile. He was squatted on the top step, looking as though he would leap down at the slightest signal to join her.

It felt good to be released, out from under Mrs. Hillyard's disapproving eye and Jameson's oppressive presence. Not ready to go home, she walked down Main Street. Although it was almost nine o'clock, the temperature hadn't dropped and the air had taken on a spongy feeling. The moon, past full and shrouded in a misty glow, warned that it was going to be hot the next day.

Sarah felt lonely. Really, there was nothing to go home for. Her father, while not so outwardly disapproving, had retreated into a distant moodiness. Her mother, always eager to talk, lingered on the happier days of Sarah's childhood. Now that she was no longer the center of her parent's lives, perhaps things between them were coming unraveled. Were her parents subconsciously resenting the loss of her childhood? But wasn't that the plan? To have her grow up and become her own person?

Although the evening with the Hillyards reminded her of a poorly written sit-com episode, she had to admit that they had a cohesiveness that united them and a degree of certainty that bound their lives into a neat package. Jameson destined to take over the family business, and Hanna already planning her life's course on the pattern set by her mother. Mrs. Hillyard would remain the opinion-maker and Mr. Hillyard would carve the roasts and bury himself in the newspaper, always present but seldom involved. And Arnold, his summer visits forever providing the comic relief to an otherwise mundane life. Perhaps JoBeth was right, throw your lot in with the group, obey the rules and hope for the best. It didn't work out so well for her, but that's how the herd survives.

She'd been home for almost a month but still had no friends. If Marney were here, she'd have someone to distract her. She'd not be so whacked out over Al. Maybe she'd ask Janet to dinner. Unlike the Hillyards and Weebers, she and Janet had something in common. And she might have some inside scoop on Al. Could make an interesting evening.

"Sarah, Sarah Wasser. Wait up." Al, tieless, his shirt sleeves rolled to the elbow, and his suit coat over his arm hurried toward her from the doorway of the Agusta Hotel. She stopped and waited. "What're you doing out by yourself so late at night?"

"And what are you doing following me?"

He threw his head back and surprised her with a hearty laugh. It was annoying that her suggestion hadn't taken him off stride. He took her arm and turned her toward the hotel door.

"Come on, let's have a drink. It's Saturday night."

This would be a great opportunity to tell him to tap dance all the way home by himself but she had nowhere else to go. He steered her toward the bar at the back of the lobby and held the chair until she was seated. The bar tender nodded to Al. Except for two men in the far corner, they were alone.

Al handed her a menu. He seemed to be scrutinizing her face. Why hadn't she worn make up, polished her nails, anything that made her look different than everyday-Sarah-at-the-office in a dress taken from the Goodwill box? Annoyed, she glanced around, feigning interest in the surroundings. It wasn't like her to be concerned about her looks.

"What'll you have to drink?" Al asked.

"White wine, a chardonnay. No, wait. A gin and tonic."

"Back so soon, Al?" The waitress held a tray in one hand and placed the other on Al's shoulder. Something passed between them; a pang of possessiveness gripped Sarah. She looked down and examined her fingernails.

"Two gin and tonics, Megan. Make them doubles."

Sarah watched the waitress saunter back to the bar, trying to shrug off the feeling that Al belonged to the office and, by extension, to her. "Did you see Ian Dunning's bio in the newspaper?"

Al nodded.

"What do you think?"

"Impressive."

"Do you think he'll be a tough opponent?"

"I'd be disappointed if he wasn't."

Megan returned with their drinks. "Running a tab?" she asked. She was bent over, almost eye level with Al.

"Not tonight." Megan gave him a private smile that excluded Sarah.

"What were you doing out tonight?" Al asked. He stirred his drink with a swizzle stick, but kept his eyes on her face.

She pushed some stray hair behind her ear with her forefinger and cleared her throat. "I told you I had a dinner invitation. It was at the

Hillyards."

Al nodded.

"They own the drug store here in town." She sipped her drink, waiting for him to say something. She gave in. "I went to high school with their son, Jameson."

Al held up his glass and looked at the light through it.

"You should meet the nephew, Arnold. He was a kick. Made the whole evening worthwhile."

Al raised his eyebrows. His shirt was open at the neck and she could see some black hair escaping the top of his undershirt. She wondered if his chest was covered and imagined what it might feel like to lay her cheek against it.

"What about Arnold?" he asked.

She tore her mind away from the image of Al's chest and described Arnold's exaggerated attempts to get her attention. They laughed, agreed that the nephew was the most interesting person in the family and talked about overbearing mothers and sons who had trouble leaving the nest. Her glass was empty and he asked if she wanted another drink.

"No thanks." She didn't want the evening to end but she didn't want another drink, either.

Al threw some bills on the table. "Monday, don't forget. JoBeth, at nine. See what you can get out of her about this molesting thing." He stood behind her chair. "Let's go."

He didn't ask if he could walk her home and she didn't say it wasn't necessary when she understood his intention. At her house, Al turned up the front walk.

"We always go in the back way." She pointed to the side where the rhododendron bushes overlapped the driveway, their purple color subdued by the darkness. Al broke off a small bunch of blossoms.

When Sarah reached for the key to the back door, he took her shoulders and lightly brushed her lips with his.

She stiffened. "It's been a long time since anyone has done that," she blurted.

Al smiled, undid the clip that held her unruly hair, arranged it about her shoulders, and pushed the flowers through the tight curls above her ear.

"I wondered what that hair looked like when it wasn't tied up in a knot." He placed the clip in her hand and closed her fingers around it. "Good night, Sarah. And don't forget Monday. Be on time."

Her glasses steamed as she watched him stroll down the driveway, his hands in his pockets. She took off her glasses and wiped them with her dress. Untamed thoughts urged her to run after him and demand an explanation. Why did he kiss her? Would this change their professional relationship? Al reached the end of the driveway and disappeared.

You goof-ball, she chastised herself. He kissed you as he would have kissed his little sister. One drink, one kiss and you're in fantasy land. Still, she curled up in bed that night and, like a love-struck teenager, relived that kiss again and again until she fell asleep.

Chapter Ten

*S*arah stared at the list of questions she had prepared to ask JoBeth while she waited for her to appear but she couldn't bring the words into focus. This wasn't going to be easy—jumping right into the sensitive topic of Howard. Despite what Al expected, this couldn't be all business, not after having been JoBeth's best friend. Go slow. Wait to see how she responds. The door to the interview room opened and the deputy walked JoBeth to the table.

She fell into the chair and glanced about the room. Her uncombed brown hair, already graying along the hairline on her forehead, hung listlessly about her shoulders. Dark circles hemmed her eyes and worry lines were etched into the pale skin on her forehead. Without makeup, she appeared older, worn, and tired. Sarah wanted to reach across the table and take her hand but touching was prohibited.

"I'll be right outside the door. Call if you need me," the deputy instructed. The door closed heavily behind him.

Weird how things change. A few years ago, she and JoBeth were sharing confidences, planning their lives, looking forward to the future. Now, there was more than a table between them: Sarah's life in academia, JoBeth's failed marriage, and the murders. They were no longer just friends, JoBeth was the defendant, Sarah her defender.

Sarah smiled, and tried to make eye contact. "How are you JoBeth?"

JoBeth, avoiding Sarah's gaze, reached into her coveralls and pulled up her bra strap, a gesture that brought back high school. She had always said that her shoulders were too narrow to carry the burden of her big boobs. The gesture blindsided Sarah, shaking her professional exterior. It took several seconds to regain her footing.

"It's good to see you, JoBeth."

She looked up quizzically. Moisture glazed her cheeks. Sarah pushed a box of tissues to the center of the table and took a note pad and pencil from her briefcase.

"Did you get the magazines we sent over?" she asked.

JoBeth sat mute, concentrating on her finger nails.

"You know, I'm working with the defense team."

She nodded.

Sarah decided to jump right in. "I need to ask you about the complaint you made against your stepfather. In the seventh grade, wasn't it? It might help if you're able to tell me something about it."

JoBeth wiped her face with the collar of her prison coveralls. "Nothing can help me now," she mumbled and covered her eyes with her hands.

"Remember how you used to tell me about your problems in algebra and geometry? You always came to me for help back then, and we always got you through the tough stuff. If you talk to me now about what happened with Howard, John-Two and Al will have a better chance at working up your defense."

JoBeth's hands dropped away from her face. "Why are you asking me about my step-daddy?" Is that lawyer talking behind my back, too?"

"No one seems to know much about what happened. Besides, if there's anything to tell, I'd much rather hear it from you than from a bunch of lawyers."

"They can see us, you know," JoBeth said, pointing to the camera placed in one corner of the room.

"Please, JoBeth. You can still trust me. What happened?"

JoBeth slumped, looked at the far wall behind Sarah, and retreated into her memories. Her tear-filled eyes were half closed and her hands gripped the edge of the table. Sarah searched for something to penetrate JoBeth's sadness.

"Do you remember the time we broke into that old kudzu-covered shack? I ripped my brand new pants on the broken window sill and you were so scared you wouldn't let go of my hand."

"Yeah." JoBeth brightened a bit.

"It was for history class. Something about early settlers in this area. We thought that old shack was full of secrets." Encouraged by a smile that crept onto JoBeth's lips, Sarah said, "Please tell me about the complaint?"

"I don't have anything left. My marriage is done. My children are gone." Tears came to her eyes once more.

"You still have your life and I want you to fight for it."

She looked at Sarah, then up at the camera peering down at her. "Can they lip read?"

"Go on, JoBeth," Sarah coaxed. Tell me how it started?"

"When my momma and me moved into my step-daddy's house over on Middleford." Her voice was small and tiny, like a small child. "Ya'll know the one, the biggest house on that old street."

"Go on," Sarah said.

"Momma said, 'Little Darlin, we're going to be real happy here.' We had a housekeeper and Momma never had to touch a vacuum cleaner. I had my own bedroom. Momma wanted me to sleep in the room next to her in case I needed something at night, but my step-daddy said that the bedroom at the end of the hall was for me because I was already a big girl and needed a big girl's room."

"How old were you?"

"Almost seven. And right from the start, my step-daddy loved me. He was always hugging and petting me like I was his favorite little kitty. My momma kept telling me your step-daddy loves you like you was his real daughter."

"Remind me about the bedroom your stepfather chose for you."

"It had windows that overlooked that big old side lawn. It had a closet I could walk into and a grown-up bed that I didn't have to share with momma. And there was a mirror so big that, if I stood on a chair, I could see myself in it all at once."

"What happened to you in that bed?" Sarah asked.

"What are you talking about?" JoBeth's eyes became cloaked with suspicion.

"Did someone come to your room at night?"

JoBeth slowly traced her finger back and forth along the edge of the table, staring intently at it as it moved. Dirt, ingrained in the table, came off in small black rolls and dropped to the floor. JoBeth jiggled her foot. Sarah could feel the tremor through the table.

"One night, one side of that big bed moved down the way it does when someone sits on it. Like when you're sick and your momma comes to take your temperature. The shades had been pulled. It was dark and I couldn't see. I tried to call my momma but my voice got stuck, like it was too scared to come out." She paused. Her foot jiggled faster.

"Did you know who it was?" Sarah asked quietly.

JoBeth rocked slowly from side-to-side, eyeing Sarah with a half-lidded gaze. She seemed to be retreating, her voice took on a muffled tone, sounding as if she was speaking through a gauze mask. "I couldn't see. I told you, the shades were pulled and it was real dark."

"Did something happen?"

"Something brushed against my arm, something with hair on it."

"Who was it?" Sarah prodded.

JoBeth giggled. "I thought it was the lion come out of the wardrobe to take me way to Narnia. Just like Lucy, the little girl in the book."

"Yes, I remember that story."

"The lion lay next to me, holding me close, saying shhh, shhh, shhh, you know the way lions do when they're happy and purr like kittens. He rubbed my tummy. Gentle like. I couldn't even feel his claws, that's how gentle he was. He touched me where my momma always told me that I shouldn't touch except after I pee because it was bad to do that." She stopped talking, took a tissue and shredded it. "I tried to reach up to find his hairy mane, but the lion took my hand and held it against his body. He rubbed my hand against him all over, not purring anymore, just making little grunts like he was a pig instead of a lion. I wanted to laugh, but I thought if I did, I would scare him away and I wouldn't get to Narnia."

"What happened after that?"

"He went back into the wardrobe."

"Did you tell your mother?"

"Yeah. She got awful mad and said 'My, my, what a great big imagination for such a little bitty girl.' I said, No, it was real." But she just waved her hand and said things like there wasn't no wardrobe in that room and that I wouldn't know a wardrobe if I saw one."

"When did you find out that it wasn't a lion that came to visit you?"

"Not for a long time. Up until then, we just rubbed on each other, making each other feel good. I kept telling my momma, but she kept getting mad and saying I was dreaming."

"What changed?"

"When he tried to put his thing inside me. It hurt, and when I reached to push him away, he spoke for the first time. That's when I knew it was my step-daddy, not the lion come to take me to Narnia, and I started to cry, tried to call out, ask him what he was doing, but he put his hand over my mouth saying shhh, shhh. He whispered that this was something he did only with people he loved, that he loved me, really loved me. Loved me more than he loved my momma. Now that was something, wasn't it?

Loved me more than my momma, that's what he said. When he left, he told me not to tell. He said that I was old enough to have such a big girl secret."

"Did you tell your mother what happened?"

"I started to. I said that Daddy came to my room last night."

"What did she say?"

"You're dreaming."

"How did it feel when she wouldn't listen?"

"It wasn't no big deal. All I knew was that my step-daddy kept telling me that he loved me and that everything would be all right if I kept our secret."

"When did you decide to go to the school nurse?"

"When I was in the seventh grade. I started to bleed and I got real scared. I thought I was going to die, so I told the nurse that I was bleeding because of what my step-daddy was doing to me. She took me to the principal's office and he called my momma."

"What happened?"

JoBeth's face tightened, her voice became harsh and belligerent. "It was a bad mistake."

"Why?"

"They had some kind of meeting. My momma told them I had started to menstruate, that the bleeding had nothing to do with my step-daddy, and she told them about the lion dreams I was having. She said everybody at the meeting agreed that I was sexually advanced for my age and that I would grow out of my fantasies. That's what they called it, fantasies. My momma warned me never to say anything more about it and I never did."

"After the meeting, did the nurse ever talk to you about what happened?"

"Yes, she explained that I might be menstruating. I was too ashamed to ask her what that was. When I asked Momma about menstruating she said don't worry, you'll find out some day."

"Did your stepfather ever talk to you about what was happening?"

"He told me to pay them no mind, that he loved me and that I was his very own best friend, and that we would be together forever. After that, he always brought me chocolates when he came to me. Not the skinny candy bars you buy down at Bi-Lo, either. He brought those big thick bars wrapped in fancy paper that came all the way from Belgium. He had the candy store down in Myrtle Beach send them directly to me. He's the sweetest man you could ever meet, Sarah."

Oh, god. Candy bars. Sarah drew a breath and continued. "How long did this go on?"

"Forever." JoBeth stopped, covered her face with her hands. When she looked up, she said, "I know this is hard to believe, but my step-daddy said it was right thing for me to marry Phillip. That way, I could have babies. But he said that no matter what, I would always be his special friend. And I was. His special friend. He never left me. He always loved me."

"You continued to see Howard during high school and after you married?"

"High school. But not while I was married. Only after Phillip left." JoBeth gave Sarah a sly glance. "You have to understand. My step-daddy says he can't live without me."

"Did he take you on trips?"

"We went to motels. He has plenty of money and he just loves spending it on me."

"Where did you go?"

"To some pretty snazzy places. That's the actual truth. It was like we was going on vacation every time. Swimming pools, fancy restaurants, tennis courts. I liked pretending I was there with my rich husband and could swim and play tennis any old time I wanted. We never did, of course. Mostly, we stayed inside. My step-daddy liked to order room service. I never had room service before. It was something else. Sitting in bed, eating, and watching TV."

"Who took care of Daniel and Casey?"

"Oh, they were just fine. Mrs. Sequieda, the lady next door, didn't have a car, so I took her to BiLo's every time I went. She baby sat as a favor. She was good to those little ones." Tears came to JoBeth's eyes, she reached out to Sarah. "Oh God, what did I do?"

Sarah spoke quickly, trying to divert JoBeth. "Can you remember which motels?"

"One that had one of those hot tubs right in the room. You know the kind, with water shooting out of the jets all around the sides. We put in bubble bath and did all sorts of things in that tub. You should've seen the foam. My step-daddy kept ducking under the water and coming up with a head full of soap bubbles. He said he was the lion from the wardrobe." JoBeth startled Sarah by laughing outright.

"Do you remember the name of that motel and where it was?"

"That one I really remember. I always wanted to go back, but we never did."

"What was the name of it?" Sarah prodded.

"The Double Experience Motel, a real classy place near Charlotte." JoBeth closed her eyes and spoke softly. "It had a bright red bedspread, free bottles of shampoo and lotion in the bathroom, and mirrors on the ceiling. I took home all those little bottles of shampoo and stuff as souvenirs. We drove a long way to get there. My step-daddy never did mind driving.He'd say we're going to our trysting place and drive and drive. That's what he called it. Our trysting place. Sounds secret, doesn't it? I sat close to him, sometimes he'd unzip his pants and, you know, put my hand on it. I liked sitting there, holding it, and driving along."

Disgust swelled Sarah's stomach and acid burned her throat; its bitterness lined her mouth. She reached for a tissue and wiped her lips. JoBeth had changed from a frightened child reduced to fantasies to a grown woman who derived pleasure from an illicit sexual relationship. Something else law school hadn't prepared her for, how capricious human behavior can be. If JoBeth recounted these episodes on the witness stand, the jury's reaction would be predictable.

Full of impressions of the meeting with JoBeth, Sarah found herself at the office without remembering the walk back from the jail. Janet greeted her with her usual smile. Sarah, eager to see how Al would react toward her after last night's kiss, immediately asked to see him.

"He's gone for a few days. Business in Columbia. Is there something I can help you with?" Janet stopped typing and waited for Sarah's answer.

Strange he hadn't told her. He had plenty of time to say something last night. She lowered her head, sure that her feelings were visible and that Janet could see how much that one, insignificant kiss had affected her. She placed her briefcase on Janet's desk, compelled to offer evidence that she actually had something to show other than her sappy behavior. "No. I just wanted to brief him on my meeting with JoBeth."

"John-Two will be in soon. Why don't you meet with him? I'll tell him you have something you want to discuss."

Sarah retreated to the library and threw her briefcase on the desk, knocking over the pencil caddy. A few days ago she couldn't even stand to be in the same room with the guy. A pencil shattered underfoot. She kicked it under her desk. Now she was distracted by one kiss, a kiss he has most likely forgotten. She scooped up the pencils and returned them to the caddy.

Before long, Janet called to say John-Two was in. As soon as Sarah entered his office, she handed him her typed notes. He penciled his thoughts as he read, his cramped writing jumped above and below the blue lines of the yellow pad. When finished, he reread everything, and nodded his approval.

"What was she like during the interview," he asked.

"Nervous at first, then childish and wispy. Cried some. Changed from poignant fantasies about her childhood to actually relishing the memories of the motel encounters. Watching her change in a short time from an innocent victim to a sensuous adult was quite an experience."

"Seems we have enough to put Howard and JoBeth together. If only we had hard evidence of the complaint she made to the school nurse. That would help make the case for victimization, maybe enough to create doubt in the jury's mind that she intended to murder her children. Al will be happy. Good job, young lady."

She gathered her papers, placed them in her briefcase, and stood.

"Wait. I'd like your opinion about putting JoBeth on the stand."

This was her day. Her report was well-received and now, the senior partner was soliciting her opinion. John-Two had taken out a pair of clippers and was concentrating on his nails; the clippings flew onto the desk and floor.

"It'll be difficult," she said. "No doubt she was victimized by her stepfather, her mother, and the school authorities. So far, so good. But, as she got older, she clearly began to enjoy her liaisons with Howard. After Phillip left, she continued to meet her stepfather at motels. If the prosecution gets hold of that, they'll suggest that she is not only sexually promiscuous, but an irresponsible mother."

"I suppose you're right," John-Two mused. "If we could split her in two, put the young JoBeth on the stand and send the older one off somewhere, we might let her testify." He smiled and shrugged. "But no can do. At any rate, we can't let the adult relationship go uninvestigated. If we can dig up the motel evidence, so can the DA."

"Even the young JoBeth's story has problems," Sarah added. "If we raise the school complaint, we could argue that the lion and the wardrobe was just a child's way of deceiving herself so that she could believe she wasn't doing anything wrong. However, the DA could take the same evidence and argue that JoBeth was, as her mother apparently claimed, sexually inquisitive at an early age and corrupted by her own sexual fantasies. My mother told me that many women in town believe that she solicited Howard's attentions, even when she was a young child. As unbelievably sick as that is, a jury could go down that road, also."

"Any suggestions?" John-Two asked.

"We could have the psychologist testify that JoBeth is ill, perhaps suffering from erotomania."

John-Two returned the nail clipper to the drawer. "Where did you find that word?"

"Psych101," Sarah blushed.

"I can't see a jury in this state finding her a sympathetic figure on the grounds that she's a sexual deviant. Good try though, young lady. We don't have to make that decision yet. We can put her on the stand at the last minute if it'll help. Looks like we'll have to follow Al's suggestion; go after the old man and see if we can break him."

"I don't get it, though. You'd think she'd loathe her stepfather. But she happily describes the times they were together and talks about how much he loves her. She even kept the bottles of lotions and shampoo from the motels as souvenirs. What do you make of that?"

"I'm a lawyer, not a psychiatrist. I have long ago stopped trying to figure out human nature. Just when you think you've got it right, the clients change and prove you wrong."

"You never try to figure it out?"

"In the courtroom, the facts dictate guilt or innocence and the jury decides which it is. The attorneys' creativity begins at the sentencing stage. Stick to that formula and you can go home to a good night's sleep." He opened a folder and began writing.

Before leaving, Sarah muscled up enough courage to ask him why Al had gone to the capital.

John-Two spoke without looking up. "He's talking to a firm in Columbia about jury selection."

"When will he be back?"

"Ask Janet."

It was clear that John-Two didn't give two hoots about her or any of her interests outside the case, and that he probably didn't care anymore about her as a person than he did about JoBeth. It was all business to him. Anyway, it wasn't all bad. He did treat her as a colleague this morning, even her half-assed idea about erotomania.

When she took Sarah's notes to prepare for Al, Janet said, "Wait, I have something for you." She pulled a piece of paper from under the desk blotter. "Al liked your suggestion. After court on Friday, he wants you to interview Bendhurst. You'll have to drive up to Charlotte."

"Thanks." Sarah hesitated. Maybe this was a good time to get to know Janet better. "Are you free this evening?" she asked. "How about dinner?"

"Sounds like fun," she said. "It's about time the girls had a night out."

"The Pinker Dot or the Agusta dining room?" Sarah asked.

"Neither. Some place much nicer than any in town. I'll drive."

Janet's Ford Festiva rounded the mountain roads with the self-command of a much more elegant car, heading northwest toward the higher Appalachia. Sarah couldn't remember if she'd been on this road before. She watched the scenery in the fading daylight, trying to identify landmarks and wishing she had brought her map so she could follow the route they were taking.

As the day ended, tiny stars hailed earth from the sky; roadside stands and houses responded with yellowed lights of their own. Darkness hid everything else. Sarah was mesmerized by the drone of the engine and the reflecting stripes sliding under the car. Road signs flashed, suddenly filled with words and numbers and, just as suddenly vanished, as if some magician had swiped them away with his wand.

"Do you eat at this place often?" Sarah asked.

"Yes, quite a bit."

Janet didn't seem to want to say anything more so Sarah let it rest. She was content to be away from home, the office, and to share the evening with someone she didn't have to impress.

They turned onto a dirt road and passed through iron gates held in place by stone walls constructed of rounded river rock. The sign embedded in the wall read "Welcome to Mountain Winery." An arrow pointed toward a building surrounded by rows of grape vines warmed by the light of carbon arc lamps. Janet stopped the car beneath an overhang draped with purple passion flowers. A red-vested valet stepped to the driver's side and greeted her by name. When they entered the restaurant, Sarah was surprised to find the dining room crowded.

"Evening, Miss Ciminio," the hostess greeted Janet and led them to a secluded table near a window that overlooked the grape vines climbing up the mountain slopes, and disappearing into the darkness. A busboy approached the table, towel over his arm, water pitcher in hand.

"Good evening, Miss Ciminio," he greeted her. "Nice to see you again."

When they were seated, Janet asked, "Okay if I order the wine?"

"Better you than me. Wine's not my strong suit." Especially since that night with her father. She wanted to remove that memory from her mind, but it wouldn't budge. Like an aging overstuffed chair, it remained in place, too heavy for her to dislodge.

"Let's have your Merlot Elderberry blend," Janet said to the waiter.

She turned to Sarah. "That's a southern specialty; you'll only find it in these mountains. One of my favorites."

Now that they were out of the office, Sarah was seeing Janet as if for the first time. She noticed her round face, tiny nose, and lively brown eyes hopping merrily about behind her rimless glasses. Instead of the black velvet band that usually kept her hair behind her ears, tonight she let it fall loosely about her face, her long silver chain earrings making an appearance only when she bent forward. She looked younger, less like an office fixture, more like someone you'd immediately notice when you entered a roomful of strangers.

"Have you always lived in Eight Mile Junction?" Sarah asked.

"I was born over in Pioneers Rest. My folks sent me up to Washington, D.C. to secretarial school. It was a compromise. My father wanted me to be educated in the North and my mother wanted me to stay in the South. They had their own civil war going on. I came back here to work for William fifteen years ago."

"Then you knew Allison."

"Wonderful woman." Janet held her wine glass up to the light. "This wine has a rich color, don't you think?"

The busboy refilled their glasses with water and delivered bread neatly wrapped in a napkin embroidered with the winery's logo. Sarah helped herself. "Mmmm, it's nice and warm." She passed the bread basket. "Clayton seems to have loved her dearly."

"They bake it here," Janet said as she took a slice. "Did Clayton tell you about John-Two and me?"

"Alluded to something about John-Two's life after Allison died, but never said anything definite. He was discreet and I didn't ask."

Janet nodded.

"Your last name isn't common in this region. We share something, you're the only Ciminio and I'm the only Wasser in the Eight Mile Junction phone book. Let's drink to that." Their wine glasses clinked. Notes of berry tingled the back of Sarah's tongue. "Not bad."

"No, there aren't many Ciminios upstate. My father came down from New York City with an engineering degree to work in the mill at Pioneers Rest. Married, had children, lived, and died here."

"And your mother?"

"In a nursing home over in South Cherokee. I see her every Sunday but she doesn't know me. My visits don't do much for her but they make me feel good."

"And you? Never married?"

"Never. Ever since Allison died, John-Two has been my only interest."

Sarah raised her eyebrows.

"I could never take Allison's place," Janet answered Sarah's quizzical look. "They grew up together and when they married, they joined the names of the town's two best families. No one could ever replace her, especially an older, unmarried, Italian Roman Catholic."

"Do folks know about you two?"

"They do. As long as we don't do anything official, they don't care. That's the way things are here. Don't flaunt it and you'll get space. But don't cross the line. That's when civility turns to cruelty and you might as well leave town."

"Doesn't it bother you? I mean, having to pretend."

"Are you thinking he should make an honest woman of me?"

"Well, I thought…"

"What makes you think I want to get married?"

Janet was more spirited than she thought. Their dinner came and they fell silent. The nasally voice of a female ballad singer snaked its way around the room, filling the air with the lonesomeness of the mountains. Al's face came to Sarah's mind, his black hair falling onto his forehead. She picked up her fork and moved her food around her plate. Her heart swelled, leaving no room in her stomach. The voice stretched the last note and the music quietly left the room. Sarah was glad to see it go.

"What do you think of Al?" Sarah asked.

"Bright. John-Two's happy he came with us. Takes a lot of pressure off him."

"I mean as a person. What's he like?"

"Not interested, are you?" Worry lines crinkled Janet's forehead.

Sarah wiped her mouth with her napkin to hide her discomfort. She had started something she couldn't finish, knew that telling Janet about being moonstruck over a friendly kiss would ruin the image of a dedicated attorney she was trying to maintain. She shrugged.

Janet's voice took on a note of caution. "Al has a lot on his plate. And, he's a very private person."

Sarah heeded the warning and pushed the conversation from personal to professional. "Just wondering. From your perspective, I mean. Sometimes he's a little hard on me."

"We're all a little tense right now. There's a lot going on. I wouldn't take anything he says or does too seriously." Janet motioned to the waiter to refill her water glass. "And what about you? How did a nice Jewish girl like you come to work at the Williams' firm?"

Sarah was grateful. Sick of dealing with her rampaging hormones, playing biography was a pleasant relief.

The two women didn't have much to say on the way back to Eight Mile Junction. The haunting melody of the folk song kept invading Sarah's mind, keeping her focused on Al and that damned kiss. When they got to town, Janet stopped in front of Sarah's house. As she stepped out, Sarah leaned into the car. "It's been a great evening, the best since I've been back.

"Let's do it again. Before I forget, my niece, Laura is coming. I want you to meet her. I know she'll enjoy your company." Janet put the car in gear, and drove off.

When she entered the kitchen, Sarah found a note on the refrigerator. "Chewie still not eating. Took her to the vet. She's staying the night. Sleep well. Love, Mom." Ellen hadn't forgotten to include the X's and O's.

Chapter Eleven

While they waited outside the courtroom for the start of the change of venue hearing, John-Two confronted the assistant DA, Colin Kearney. "When do I get those documents I requested?" He stood close to the younger man, jabbing his finger toward Kearney's chest. Sarah could see that Kearney was trying to back away, but the crowd in the hallway kept him from getting too far. She hunkered down on a bench along the wall, going over her report.

One answer to the survey questions grabbed her attention. The respondent had said, "I watched her change from the apple of her step-daddy's eye to a grown woman who was always running after something more than what she had, and that something was never anything good." The comment reminded Sarah of the changes she had seen in her friend when she had visited her during a school break. That had been almost a year after Casey was born. JoBeth and Phillip had separated, and she had started working at the plant, the one managed by Sarah's father. She and the children were living in a tiny apartment over the hardware store.

"As soon as Casey gets a little bigger, I'm going to get myself to college," she had told Sarah. "Your daddy promised me a promotion over at the plant if I went back to school. When I told him I didn't have any money for that kind of thing, he said the company could help."

Good old dad. Always stepping in to manage the situation. "That's nice," Sarah remembered saying. "It's good that you have a plan."

"Let's go," John-Two called.

The courtroom was almost empty except for a few attorneys waiting for their cases to be called. Sarah sat at the defense table for the first time.

JoBeth, sitting between Sarah and John-Two, looked vulnerable, more like a lost child than a murderess. Sarah reached under the desk and patted her thigh. Their case was first on the agenda.

Sarah's stomach twisted nervously when she was called to the stand. The facts of her report circled her brain wildly, and she feared she would be unable to remember anything. Her voice stuck at the swearing in. The judge asked her to speak louder. Bad start.

"Proceed." The judge motioned toward the defense table.

John-Two and surreptitiously gave her a thumbs up. "Please state your credentials for the court," the judge said.

"I have completed two of a three-year program that combines a J.D. with an MBA. My work experience includes legal and survey research, statistical analyses, as well as interviewing and report writing for private and public agencies."

The judge nodded. "What did your research on this case show?"

"The defendant is unlikely to receive a fair trial in Eight Mile Junction. Over 93 percent are convinced that the defendant went to the lake intending to murder her children." The judge was the one she had to convince, so she spoke directly to the bench. He leaned toward her, tilted his head as if he was putting his good ear forward. A hard-of-hearing judge. Just my luck. She raised her voice. "As important, the respondents agreed without exception that in a case such as this, the death penalty is appropriate. Therefore, the defense concludes that the trial should be moved to another county."

The judge nodded again and looked toward the assistant DA. Does the prosecution have any questions?"

"Yes, Your, Honor." Kearny remained behind the prosecution's desk. "Ms. Wasser, how do you know the results of your study are representative of the folks here in Eight Mile Junction?"

She answered slowly, giving the statistical significance of the findings. Her palms were sweating but she kept her voice even.

"When the respondents to your survey said they followed the case in the newspaper, did you ask if they read the entire article or only the headlines?"

"We didn't ask that question."

"I see." Kearney walked toward the stand, scratching his head as if perplexed. "Then you might say that there's a possibility that the respondents to your survey might *not* be fully aware of the details of this case; that prospective jurors may know only what they saw in the headlines but, once impaneled, could hear evidence previously unknown to them?"

"Objection, leading the witness."

John-Two's intervention gave her a few seconds to prepare for the barrage of questions and insinuations she knew was coming. Without waiting for the judge's decision, Kearney continued.

"When the respondents said they knew the defendant, did they tell you how *well* they knew her?"

"We divided the survey results into two parts, those who considered her a friend and those who said she was an acquaintance. The results of the opinion questions were tested by group. There is no difference in their knowledge about the case, and no difference in their opinion about the death penalty. The same percent in each group stated that it is an appropriate sentence for this crime."

"Did you have a measure of friendship?"

"No."

"Did you differentiate by asking if they saw her every day, every week, or every month?"

"We didn't ask that."

"Then you *don't* know *how well* any of the respondents who said they were friends of the defendants actually knew her, do you?"

"Objection," John-Two's voice rang out.

After Kearney retired, Sarah feared a negative outcome. The assistant DA had nit-picked every sentence, carried out each conclusion to its extreme, and at every turn, made it appear that her findings were faulty.

As John-Two approached the witness box, he unbuttoned his jacket and placed both hands in his pants pockets. He stopped in front of Sarah and smiled. Despite the chastening Sarah had endured, John-Two looked confident.

"It seems that the prosecution missed the objective of the survey," John-Two spoke condescendingly. "The defense would like to remind him that it was to show the public's familiarity with the defendant and the case, as well as their predilection to convict, not to submit evidence that the defendant could win a popularity contest."

"Counselor, do you have any questions for the witness?" the judge asked.

"Yes, Your Honor. Ms. Wasser, did your research show that the public's familiarity with the defendant and their penchant to prejudge might interfere with the defendant's getting a fair trial?"

"Yes, the findings suggest just that."

"And are those findings statistically significant?"

"Yes, they are."

"That's all, Your Honor." John-Two returned to his seat.

"Thank you, counselor. Miss Wasser." The judge bent forward and looked directly at her. "I must compliment you on a thorough and well-written report, one that would be convincing under other circumstances. But in my court, when I tell the jury to be fair and open-minded, they are fair and open-minded. Change of venue denied." He gave Sarah a half-smile dismissal, and left the bench in a swirl of black-robed self-importance.

On the way back to the office, John-Two ushered Sarah into the Pinker Dot. It was late morning and the breakfast crowd had left. The waitresses, preparing for lunch, were replacing the condiment bottles and filling the napkin holders. John-Two took a seat next to the window and asked the waitress for two cups of coffee.

"I guess we took a beating this morning."

"It was an outside chance he'd move the trial. You made a convincing argument. That's all we could do. It was a good report."

The waitress brought coffee. "Anything else?" she asked. John-Two shook his head and asked for the check.

"Is that the only thing we can offer as a defense? Do what we can, and let it go?"

"We do our best," John-Two spoke softly, not his usual blustery self. "But JoBeth murdered her children. No one in that courtroom will ever forget that. But we have extenuating circumstances on our side, and we'll exploit them."

John-Two offered Sarah the sweetener and, when she refused, emptied three packets into his coffee. He seemed at ease, even content with the morning's proceedings, but it didn't make Sarah feel any better. She'd gone into that courtroom to win.

"What do we have besides Howard?" Sarah asked. "Will the DA let him testify to anything that would connect him with pedophilia?"

"Al is working on it. Your interview this afternoon may be another critical piece. We might be able to show Bendhurst as someone else who used JoBeth and dumped her. Help sway the jury away from the charge of intentional murder. Have them see her as a woman whose judgment has been battered by abuse. See what you can get from him. Keep going back to the reason he broke up with her."

"I'll do my best.

"That judge was a pisser, wasn't he?" John-Two pointed to her coffee cup. "Finish up. I've got some stuff to get ready for Al." He tossed his napkin onto the table.

"When is he coming back?" She hoped he didn't remember that she had asked him that question before. Couldn't have him think she was anxious.

"Sometime late today or tomorrow morning."

Sarah's heart lifted. She pushed it back down with a deep breath. When she got back to the office, Clayton was in the library.

"How'd it go this morning?"

"Judge clobbered me. Said he'd see to it that the defendant got a fair trial."

"First experience with judicial discretion crossing over to judicial arrogance?"

"It wasn't pretty."

"Get used to it." Clayton advised. "It's the bane of every attorney. I'm sure you did your best, Sarah." He squeezed her shoulder, selected a book, and left.

She could always count on Clayton to make things look brighter. John-Two was right. It was stacked against them from the start, and but she had done a thorough good job. She went to her desk and prepared for her meeting with Bendhurst.

That afternoon, Sarah drove to Charlotte and waited in the company lunchroom. Bendhurst entered, ignored the hand she held out, and tossed a greasy rag onto the table. The smell of oily residue overpowered the stale cafeteria odors of leftover food and standing dish water. He was a large fellow, solidly built, broad and muscled. His hair was tied in a skinny pony tail that hung between his shoulder blades; a large glass earring in his left ear flashed each time he turned his head. A snail tattoo, seeking a more secluded spot, crawled down his neck toward the collar of his shirt. He was the antithesis of Phillip.

"You the one they sent up?" He looked past Sarah at a cafeteria worker wiping off the lunch tables. "I'm not saying nothing bad about her, if that's what you're after."

Sarah slid a business card toward him. He glanced at it but didn't pick it up. "Sarah Wasser," she said. "I'm with JoBeth's defense team. We're asking you to help us defend, not condemn her. Do you mind if I record this?" She pointed toward the tape recorder.

He shrugged. "Okay with me."

"Let's start with how you met JoBeth."

"At the Little Glass Shot House," he answered, still watching the cafeteria worker. "Out on Route 20 between Eight Mile Junction and Bootville." He waved his hand, perhaps in the direction of the bar. "The bikers hang out there. She came with a bunch of other women one night and, as soon as she saw me, walked right up and introduced herself. Back then, she was always laughing and flirting. I liked her right off."

"Did she ever seem depressed or unhappy?"

"Not that I can recollect."

"How often did you see her?"

"Most Fridays when her old man had the kids."

"How long before you got serious?"

"She got serious right off, wanted me to move in. Told me she and Phillip were finished. At the time, I wasn't wanting a steady old lady."

"Did you ever get serious?"

"More like comfortable. Got to liking regular booty, and she sure was a witch in bed. Hung around her place a lot, stayed over a night or two during the week. She liked the bike and was always making a big fuss over me. I got to liking that, too." He rubbed his eye, leaving a greasy smear on his cheek

"You weren't ready to make a commitment. Am I right?"

"Yeah. Those kids was treating me like I was their daddy. When I came, they'd hug me and pull on me and, when I sat down, they'd crawl all over me. Liked that plenty but wondered if JoBeth was putting them up to it."

"When did the relationship end?"

He took out a pen and pushed the trigger, distracted by the point appearing and disappearing.

"Did you end it?" Sarah prodded, hoping she wasn't pushing him too far.

"I always had one foot inside and the other out the door. She knew that. Didn't want no kids that weren't my kin."

"How did she take that?"

"Said she'd have my baby. I wasn't ready for that either. She said she needed someone of her own and that she wanted me to be that someone."

He stopped talking and wrinkled his brow. Sarah gave him time to think.

"That was when she told me about her and her step-daddy." He frowned, and shook his head.

"He was doing her." Bendhurst looked at Sarah. "Did you know that?"

She kept her face impassive and remained silent. He averted his eyes; they came to rest on Sarah's briefcase. He fingered the latch.

"Been doing her since she was a little girl. That's how she knew all that sex stuff. Learned it from that pervert." He jerked himself upright, crossed his leg over his knee and then uncrossed it. The buckles on his leather boot jingled.

"Why do you think she told you about her stepfather?"

"Maybe to make me jealous. I don't know. When I found that out, I didn't want to see her no more. I stayed away. She kept calling me, but I wasn't into it."

Sarah hesitated. Would he be forthcoming if she asked him about the murders? She quickly reviewed her list of questions to make sure she had covered everything. Just in case he stalked out. She held her breath, and asked, "Mr. Bendhurst, why do you think she drowned her children?"

"She was a good momma," he blurted out. "Don't you never think nothing else. She loved them and took good care of them."

"Then why did she let them drown?"

Bendhurst closed his eyes, and shook his head. "Maybe she was putting them to sleep forever because she knew they'd never get growed up right without a daddy. Thought they'd be in a better place with the Lord. She was a good momma, and I know she wanted the best for them."

There it was again, that "Lord" stuff. She wanted to ask him if he was kidding, but held it. Might need him as a witness. Besides, his explanation for the murders might fly in Eight Mile Junction.

"Is there anything else you can tell me about JoBeth?"

"She was a good momma. She loved them kids."

They sat quietly. Then Bendhurst asked, "You got everything you wanted?"

Sarah nodded and he left. She sat for a short while, thinking about what he said. JoBeth loved her kids. Sarah was sure of that. If what he said was true, then she could have murdered the children because she loved them and wanted to protect them from a world that had become more than she could manage.

John-Two called to Sarah as she entered the office. "What did Bendhurst say? Anything new?"

"He knew about her stepfather. He broke off seeing her after he found out."

"So, we have a biker with principles."

"What good did it do to tell him? It's as if she isn't able see the impact that her relationship with Howard has on everyone."

John-Two cleared his throat. "As a witness, would he show her as sympathetic?"

"Finding out about what Howard and Vera did to her alone should wring every ounce of sympathy out of any jury."

John-Two raised his eyebrows and wagged his head. "Bendhurst. What about Bendhurst?"

"He seemed fond of her and the children but wasn't ready for marriage. He said that she was looking for a father for the children and that failure to find one might have led her to seek someplace safe for them. Instead of murder, he referred to the drowning as 'putting the children to sleep."

"Did he say how she felt when he broke it off?"

"She kept calling him but he refused to see her. She must have felt used and dumped."

"Do you think any of this is useful?"

"Worth pursuing. It might show that she was looking for a way to save her children, not murder them. He kept repeating that she was a good mother." She stopped and thought. "Far-fetched, but it may fit somewhere in this puzzle. If we argue that, in her confused state, the only way she could save them from what seemed a disastrous fate, was to lay them to rest. You and I can't buy it but the locals might really get into it."

"And what was the disastrous fate?"

"Searching for the love of a husband and father and continually meeting rejection. Let me talk to her again. I still haven't asked her why she did it."

"Okay. Ask Janet to set you up."

After she left John-Two, Sarah dropped the Bendhurst tape on Janet's desk. "John-Two wants a copy of the transcription."

"What about him?" Janet jabbed her thumb toward Al's office.

Sarah could see Al seated at his desk. She raised her voice in case Janet couldn't hear her above the words "he's back" reverberating in her mind. "I'm sure he'll want to see it."

On her way past his office she stared ahead, pretending she was in too much of a hurry to notice that he had returned from Columbia. Her racing heart preceded her into the library, but before she could capture and calm it, Al sauntered in and settled across from her desk as though he was there to stay.

"Doing anything tonight?" he asked. "Thought you might like to go to dinner."

"I can't."

"Date with Jameson?"

"No, not that it's any of your business." Al laughed, apparently delighted at her brashness. "I promised my mother ..."

"Does your mother mind company?"

"I ah, I ah could ask her." She rearranged the tape dispenser and stapler on her desk, opened a drawer, pulling out folders as if she was looking for something. Her mother would be happy to have her daughter's friend for dinner, especially a male friend. Her father? That might not be so good. He would circle him like an alpha dog establishing his dominance. No warm and fuzzy time for Al to get his bearings. She took papers from a folder and tapped them against the desk, aligning their edges.

Al pointed to the telephone. "How about it?"

She punched the speed dial.

At dinner, they stood around the table as Ellen lit the two candles welcoming Shabbat. Her hands circled above the flames then, beckoning the sacred smoke, brought her palms toward her breast. She covered her eyes, and recited the blessing.

Barukh atah Adonai, Eloheinu, melehk ha'olam
Asher kidishamu b'mitz'votav v'tzivamu
L'had'lik neir shel Shabbat. Amen.

Sarah eyed Al through her half closed eyelids, wondering what he was thinking. If he was surprised, he didn't show it. Immediately after the blessing, Al turned to Ellen, speaking as if he had always known her.

"It's been a long time since I've been invited to a table as fine as this."

Sarah thought fine was a just-right word. Ellen blossomed; her smile folded the worry lines around her eyes into crinkles of happiness. Al was on the right track, perhaps following the path her father had travelled many years before. Was he courting approval? A glad-all-over feeling consumed her. The evening was headed in the right direction.

Al turned his attention to her father. He asked about the plant, its operations, and prospects for future employment growth in the region. His knowledge about her father and his business was amazing. Sam was engaged. Sarah listened to the animated talk between the two men and watched her mother make the most of her role as hostess. It was like watching a movie in which you knew everything would come out all right. She sat back and waited for the ending.

Sam's voice jolted her out of her complacent woolgathering. "How did it go today? Did you hit one out of the ballpark?"

There he goes with the ballgame stuff. Play to win. She hadn't hit one out of the ballpark and she didn't want to talk about it. But everyone was waiting for her answer. No hedging tonight. Al was here and he knew the scoop.

"The judge denied the motion," she answered matter-of-factly.

"What did you do wrong?" Sam asked.

She struggled to answer but got hung up on the word wrong. She really hadn't done anything wrong, but the way he asked the questioned made it a damned if you did, damned if you didn't situation.

"Well, did Williams go over the hearing with you and point out your mistakes?"

"He didn't. In fact, he..."

Sam took off his glasses and laid them on the table. "If Williams didn't point out your mistakes, how do you expect to get it right the next time?"

Sarah fidgeted with her napkin, twisting it around her wrist as if she was stemming blood flowing from an open wound. Ellen rose.

"Anyone want more rice pudding?" she asked brightly. No one answered. She began to clear the table. "I'll put on the coffee." She retreated to the kitchen.

"You see, Dad..."

"I thought the objective was to win. You can't keep JoBeth out of the chair unless you win every milestone." He turned toward Al. "Am I right?"

Al shrugged. "In this case..."

"Besides," Sam continued, "Sarah's not doing herself any favor working on this trial. She's going to be a corporate attorney, not some social worker like my sister, Rebecca—up there in New York trying to save the world." He gave a grunt of disapproval.

If Sarah's hostility toward her father had a sound, it would have shattered the crystal chandelier. No amount of reasoning could deter his attack. He enjoyed the chase, smelled blood, and would pursue the wounded to ground, even if it was his daughter. She twisted the napkin-tourniquet tighter.

"Mrs. Wasser, can we have coffee in the living room?" Al asked. "I'd enjoy sitting on a softer chair." He brushed his hair off his forehead as he slid his chair away from the table.

Ellen clung to Al's words as she would a life preserver, ended the meal, and hurriedly brought the silver coffee service into the living room. Sam acquiesced. Even he knew when to retreat. Silently, they shuffled into the living room.

Sam sat in his favorite chair and motioned for Al to sit beside him.

Sarah sat across from Al, not daring to meet his gaze. Why had she let him talk her into taking him home? She had worried that the evening might end in disaster, but she'd thought Al would be the butt of her father's sardonic nature. How could he strip her naked in front of her colleague? Was it revenge for going against his wishes, or had he found out about the internship? She shrouded her thoughts in a white fog of disengagement.

Al began speaking before Ellen finished pouring the coffee. Not mentioning Sarah's name, he spoke technically, looking directly at Sam. "The primary objective of the motion was to move the trial out of town, but we were pretty sure that the judge wouldn't grant it. Moving a trial is an expensive proposition and this is a poor county with insufficient funds. And judges have personal reasons. No one on the bench wants to lose out on presiding over a case that could make his reputation and increase his chances of being considered for an appointment to a higher court."

"Then why in hell did Williams decide to do it? Waste of time and money in my opinion." Sam stirred his coffee, lifted the cup to his lips, and studied Al over the rim. Sarah knew her father was being intentionally confrontational. Couldn't he be pleasant just this once?

"Anyway," Al continued, "if the verdict goes against us, the denial could be grounds for an appeal. Furthermore, data gathering surveys, such as the one Sarah conducted, collect information about community attitudes. The results can often give direction for selecting jury members. Kind of tells us where the hidden hazards lie."

"I've been talking to people around here," Sam cut in. "I know how they feel. Why didn't you ask someone like me?" He sounded peevish. Al had usurped his position as leader.

"In-person interviews are time-consuming and costly. They're reserved for persons we expect to call as witnesses." Al returned to the original topic. "Sam, change of venue is a strategy attorneys adopt early in the process, when things are the most uncertain. The defendant is assured that the team is doing everything it can. It can forestall accusations of incompetence."

The tension eased; Ellen smiled. Sam studied the young man, perhaps wondering how he could co-opt him into his business. Sarah rallied. Al was defending her without alienating her father.

"Since you mentioned it," Al continued, "I'd be interested in your opinions about the defendant."

Sam put his coffee cup aside, sat back and glared at Al. He appeared to be searching for the right words. When he spoke, his voice was cautious.

"She was my employee for some time."

"How long?"

"I don't keep track of that. You'd have to look in the personnel files."

It must be the only thing he doesn't keep track of, Sarah thought. He's being cagey. Maybe he wants to see where Al's going before he commits himself.

"Dora Channing told us that JoBeth actually worked in the front office."

"Yes, yes. If I remember correctly, she wasn't there very long."

"Did she work directly for you?"

"I wouldn't say directly."

"Was she a good employee?"

"I never heard any complaints. I don't interfere in personnel matters at that level. Joe Appleton in human relations takes care of that. Ask him if you want details. Tell him I sent you."

Wow. Something her father doesn't interfere with. That must be another first.

"Why did she leave for a job in the warehouse? Wasn't that a step down for her?"

Sam slammed his cup on the table. Startled, Ellen jumped. "Sarah," she said hurriedly, "why don't you two go downtown? You can't sit around all night with us old people. It's almost our bedtime."

Al rose and handed his cup to Ellen. "Thank you for a lovely evening, Mrs. Wasser. Perhaps you and your husband will let me treat you to dinner sometime."

Sarah feared he was going to walk out, rejecting her mother's suggestion that they go downtown for the evening, leaving her alone with her father's contempt. She tried to catch his eye, but he walked ahead into the hallway. There was an awkward silence.

"Did you bring anything with you?" Ellen asked, wringing her hands as she spoke.

"No," Al answered. "But Sarah may need a sweater."

They were seated in the lounge of the Agusta Hotel before Al spoke again. Sarah had been grateful for his silence and the shelter of darkness that helped soothe the bruises left by her father's caustic remarks. If her mother was right, and he always had her best interests at heart, he had a funny way of showing it.

"Did you sprain your wrist?" Al asked, pointing to the napkin.

Sarah unwound it and stuffed the napkin into the seat behind her, happy that Meagan wasn't on that night. Right now, she didn't need anyone who would make her feel any more inadequate than she already felt. She wondered what Al thought about her now, after her father's dreadful attack. He probably thought she was like one of those battered women who continually returns to their abusive husbands.

Why should she care what Al thinks? Really, he is very much like her father. Critical, but not in the same way. Up until now, her father had been tough, but always her mentor. On the other hand, she has never known exactly where she stood with Al. Except for tonight, when everything went to hell. Was her father really that angry with her, or was he showing off in front of Al? Whatever. She should have known better than to let the two of them get together.

"Is your father always that rough on you?"

"Only recently," she answered carefully. The hint of criticism brought back her loyalty toward her father. "He wants the best for me. I'm his only child and he has high hopes for my career." As angry as she had been with her father, she wasn't going to trash him in front of Al. "What happened in Columbia?" she asked.

"Hired two consultants for jury selection. What are you drinking?"

"I'll have a coke. That Dunning is pretty damned sure of himself."

"Ivy Leaguer." Al said the words as though they explained everything. He gave the waitress the order and sat back. No flirting with this one.

"Where did you get your law degree?" she asked.

"UNC."

"Why did you go there?"

"Started as an undergraduate."

"I mean, why did you decide to go to North Carolina in the first place?"

"Scholarship."

"Did you come back to Columbia right after graduation?"

"No, clerked for a year."

"I went to Chicago because my parents are alums." She wanted to tell him she had a scholarship, but it seemed gratuitous. Save it for a later time. "I never considered any other school."

"That figures."

"Ever get tired of being sarcastic?"

"Finished?" he asked, pointing to her drink. "Let's go to my place."

Sarah shut her lips tightly so the words "what for" didn't leap out and land on the table. Sex immediately came to mind, sex on the messy futon, the wisdom of sleeping on dirty sheets, and whether he had condoms available. She should tell him she wasn't on the pill, but he hadn't mentioned sex. Was she jumping the gun? Maybe it was just for a glass of wine and some more Mahler. Don't be dense. It's sex. What if they stopped at the pharmacy for condoms and Jameson was working late? What if he wanted her to stay all night? Jesus, why didn't she just give him a questionnaire to fill out?

"I didn't ask you to go to the moon; I just asked if you wanted to go to my place."

"Well," she stalled. "I hadn't thought of it."

"I know you didn't. I did." He grinned, finished his drink, and said, "Come on, let's go." He grabbed her hand and pulled her up.

When they passed the drug store, Sarah hung back. "Al, ah, I don't use birth control pills."

"I've had a vasectomy."

"Really?" Sort of young to have a vasectomy. Maybe he never wants kids. She hurried to keep in step with him, flooded with relief that she hadn't misread his intentions, made a fool of herself.

"Really," he said. "I wouldn't lie about that."

The apartment was as she remembered except the futon was neatly covered, the room tidied, and night air blew in through an open window and rattled the beaded curtain. Had he cleaned up because he had been expecting her? Was she that easy?

"Want a glass of wine?" He hung his jacket on the pipe rack, keeping the futon clear.

"No," she said a little too firmly. She stood with her hand on the door knob, as if contemplating an escape. He placed his hands on her shoulders and brushed his lips on her cheek.

"Scared?" He stood back, watching her, grinning.

Out of my mind, she thought. Am I doing the right thing? Please don't let me ruin this.

He drew her away from the door and led her to the bean bag. They sank deeply into its center, the sides coming up and around them, pushing them closer. Al turned on the stereo, picked up a joint, lit it, inhaled, and handed it to her. "Hotel California" filled the room, and the words "such a lovely place" massaged Sarah's misgivings. She took the joint, inhaled largely, and coughed out a lungful of smoke.

"Don't get greedy."

His voice was soft and reassuring. She tried to retain her logical footing, remember if that was the voice he'd used in the office, but couldn't bring up the office setting, doubted that she had ever seen him there. Her memory didn't seem to be working. There was only this moment and the worrisome future—getting out of the damned bean bag chair. She inhaled again, wrapped her tongue around the smoke, held it down, let it burn her throat, rush to her head, and gradually spread through her body. She exhaled, the practical Sarah pushed to the background, wondering if pot caused lung cancer.

He placed head phones over her ears, she eased back against his arm, and the music wandered, each nerve ending in her brain jingled as it passed its music message across the synapses, pushing out thoughts of her father, work, even Al. She drifted, wondered if she was alone, grew anxious, feared she was lost. But before she could marshal any effort to find herself, the words "such a lovely place" sheltered her in a cozy little chrysalis that guaranteed everything was good and as it should be.

She didn't remember how she got out of the bean bag chair and into bed. All her fears about rising gracefully from that ass-cradling monster didn't matter in the end. It was her orgasm that brought her back from the void that had been steaming with uninterrupted sensations produced by drugs, music, and closeness to Al. It began slowly, heating her body and lasting so long she feared it would never stop. A terrifying and exhilarating thought, but one that refused to linger. A light flashed in the corner of her eye. Anxious, she groped for something to cling to, found his shoulders, then his hands. They were as experienced and disciplined as his mind. She melted into the mattress.

He held her tightly, his body rhythmically soothing hers. He groaned, exhaled, and stretched so that his body covered hers completely. Her fingers, finding a mole on his shoulder, traced circles around it. He fell asleep; she lay wide-eyed, thinking of ways she could get out from under the weight of his body without waking him, smiling at the thought that she might have to call in a bulldozer. But when she moved, he didn't stir. She gathered her clothes, dressed, and crept out the door.

On her way home she wondered if he would be disappointed when he found she was gone. Probably not. He'd most likely be relieved. Got what he wanted and he wouldn't have to cook breakfast. Probably mac and cheese again.

And what did she want? She wanted Al to care. Things had gone further than she ever imagined, but she still didn't know if he cared or not. Perhaps she should have stayed and hashed things out. That was her way. Talk about stuff. But Al would remain noncommittal. That was his way. Now, all she could do was retreat and climb into the safety of her own bed. The eastern ridges of the mountains showed faintly light, as though someone with a flashlight was standing behind them, forecasting the rising sun. She entered the dark house quietly.

The domestic noises rose up the stair well the next morning and intruded politely: dishes clattering, a chair scraping the hardwood floor, a drawer in the kitchen closing. She reached down and felt the still sticky substance of his sex between her legs. She pulled the coverlet, examined the sheet, and was relieved to find that no yellow stains betrayed her last night's behavior. She showered, believing her parents might be able to smell him on her body and washed her underpants. Marijuana and sex. What would they say if they knew?

"Why, Sarah. Up so early?" Ellen poured her daughter a cup of coffee.

Had her mother heard her come in? Didn't Ellen always say that she never slept until Sarah was safely home? That was high school. Now that she was an adult? She waited to see if her mother had anything to add.

"The paper says that reporters from out-of-state are staying at the Agusta," her father commented. "Seen any?" Sam held the paper in front of his face as he talked.

She was annoyed that her father was forcing her to talk to the newspaper. "John-Two had an interviewa day or so ago. He gave them so little that his remarks were incorporated into another article. The store clerk at Bi-Lo's was willing to retell his part of the story, though. It must be the fourth time he's been in the paper." She wondered if her father had been subdued by his contest with Al the night before. If he had, he'd be planning his comeback. It was only a matter of time.

"Nice young man you brought home," her mother said. "He appeared to enjoy himself."

"Al?" Sarah questioned his name as if she was trying to identify him as one among many. "Yes, he's great to work with." What a farce. Her mother could probably see right through her, but was too civil puncture her daughter's story.

Her father, having enough of the nice-nice talk, interrupted. "Seems pretty cocky." He folded the paper and handed it to Sarah.

"That's Al."

If her father was looking for an argument, he'd have to try harder. She wasn't biting at snide remarks, not anymore. She poured herself a glass of Ellen's freshly squeezed orange juice. The sweet, pulpy mixture soothed her parched throat. Did smoking dope make you thirsty? She knew about hungry, but...she gulped the juice.

"Nice guy but doesn't get the point." Sam looked at his watch, sat back, and challenged her with that little squinty look he got when he was sure he had the upper hand. Certain that he wasn't going to let it go, Sarah waited.

"The point is," he directed the tip of his fork at her, waving it in tiny circles, "that when you're in court, you're there to win. If you forget that, you'll never be a successful attorney. The name of the game is to win at any cost."

"More coffee?" Ellen placed her hand on her husband's shoulder, as if she was holding him back. He ignored her. She refilled his cup and glanced at Sarah. Her face was bleak.

"As Al said last night, the objective is ..."

"I don't care what he said. You don't need anyone making excuses for your failures."

"Sam, please," Ellen coaxed.

"It's okay, Mom." Sarah smiled and turned to her father. "I don't have to make excuses."

Sam cleaned his glasses with his napkin, then returned them to his face. "If you're so sure of yourself, then tell me, what good did it do?"

"As long as John-Two and Al are satisfied, I'm okay with the job."

"Failure? That's satisfactory?"

"You know, Dad, maybe you don't know what you're talking about."

Ellen caught Sarah's eye and wagged her head toward the kitchen. "Let's clear the table."

"Not yet." She turned to her father, reminding herself to keep her voice low. "I respect you Dad. And I love you. I know how much my career means to you, and how hard you've worked to make things easy for me. But I'm ready to take responsibility for what I'm doing. No need for you to second guess my work." She stood up. "Mom, let's clear the table."

Sam slammed the door as he left. Ellen smiled behind her hand, her eyes sparkling as she looked at her daughter. She turned to the sink and began to rinse the dishes, pushing little gusts of air through her lips that suggested she was whistling. Sarah knew she'd won the battle, but it didn't feel very good.

Chapter Twelve

The interview room at the jail, devoid of any hint of warmth, promised little other than a negative outcome to the upcoming interview. Asking JoBeth why she drowned her children was going to be more difficult than eliciting the details about Howard. The stale smell of ancient cigarette smoke drifted downward with the incoming air, assaulting Sarah's nose. She shivered, pulled a sweater from her handbag, and draped it across her shoulders.

When JoBeth entered, she was chatting with the stone-faced deputy who held her arm as he led her to the table. "That dress," she was saying, "has a sweetheart bodice." Her voice was a strained remnant of what Sarah remembered from high school. Rather than happiness, it was shaded with desperation. Sarah was taken aback by the change in JoBeth's demeanor.

"I never even got to wear it," JoBeth said to the deputy. "I hope it still fits me." She sat in the chair he pushed in her direction, and facing Sarah, gave her a tiny four-finger wave. "Do you think I've gained weight since I came here?" she asked, patting her waist.

The woman sitting across the table was a caricature of the JoBeth that Sarah had once known. She seemed to be reaching into the past, retrieving parts of her younger self, trying to put her life back together, infusing the room with a strong desire to return to the time before the murders.

"What do you think, Sarah? Should I go on a diet?" JoBeth glanced back at the deputy as he opened the door to leave. She started to stand.

"Remain seated." The deputy frowned and left the room. She made a funny face, shook her head, and dropped back into the chair.

"How are they treating you?" Sarah asked.

"That deputy is cute, huh? Did you notice the way he looks at me? I look just awful in this orange." She looked down at her coveralls, pinched up a piece of the fabric, and wrinkled her nose. "Can you bring me that dress I was talking about? It's blue, like the duster your momma used to wear. Remember that old thing? I'll bet she still has it. Blue makes my eyes look like the sky. That's what everybody tells me."

She smashed one sentence into the next as if fearing that if she stopped talking, the reality of the situation would overwhelm and crush her. Sarah, overcome by a feeling of protectiveness, wanted to take JoBeth's hands and warm them in the cradle of her palms, assuring her that everything would be all right.

"The next time I see Al, I'll ask. Can we talk about something else?"

JoBeth bit her lip and nodded. Her chin was covered with a nasty red rash and Sarah wondered if a doctor had seen it. She'd ask John-Two when she got back to the office.

"I want to talk about that night at the lake."

Sarah couldn't bring herself to mention the kids by name. Perhaps JoBeth would catch on and be able to talk about what happened. But she appeared unable to concentrate and kept picking at the rash with her fingernails. A small spot of blood appeared near the corner of her mouth. The silence in the room hung heavily about them. "The lake?" she asked vaguely.

"Were you angry the night it happened?" Sarah prompted.

JoBeth looked up sharply. "I never was angry with my little treasures. I loved them more than anything else in the world. You know that, Sarah. You didn't need to go ahead and ask me that."

"We sometimes get angry, even at those we love and things get out of control."

JoBeth retreated once more, fingering the sleeve of her coverall, her chin buried deep into her neck.

"What about Phillip, had he done anything to upset you?"

She sighed. "Phillip was gone. He wasn't ever coming back to me and the kids. I was past being angry with what he'd done. I was trying to build myself a new life."

"Then what happened that night?"

"Believe it or not, I wanted to die. There was not one reason left in this here world for me to go on living."

"Why?"

"No matter how hard I tried, nothing good came my way. There's hardly a person living in this here town that has any use for me anymore. Maybe there's nobody in the whole world that could ever love me again. I turned out to be the kind of person even I hate." Tears welled in her eyes. The spot of blood near her mouth dried, and the sore covered over with a small brown crust.

"What about the children? They loved you."

JoBeth sat forward and spoke slowly, as though she was explaining a hot stove to a small child. "It was never about them. It's about me and who I am."

"Then tell me how it happened."

"I drove to my step-daddy's house to ask momma to watch them. I was going to go to the lake and drive myself into the water."

"And what happened?"

"The maid said they weren't home. The kids were sleeping in the car. I didn't know what to do. There was no one left to help me. I got to thinking that I didn't want strangers to be raising my kids. Without me, there was not one person left to love them the way I did. Especially that Jaynelle. What kind of mother would she be? A god-damned shitty one. That's what she'd be. I couldn't go and leave them with the likes of her." Her voice softened. "That's when I decided to take them with me. You understand. I couldn't leave them behind."

She leaned forward, her arms outstretched, her fists clenched. Sarah had never known JoBeth to speak with such intensity. She had always been a go-along to get-along kind of person, someone who could find something to like about everyone. Now, she had found someone on whom she could vent her anger and frustrations, her ex-husband's soon-to-be-wife. Maybe the wrong person on which to place her resentment, but easier because Jaynelle was one person on whom she had never placed her love.

"When you left your stepfather's house, where did you go?"

"I drove to the lake. I wanted us to be together forever. In the end, I watched them go alone."

JoBeth stopped speaking. She seemed to be reliving that night, hearing the lonely sounds of the night creatures and watching the car sink below the surface of the water. Tears spilled and ran down her cheeks. She made no attempt to wipe them away. Sarah pushed the box of tissues toward JoBeth.

"All I wanted was to marry and have a family."

"I know."

"I loved Phillip and the children."

"I understand."

"Now look at me." JoBeth's voice rose. She began to talk through her sobs. "Everybody in town h-h-h-hates me. They're all talking about me and what I did." Her voice became hysterical. "They're all wishing I was dead. I'll do what I have to do and then they'll get their wish."

JoBeth stood and walked toward the door. The deputy's face appeared at the window and, when he saw her approaching, entered and took her arm. She stumbled after him. Before they reached the door, she pulled back. "I'll sit down. I promise. Tell him to wait, Sarah," she pleaded

"Give us a minute, deputy," Sarah asked.

He released his grip and stood aside.

"Alone please."

The deputy left the room. JoBeth remained standing by the door.

"What is it you have to do?" Sarah asked.

"Someone had to tell about all the things that happened to me, and I'm the only one who knows about that. Make everyone understand why I had to do what I did. After they find out, I'll be ready to die. I'm just sorry I brought those two innocent children into the world I created."

"Is there anything you haven't told me?" Sarah asked.

"Without answering, JoBeth turned and rapped on the door, signaling that she was ready to leave.

"JoBeth, wait…"

The deputy entered again and led JoBeth from the room; the door closed behind them.

When she entered the office, Janet handed Sarah a message from her mother. She stuffed it into her pocket and went directly into John-Two's office.

"Something's going on that we may not know about."

"What's that?" John-Two asked. He pushed aside the brief he had been reading.

"JoBeth told me that she couldn't go on living and that she contemplated suicide, but didn't want the children to be raised by a stranger. When I asked her why she let the kids drown while she decided to live, she said that she had to stay alive to tell her story. Do we know everything? Is there more than Vera's betrayal, Phillip's leaving, her stepfather's disgusting behavior, or Bendhurst's rejection."

John-Two shrugged and buzzed Janet. "If there's something else, she may tell you later. Al expects to finish jury selection by the end of the week. He wants to get started as soon as he can get the DA to agree to a date."

Was he was brushing her off? Before she could pursue the issue, Janet entered and placed a folder on John-Two's desk.

"We want you to see Vera Maitlan this afternoon," John-Two said, pointing to the folder. "Sorry it's such short notice, but it took a while to get Margaret Standcroft to agree to let Vera talk to you without her being in the room. You know how protective she's been."

"Are you calling Vera as a witness?" Sarah asked.

"Before he decides, Al wants a heads up on what she might say. He knows what he wants to ask her, but he also knows she'll be defensive. Wants you to soften her up. You know. Make her feel you sympathize with what she's going through. Can you do that?"

"Sympathize with her? Huh! But it might be interesting to see what makes her tick."

"Careful, we don't want her to turn into a hostile witness. See if she has any doubts about her husband. Maybe you can plant a few and she'll slip. We trust you to pull it off."

Sarah picked up the folder. "See what I can do."

Before heading to the Mailtlins, Sarah returned her mother's telephone message.

"Dr. Rose has bad news about Chewie," Ellen told her.

"Bad news?" Sarah looked at her watch.

"She has a tumor in her throat. That's why she hasn't been eating."

"Can they operate?"

"No." Her mother's voice wavered.

"Then what are they going to do?" Her mind raced through the possibilities: medication, radiation, something? She placed her tape recorder in her briefcase.

"There's nothing they can do."

"Are you sure there's nothing?" She looked at her watch again, wishing she had more time. "Where's Chewie now?"

"Home. So you could see her one last time. Then…" Ellen's voice faltered.

Sarah's appointment with Vera was for one-thirty. If she didn't leave now, she'd be late. "Mom, I've got to run. There must be something someone can do about the tumor. I'll take care of it when I get home."

What next? Sarah left for the Maitlins' home with her concern for Chewie gnawing away at the edge of her thoughts.

The Maitlins lived in a large house on the edge of town. When Sarah arrived, two men, each riding a mowing machine, were manicuring the lawn, working systematically, travelling in smaller and smaller squares. Vera met her at the door, opening it before Sarah rang the bell. She wore a red and blue geometric-patterned caftan with a red floor-length, sleeveless over-cloak and was smoking a cigarette plugged into a charcoal filter. She held the cigarette between her middle finger and forefinger, slightly above her shoulder, like she might be crecreating a scene from she a1930s movie.

She motioned with her cigarette for Sarah to follow, walked through a library, toward the screened porch that overlooked a spread of softly undulating lawn that followed a downward slope, stopping unseen at the edge of a wooded rise. As soon as they were seated, a maid wearing a black dress and a white apron served sweet tea and cookies.

A Skye Terrier, its eyes hidden behind long strands of gray-black hair, jumped up next to Vera and settled against a pillow. Sarah got it. Myrna Loy and Asta, sitting on the couch. But where was the Thin Man? Or was it Fat Man? Out molesting children?

"Anything else, Mum?"

Vera waved her away with her cigarette.

Sarah expected the maid to curtsy. She eyed the Madeleine cookies artfully arranged on the plate and decided against taking one. There was no eating one. She knew that.

Vera inhaled, looked out over the lawn, and spoke with the scratchy voice that accompanies a lungful of smoke. "I know why you're here. You want to ask me about JoBeth's crazy accusations against her step-daddy."

"Mrs. Maitlin," Sarah began slowly, "I'm here because we want to defend JoBeth, not persecute anyone. We hope you might help us." Actually, Sarah thought, I hope you spill your guts about fat man. She placed the tape recorder on the table between them and pointed. "I'm going to record our conversation, if it's all right with you."

Vera shrugged and nodded. Her hand shook as she took the cigarette from the holder: the wicker couch creaked as she leaned forward and ground the butt into the ash tray. The rubies in her ring and bracelet captured the sunlight and sent ribbons of color around the room. Disturbed by her movement, the dog turned around several times and flopped back on the pillow. It made Sarah think of Chewie. It took a few seconds for her to find her voice.

"Let's go back to when JoBeth and Phillip decided to get married.

How did that go?"

"Just as I expected. None too good. She was pregnant already and everybody in this town knew it. I was so embarrassed—it took everything I had to get back into Wednesday's bridge club."

"Did you like Phillip?"

"How could I? He got her pregnant." She patted her knee; the dog climbed onto her lap.

"They were in love before she got pregnant, weren't they?"

"I suppose. But the folks he came from didn't live up to the standards that Mr. Maitlin had set for us."

"What do you mean?" Sarah hoped that Vera wasn't referring to moral standards.

"Y'all know what I mean. His family lived over there in those government tract houses they built after the war. Not much better than the factory homes in Millside."

"You mean standard of living, is that it?" Sarah reached for one of the cookies. Just one, she promised herself.

"Uh huh. His father was some kind of carpenter or something. Hires out to the folks in this part of town. We see them at the church every so often. They aren't regulars. Not like Mr. Maitlin and me. What can you expect from a boy raised like that?"

"I don't understand."

"That kind ain't," she paused and corrected herself, "aren't brought up to do the right thing." She raised her eyebrows and cocked her head to one side, challenging Sarah to disagree.

"He married her. And in the beginning, they seemed happy."

"If you want my opinion, I don't think Phillip ever wanted to marry my daughter. I told her as soon as he finds out you're pregnant, he's never going show any respect. No man wants to feel as though he's been trapped and has to get married. Turned out I was right." She gave a self-satisfied nod.

"They must have shared some happiness," Sarah pleaded for JoBeth. Not something she should be doing, but she couldn't help it.

"They shared sex, that's what they shared. As soon as he could, he ran off with that Jaynelle. I told my daughter she should've known that would happen. Every man wants to do the picking, not get forced to marry. Why, Mr. Maitlin picked me, and we've been happy ever since. I don't know what she was thinking. That girl never used the good sense the Lord gave her."

Vera rang a little bell. The maid appeared with the sweet tea so quickly that Sarah thought she must have been standing in the library, waiting to be called. Vera pointed to the glasses. They waited for the maid to leave.

"So you think Phillip had good reason to leave your daughter?" Sarah reached for another cookie, took a small bite, and surreptitiously folded the rest in her napkin, hoping Vera hadn't noticed.

"I'm not saying anything of the kind. I'm only saying that a man wants a pure, Christian woman, not some slut who'll let him have his way with her.

The word "slut" hit Sarah like a slap on the face. She fiddled with the tape recorder, giving herself time to recover. Is that what Vera really thought?

"Let me see," she stalled, trying to remember where she left off. "We were talking about the separation. How did JoBeth react to Phillip's leaving?"

"The way you'd expect someone with her kind of morals would. Why he was no sooner out of the house than she started traipsing around on the weekends Phillip had the children. Ask anybody. There's no goodness left in that girl."

"What do you mean?"

"She went directly to the bars. Wasn't long before she was hanging out at that place where the bikers go, over there on Route 20. Started going with that Bendhurst. Now there's another one for you. Someone right out of one of those movies the Reverend Waldfield preaches against on Sunday mornings."

"Did you ever meet Bendhurst?"

"Absolutely not. I told her if she brought him here, it'd be over my dead body. I don't know what got into that girl. When she was little, she was sweet natured, like her natural daddy. After he died, she was my best friend. It wasn't until I married Mr. Maitlin that she went god-awful crazy. Phillip's leaving only made it worse."

"How's that?

"She wanted me to watch Daniel and Casey so she could go riding with Bendhurst on that bike. Out where everyone could see them. A grown-up woman with two children riding around on a motorcycle with a man the likes of Bendhurst. Now you tell me what that says about her."

"Did you?"

"Did I what?"

"Did you babysit for her?"

"Lord help me, no. I knew what those two were up to."

"Which two?" Sarah asked, thinking Vera might be talking about the children.

"Well, who'd you think? My daughter and that Bendhurst."

She stuffed another cigarette into the end of the holder and lit it, inhaling deeply and blowing smoke through her nose. The acrid smell of lighter fluid and burning tobacco filled the space between them. Sarah sneezed. Vera gave a little cough and quickly inhaled again.

"I heard Mr. Bendhurst left town."

"I guess. Went off to some mechanic's school. Good riddance to that, I said." She flicked her hand. Ashes from her cigarette drifted to the floor. "One thing you can say about him though. At least he didn't get her pregnant."

"Was JoBeth unhappy when he left?"

"Not for a minute. She was back in those bars before the door closed behind him."

"Dora Channing, her supervisor at the plant, said that JoBeth did very well on her job."

"Never said she wasn't smart. Quick like her natural daddy, she was."

"Did she tell you about her promotions?"

"Not that I can remember."

"Did she like her job, get some satisfaction out of working?"

Vera shrugged and took another drag on her cigarette. When she spoke, smoke shadowed the words out of her mouth. "We never talked about that either."

"JoBeth once mentioned that the company was willing to help with her expenses if she went back to school. Did she mention that?"

"Why would they want to do that for someone the likes of her? That was probably another of her fantasies. That girl was full of those silly ideas of hers right from the start and right on up until the time . . ." Vera stroked the dog, and murmured, "You're my little sweetness now, aren't you?" The dog yawned.

"Mrs. Maitlin, I know you've been through a lot, losing your grandchildren and your only child accused of murder. But I have to ask you this one last question. Why do you think JoBeth drowned her children?"

"I wasn't one bit surprised when it happened, let me tell you that right now. She's been full of crazy notions from the time we moved on over from Millside and she started spreading lies about people." Vera stood up so abruptly that the dog tumbled off her lap onto the floor.

It scrambled and followed Vera as she walked to the window. When she spoke again, Vera's voice hardened and the country dialect that she had so carefully worked out of her speech crept back. "No righteous person goes around sayin' the things she was always pretending happened. Like those things she said about her own step-daddy. My Lord, wherever did those ideas come from? Not from me, I'll tell you. Almost destroyed my marriage, and after all Mr. Maitlin did for her all her growin' up years."

"Why do you think JoBeth said those things?"

Vera turned and pointed her cigarette at Sarah. "It came upon me that she was a bad seed. You know what the Bible says about the sins of the father being visited on their sons? More'n likely in her case, the sins of the mother was visited on her two innocent babies."

She returned to her chair and snuffed out her cigarette. "More sweet tea?" When Sarah shook her head, Vera stooped and gathered the dog in her arms. "I have things to do. The maid will show you out." She left Sarah sitting alone on the porch.

John-Two was still in his office when Sarah returned. Janet had left for the day, and the place was quiet. "Find out anything?" he asked, setting down his pen and leaning back in his chair.

"Vera isn't going to be a strong witness *for* JoBeth, but the defense might get somewhere showing how she felt about her. And don't worry, I didn't antagonize her. She got herself all worked up without my help."

"How's that?"

"She is totally wrapped up in the lifestyle Howard Maitlin has given her. She acted like the Queen of Sheba, even dressed the part. She treats the maid like a trained pet. Rings a little bell when she wants something and gives her directions by waving her hand. Smokes constantly and uses her cigarette like it was Tinker Bell's wand and could grant wishes. Almost funny if the whole scene wasn't so disgusting. "

John-Two shook his head.

"She gave her daughter no quarter, mentioned JoBeth's accusations against Howard without my asking, and complained that her daughter's fantasies almost destroyed her marriage. She said that Phillip left her daughter because she wasn't righteous, even called her a slut. Vera thinks JoBeth is a bad seed. Even restated a Bible quote to suit her argument: sins of the father visited upon the sons sort of thing. And, she has no doubts about Howard's conduct toward her daughter."

"If we put Vera on the stand, how should we approach her?" John-Two asked.

The question pleased Sarah. She had been thinking about that on her drive back to the office. "I'd let her speak for herself, let the jury see how she looks and how she handles herself, let them hear the words she uses to describe JoBeth. Then call in a psychiatrist to testify about the effect that kind of relationship has on a person's maturation, on their self-esteem, on their ability to develop meaningful relationships."

John-Two nodded and smiled. "Nice, Sarah, but do you think there's enough for a psychiatrist to draw some conclusions? Might be a bit thin, don't you think?"

"Along with the implication of molestation, there might be enough."

"I'll have Al ask the psychiatrist that tested JoBeth. If he isn't right for the job, he'll recommend someone. One problem is that a pedophile usually stops molesting a child once she enters puberty. The fact that their adult sexual relations is verifiable might make the childhood abuse seem—well, at least take away some of its impact."

"It's like Al said. This is a lifetime of abuse," Sarah insisted. "Maybe each time she failed in a relationship, the only place she could find solace was with Howard. It could be that she didn't want to keep going back to him, but he was all she had. A good psychiatrist will see how it fits together. What jury wouldn't sympathize with a defendant whose mother traded her for material wealth? That's what Vera did, you know. Turned her back on her daughter to preserve her status."

"Let's talk to Al about that tomorrow." He shuffled through some papers on his desk. As Sarah rose, he looked up and winked. "Nice going, young lady."

At home, Ellen was sitting in her usual place, watching television and knitting. Sarah set her briefcase on the end table and sat down on the couch next to her. She picked up the strand of wool, watching it slide through her fingers as it traveled between the ball of yarn and her mother's knitting needles. The rhythmic clicking was soothing; she leaned back against the pillow and closed her eyes. How lucky she was to have a loving mother who took pride in her. That's one thing Vera's interview had shown, Ellen had been a great mother. Sarah was overcome with a feeling of warmth. She reached over and gave her mother a pinch on the cheek.

Ellen put down her knitting needles and put her arm around Sarah's shoulders, giving her a squeeze. "I'm afraid Chewie's not good," she whispered.

"Where is she now?" Sarah asked.

"In your bedroom. I thought she might not be eating because she had a bad tooth," her mother continued. "But Dr. Rose says it's not that. It's a tumor on the inside of her esophagus that has grown so large it's impossible for her to swallow."

"Can't they operate?"

"It's inoperable. Something about the way it's attached to the wall of her throat."

"Why not give her radioactive iodine or something like that?"

"Apparently there's not anything they can do."

Sarah searched for other possibilities. "Should we take her to another vet?"

"Dr. Rose consulted with one in Columbia. He agreed with Rose. The kindest thing to do is to put her to sleep. Otherwise, she'll starve to death."

Wasn't that what they always say? It's more humane to put a pet to sleep than to let her suffer. Hadn't Bendhurst said that? JoBeth had put the children to sleep so they wouldn't have to face a fatherless future. She kept trying to reconstruct her life, but somewhere along the way gave up. Drowning her children may have seemed more humane than subjecting them to their mother's humiliation and failures or leaving them with a disengaged father and his uncaring wife.

The thought of the house without Chewie made Sarah's heart weep. She had been so preoccupied with the trial, she hadn't—hadn't what? Noticed? Cared enough? She struggled to find a way to amend her neglect.

"I don't have to be in court until eleven tomorrow. I'll spend that time with Chewie."

Ellen patted her daughter's hand. "Maybe we'll get another puppy."

"Maybe," Sarah said. But she didn't want to think of a replacement right now. Besides, she still had something to do before she went to bed. "Is Dad in the den?"

Sam was sitting in his arm chair, reading a detective novel. He marked the page when his daughter entered and laid the book on his desk. "Saved JoBeth yet?" he asked.

"Not yet. But we're on it." She smiled and gave her father a peck on the cheek.

"Is this summer's work going to pay off for you?"

"I'd say so. At least I'm enjoying it and maybe learning something, like becoming a lawyer isn't exactly prescribed by what you learn in law school."

"Really?" He sounded unconvinced. "How's the defense shaping up?"

"I can't talk about the particulars, but I can tell you that we expect the trial to start in the next week or so. There's something I've been meaning to ask you. JoBeth once told me that when she worked at the plant, you offered to help her with the expenses if she went back to school."

"She told you that?" He placed his fingers in a pyramid, raised them to his lips and stared at Sarah. A wall went up between them and he seemed to be daring her to climb over. Pretending not to notice, she soldiered on.

"It was one of those times I came home for the holidays. She was pretty pumped up over her new job and the possibility of furthering her education. She seemed to have come to the realization that she had married too young, that there was more to life than husband and children."

"Is that so? But why would I offer a girl like that tuition when I'm having trouble coming up with the money to keep you in law school?"

His referral to JoBeth as a "girl like that" pissed Sarah off. Only a few weeks before he told Al that she had been a good employee. Now, was he implying that she was less than, less than what? A person beneath his notice? Besides, there was never any question about Sarah's tuition. Her Grandfather Solonsky had put scads away for that. What was that crap all about?

"No," she back-pedaled. "She probably meant that the company had a policy for helping employees who were going back to school and probably mentioned you because you were her boss."

"If the company has such a policy, I don't know about it."

He picked up the novel and opened to the book-marked page. Their talk was over. He was obviously offended that she inferred that he personally had offered JoBeth money for school. Did he feel caught in a bad place or had she had phrased it the wrong way? Either way, he was sulking and had put an end to the conversation before she could ask him about JoBeth's promotions. It was clear that those questions would have to wait until he cooled off. But she wasn't going to give up. His retreat just strengthened her determination to find the answer.

She whispered good night. He grunted, but didn't look up. She jammed her hands into the pockets of her jacket and went upstairs to comfort Chewie.

Chapter Thirteen

$\mathcal{S}$arah drove to the county park early the next morning where she and Chewie slowly climbed toward Lookout Point. Weakened, the dog stumbled often and labored to keep pace. Long before they reached the top, Sarah stopped and sat in the cradle of a boulder, giving the dog a chance to rest and catch her breath. Instead of chasing squirrels and browsing for delicious odors, she collapsed at Sarah's feet, exhausted and unmindful that this was her last day, grateful for the fussing sounds Sarah was making. Gnats and no-seeums bounced off Sarah's sweating arms. She absently scratched their tiny bites and sank into dreary thoughts.

The events of the past months weighed heavily. They began with Molitor's refusal to take her on as an intern and then, as if that wasn't enough, there had been the news about the murdered children. Coming home to join the defense team had strained her relationship with her father and now, caught in this thing with Al, she was spending too much time trying to figure him out. The old Sarah would have written him off after his first insult. But the old Sarah was disappearing. Her world, once defined by the certainties of her aspirations, had become shrouded by ambiguity. She lowered herself to the ground, put her arms around the dog and sobbed, glad that Chewie didn't understand the causes of her grief. The dog licked Sarah's hand with a coarse, dry tongue.

Had some strange alignment of the stars brought Sarah back to Eight Mile Junction this summer? Certainly Molitor's rejection sent her scurrying home, but that had happened so long ago. It seemed hardly worth the fuss. She would have a career and her father would get over his pique. More imminent was Chewie, lying at her feet near death, and

JoBeth's losses: her children, her freedom, very possibly her life. Really, everything else was insignificant. She dried her eyes and gently coaxed Chewie down the hill toward home.

Later that morning, Sarah made her way through the crowded hallway of thecourthouse. It was the third day of the prosecution's presentation and she was eager to hear Dunning's slant on the evidence. As she approached Department 8, someone called to her. She turned to see Janet, holding a young woman's arm, and pushing her way through clusters of lawyers, witnesses, and courtroom observers. As they approached, Sarah recognized the young woman as the one in the picture on Janet's desk.

"I tried to catch you at home but you'd already left," Janet's voice rose above the noise in the hallway. "My niece, Laura," she said drawing close. "And this is Sarah, the attorney I told you about. I wanted you two to meet." She drew a deep breath and released Laura's arm. "I have to get back to the office. Clayton's watching the phones but he won't sit still for that long. Take care of her, Sarah." She gave Laura a hug and jostled her way toward the stairs.

Laura smiled. "Aunt Janet is always busy. I guess you're stuck with me."

Laura was taller than Sarah and, in person, looked more like Janet than the photo suggested. She wore a black pant suit with a silk blouse the color of a Mandarin orange. Black onyx earrings, tastefully set in silver, hung almost to her shoulders. She looked around. "Boy, this place is something else. How can you tell where you belong?"

Sarah grinned and pointed to one of the courtroom doors. "Right here," she said. "Sorry to keep rushing you, but our case is about to be called. I have a seat up front; let's see if I can squeeze you in."

The courtroom, almost full, buzzed with excitement. The sheriff was to take the stand that morning. The D.A. had told the newspaper that Grime's testimony would clinch the prosecution's case. Sarah stared at JoBeth's back and made a wish for a favorable outcome.

John-Two was standing in the aisle talking to Ian Dunning. He was gesturing toward the bench, looking as though he was trying to convince him of something important. Dunning had represented the people of Cherokee County for more than twenty years, and this was his biggest case. He wore an expensive-looking suit, a burgundy handkerchief that matched his tie protruded from his breast pocket. He surveyed the courtroom over John-Two's shoulder, nodding every now and again to someone he recognized. He leaned in and whispered something to John-Two, who rolled his head back and laughed. Dunning smiled, his lips spread thinly, all but the tips of his teeth hidden.

Sarah pointed to Dunning. "That's the District Attorney. This is his most important case. He looks like a rooster in the barnyard, doesn't he?"

Laura laughed. "Better not let him hear you. It looks as though he takes himself very seriously."

The judge entered and the observers ceased their chatter. The session was taken up with procedural matters, and at one point, John-Two motioned that the memorials at Fenton Lake should be eliminated from the jury's visit to the crime scene. He argued that it offered no concrete evidence but did evoke a great deal of sympathy, thereby possibly biasing the jury's opinions.

Dunning countered that the emotional impact of seeing the memorials had more than likely been mitigated by the fact that most of the residents had seen pictures in the newspaper or had already visited the site. "Moreover," the DA continued, "the jurors will be guided by the judge's instructions about admissible evidence."

Dunning's play to the judge's vanity worked. He ruled in favor of the prosecution. Noting the time, the judge recessed for the noon break.

"How about lunch?" Sarah asked. "We have two hours until court reconvenes."

"Where? The Pinker Dot?" Laura asked.

"No, too noisy. Let's go to my house. Mom always has something good in the fridge."

They settled on a picnic in the Wassers' backyard. Sarah carried a tray of sandwiches and a pitcher of pineapple juice to the table on the lawn. Laura's hair, parted on the far left, fell forward onto her right cheek, hiding her eye. The bleached top, layered over her naturally dark hair, was polished by the sun. Quite a do, Sarah thought as she kneeled on the bench and struggled to raise the umbrella.

Sam's vegetable garden, tucked between the back of the garage and the fence, attracted Laura's attention. "Whoa, look at those tomatoes. Who grows those beauties? Your mother?"

"My father. They're his specialty. We can't eat them all so he gives them away. The neighbors love them."

"I should think so."

"Did you come back to visit your aunt or to see the trial?"

"A little of both. I usually visit my aunt for a few days each summer and I suppose I'm a curious about the trial."

"Do you have summers off?" Sarah asked. The ice clinked into the glass as she poured the juice.

"Mmm. Still in school. Finishing up a teaching credential this summer, starting a master's in the fall.

"Do you know JoBeth well?"

"We got together when I visited one summer. Mostly when we were in high school, but we keep in touch now and then."

"How did you meet her?"

"At Gladys' shop. I was having my hair trimmed and she worked Saturday mornings as clean-up girl. As soon as she saw me, she bombarded me with questions. Was I new in town? Where did my aunt live? How long was I staying? Would I like to go to church with her on Sunday?"

Sarah laughed. "Yep, that's JoBeth. She was a people collector, all right. Did you ever think her life would turn out like this?"

"Never. She loved and trusted everyone. My aunt always said JoBeth was uncorrupted."

Laura took out her compact and reapplied her lipstick. Bright red extensions with sparkly stars near the cuticles decorated her nails. Sarah wondered if the stars caught on her nylons when Laura dressed and kept her own chewed-off nails out of sight.

"Did you notice any changes in her recently?" Sarah asked.

Laura folded her napkin and placed it under the edge of her plate. "In hindsight, maybe so."

"What?" Sarah probed.

"I think JoBeth became secretive, more distant after she married Phillip. A few hints of dissatisfaction with life in her last Christmas letter. But doesn't everyone have a few of those feelings once in a while?"

"I suppose so," Sarah mused. She tilted the umbrella to accommodate the changing position of the sun. Laura smiled gratefully.

"I guess I wasn't paying attention at the time. Or perhaps I just didn't care." Laura shrugged her shoulders.

"When I look back, I had similar feelings," Sarah agreed. "I don't know what to make of JoBeth's behavior but, if I hadn't been so self-absorbed, I might have noticed that she was in trouble. There must have been something I could've done, something that might have made a difference."

"You shouldn't feel responsible. No matter how big her problems were, she knew right from wrong. Murder is murder," Laura said resolutely. "Someone dies and someone pays."

"But things aren't that concrete. Aren't there different degrees of murder?" Sarah asked. "Would you say murder in self-defense is different than murder for revenge?"

"Self-defense is the exception," Laura conceded.

"And what about the underlying causes of taking a life. How about a teenager who murders her newborn to hide an unwanted pregnancy? Do her parents or society bear some guilt?"

Laura shook her head. "No. Why should they? Even as a small child, everyone knows that murder is the worst of sins."

"Look at it this way," Sarah humored her. "Are the circumstances under which the teenager commits infanticide the same as the mother who stands by and watches her boyfriend abuse and eventually murder her child?"

Laura pushed the crusts of her bread to the side of her plate. "Sorry, my mother spoiled me—she always cut the crusts off." She gave Sarah a half grin.

Sarah put the crusts on the bird feeder. She looked over the tomato garden, and thought about what Laura said. "Both mothers might be motivated by fear but what they fear may have a bearing on the case. In one instance, the teen mother fears discovery and humiliation while, in the other, the mother fears life without her boyfriend. Can you see why it's so important to understand the motivation of each act?"

"Not really. It sounds like a bunch of words to me." Laura pushed her hair away from her face and tucked it behind her ear.

"But that's just it," Sarah argued. "The courtroom is a battleground of words, and it's the words that sway the jury one way or the other."

"I'm not a lawyer. You guys will have to figure that out. What time is it?"

Sarah looked at her watch. "Time to leave."

"Can I take some of those tomatoes home to my aunt?"

"Sure, help yourself. My father will never miss them."

On the walk to the courthouse, Laura asked Sarah what had happened at the trial before she arrived.

"Opening statements. John-Two told the jury that there are reasons why a person commits murder and that sometimes the reasons are not the obvious ones. He hinted that the defense was going to come up with something spectacular. You know John-Two. He can be pretty dramatic."

"I can imagine how the prosecution positioned JoBeth."

"Anger, revenge, hate, jealousy--all of the above. All except mental illness."

"Why not?" Laura asked. "It'd be easy to convince a jury that she went berserk."

"That's for the defense. The prosecution won't go near that one because the public wants her punished and in prison, not in what might be some cushy mental hospital."

"I can see that," Laura said. "If murderers can be forgiven their crimes on the basis of physical or mental abuse, very few can be judged guilty of a crime."

"It does present a moral conundrum, doesn't it?

They arrived at the courthouse at the same time as John-Two and Al. When John-Two saw them, he called out. "Laura! Your aunt didn't tell me you were in town." He placed his arm around her shoulder and she kissed him on the cheek.

"I'm sure Aunt Janet told you. You probably weren't listening." She turned to Al. "I'm Laura, Janet's niece." She held out her hand.

Al took it, glanced at Laura and quickly looked away. "Pleasure," he mumbled. He ignored Sarah.

What's up with him? Sarah hadn't expected a welcoming kiss, but a hello would have been nice.

John-Two locked arms with Laura and led her up the stairs. Al followed close behind Sarah. She imagined his breath on the back of her neck and quickened her pace to keep some distance between them. If he was going to shift into his detached mood again, she could play along. Why should she expect anything but his moody, introspective self? But she did expect something. At least a smile, or some signal that something had happened between them, that they shared a secret. He couldn't have forgotten. Confused and disappointed, she hurried inside. Get over it, she chided herself as she handed her purse to the security guard. Despite her resolve, she stole a glance to see if he was watching her. He wasn't.

Sarah and Laura took their seats, the bag of tomatoes between them. Their acrid smell reminded her of her father, how he transplanted the seedlings from the greenhouse to the garden, nurtured the plants, proudly presenting their fruit to her mother, as if he were a hunter bringing home game that would sustain the household. There was something very primitive about that behavior, so unlike her always-down-to-business father. She smiled, overcome with fond thoughts. Despite their differences this summer, she loved and trusted him. It would take more than a few tiffs to change that.

The afternoon court session began with the sheriff, Thorsten Grimes, testifying for the prosecution. His department had been called by the 911 operator, and the deputies had immediately forwarded the news to him at home.

"When did you first suspect that the defendant murdered her children?" Dunning asked.

The sheriff punched his palm with his fist. "Almost from the beginning."

"What raised your suspicions?"

"When I questioned the defendant at her parents' home the day after she reported the children missing, she said that she had visited her mother that evening, but seemed confused about the exact time. When pressed, she said it might have been sometime after eight. Maitlins' maid contradicted JoBeth's statement. She told me that it was closer to seven when the defendant showed up. If the maid's timing was correct, JoBeth had enough time to drive to Star's Crossing, roll the car into the lake, and walk back to the Bi-Lo."

"Did you ask the defendant about the discrepancy?"

"She insisted it was just after eight, closer to nine."

"Did you ask her where she went after she left the Maitlins' house?"

"She said she only remembers driving toward the lake."

"Was there anything else that made you suspect that the defendant wasn't telling the truth?"

"The defendant said she went into the market to shop, leaving the children asleep in the car. When she returned, both the car and the children were gone."

"What was suspicious about that?"

"None of the clerks in the store remembered seeing her come into the store before reporting the alleged kidnapping. When I asked her what happened to the groceries, she said she must have left them in the parking lot."

"Did anyone find the abandoned grocery cart?

"No."

"Was there anything else?"

"Yes. Her shoes were muddy. It looked like fresh mud. When I asked her about that, she said they were her gardening shoes. I didn't attach any significance to it until after we found the car in the lake. I remembered her shoes were muddied the night of the murders and suspected that she might have been at the lake." The sheriff leaned back in the chair and folded his arms over his chest. He looked pretty satisfied with himself.

"Although you thought that the defendant wasn't telling you the truth, did you pursue the possibility that someone stole the car with the Daniel and Casey in it?"

"Yes."

"Can you tell the court how you pursued the defendant's claim that the youngsters had been kidnapped?"

"We posted a nationwide alert."

"Did you get any leads?"

"As in many of these cases, we received a number of sightings. We followed every lead but none was relevant. In the meantime, we acted on the theory that the abductor might have had a waiting accomplice, and ditched the car somewhere in or around Eight Mile Junction. We sent patrols out on the back roads and dredged the lake by the dam."

"Why dredge near the dam?"

"It was the most obvious place to abandon a car."

"What made you dredge the lake a second time?"

"The defendant. After several interrogations, she admitted that she had taken the children to the lake near Star's Crossing."

"At the time, did she confess to the murders?"

"No. She remembered driving out there but couldn't remember what happened."

"When you dredged the lake, what did you find?"

"We found the defendant's car. Daniel and Casey were still strapped in their seats."

As far as Sarah could see that, while the courtroom was choked with the sadness of the sheriff's testimony, JoBeth showed no reaction. How could she not cry out? Had she retreated into a dream world, protecting herself from the reality of the damaging testimony?

"After you found the car, did you ask the defendant again about the circumstances surrounding the car entering the water?"

"Yes."

"What did she say?"

"She became hysterical."

Dunning walked to the prosecution desk and rifled through some papers. Satisfied that he had completed this line of questioning, he faced the jury and asked the sheriff, "What happened next?"

"Once the car was recovered, I called an ambulance and the coroner. After a thorough investigation and receipt of the coroner's report, I issued a warrant for the defendant's arrest."

"Exactly what that led you to arrest?"

"The approximate time of death, and the lack of any evidence that anyone other than JoBeth and the children had been in the car. Also, a thorough search revealed that there were no unidentified tire tracks or footprints in the mud, or other material evidence that suggested anyone else had been present."

"What kind of evidence were you looking for?"

"Oh, cigarette butts, candy wrappers, stuff carelessly discarded by persons in a hurry to vacate the scene of a crime. You'd be amazed at what someone under those circumstances will leave behind."

"What was it about the place and time of death that made you certain the defendant had committed the crime?"

"The entrance at Star's Crossing is largely unused now that motor boats are prohibited. And, although there is some latitude in the exact time of death, the time between the report of the children's abduction and the coroner's time of death suggests that the abductors would have had only enough time to drive directly from the Ruland household to the lake. The short time period suggests that the murderer was probably familiar with that entrance to the lake. Furthermore, it didn't make sense that anyone who stole a car would discover they had abducted two children and immediately decide to drown them."

"When you arrested the defendant and confronted her with the evidence, how did she react?"

"She cried."

"After the arrest, did you examine the muddy shoes?"

"We found that the mud on her shoes was commonly found in the lake area."

"Thank you, that's all for now."

Al slowly walked to the witness box, and began his cross-examination. "I'd like to go back to the beginning of your testimony. You mentioned the timing. If a person or persons meant to steal a car and later, found two sleeping children in it, could it be possible that the immediate reaction might have been to get rid of the car?"

"Well, yes, but. . ."

"So, the timing in this case can be explained by an immediate decision to get rid of the car and any witnesses."

"It's possible."

"And you testified that JoBeth said that she left the groceries in the parking lot when she discovered that her kids and her car had disappeared."

"Yes."

"And that no one ever found the groceries she left. Is that right?"

"That's right."

"But someone could have come along, taken them, and not admitted to the theft. That's a possibility, isn't it?"

The sheriff leaned forward, replying in a lowered voice. "I suppose it is."

"About the muddy shoes. I checked the weather that night and it had rained earlier in the evening. Do you remember that?"

"I don't remember but if the weather bureau said so, must be so."

"Although the mud on the defendant's shoes can be found around Fenton Lake, it is also present in other parts of this county. Is that not so?"

"Probably so."

"Then JoBeth could have had dried mud on her shoes, walked through a puddle left by the recent rain, and arrived at Bi-Lo with damp shoes. That could explain her muddy shoes, could it not?

The sheriff looked expectantly at Dunning, then back at Al. "Well, yes, that could be so."

"That's all. Thank you, Sheriff Grimes."

Sarah wanted to cheer a job well done. She'd have to remember to say so, show Al that she could rise above her personal feelings.

The next prosecution witness was the clerk at the Bi-Lo Market. He was a young man, barely out of his teens, his sports jacket too wide for his narrow shoulders. He kept straightening his tie, and pushing up his jacket sleeves so they wouldn't hang over his hands.

"Looks like he borrowed the jacket for the trial," Sarah whispered to Laura.

"Mr. MacGrath," Dunning said, sliding his left hand into his jacket pocket. "When did you first see the defendant on the night of the murders?"

"When she came into the store screaming. We all ran to the front, wondering what was going on."

"What time was that?"

"Around nine-thirty."

"Are you certain of the time?"

"Yes, sir. It was toward the end of my shift and I was getting ready to go home."

JoBeth whispered something to Al. He shook his head and patted her on the shoulder. She must be listening, Sarah thought, still wondering why she hadn't reacted to the sheriff's testimony.

"Did you hear what the defendant was saying?"

"At first we couldn't understand her. She kept screaming and pointing toward the parking lot. I thought she had been robbed and said so to the manager." He rubbed chin, then flexed his jaw. "The manager sent me out to look around, but I didn't see anything."

"What happened next?"

"She collapsed. Conrad, that's the butcher, ran to get a chair and a glass of water. When he got back, she had stopped screaming but she was still crying. She told us that her car had been stolen and that her children were in it."

"Can you remember what she said?"

"There was a lot of noise. Everyone kept talking, trying to calm her down. She said something about shopping and when she went back to the car, her kids were gone." MacGrath flexed his jaw again. "She kept moaning 'help me, help me.'"

"Did you see her in the store prior to the time she entered screaming, allegedly the second time that night?"

"No. But I was..."

"What happened after you found out that the children had been kidnapped?"

"The manager called 911."

"When you left the store, did you see an unattended cart of groceries in the parking lot?"

"No."

When Dunning completed his examination, Al approached the witness. He smiled at the clerk, rested his hand on the railing, and spoke in a pleasant voice.

"Mr. MacGrath, you said that you didn't see the defendant the first time she allegedly entered the store. Why was that?"

"I was out back stacking pallets of soda. I didn't come to the front of the store until I heard her screaming."

"So," Al turned toward the jury, "the defendant could have been in the store when you were in the back."

"Yes, but the check..."

"When you came to the front, how would you describe the defendant's state of mind?"

McGrath bit his lip and wrinkled his forehead. "State of mind?" he asked.

"How did she behave?"

"I already said, she was screaming and crying."

"Would you say her grief was real?"

"Objection, Your Honor. The witness is not qualified to testify whether the defendant's grief was real or not."

"Sustained."

"Then tell me, how did she sound to you?"

"Like she was real unhappy. She couldn't have carried on like that if she really wasn't sad."

"Objection."

"Sustained. Strike the testimony."

"Tell me how she looked when you first saw her."

"She looked like a wild woman."

"What did that look like?"

"Her hair was all messed up and she was out of breath, like she had been running. Her face was all red and swollen. She looked awful, like she was wrecked."

"In your opinion, could she have been pretending she was upset?"

"Nobody but a mother who lost her children could act the way she did."

"Objection, this is not evidence," Dunning called out.

"Sustained."

"Did you notice wet mud on her shoes?

"Not really."

"Thank you, Mr. MacGrath."

After the day in court, John-Two, Al, and Sarah gathered in the senior partner's office. After saying good-by to Laura, Janet joined them. John-Two took out a bottle of Chivas Regal and poured two fingers into each of four glasses, raised his glass to the others and swirled the toffee-colored liquid. Sarah caught the faint aroma of orange-honey as she lifted the glass to her lips. The scotch ran cleanly and smoothly down her throat.

"What points did we score today?" John-Two asked Al.

"Two important ones, I think. We began to chip away at the prosecution's assertion that the murders were intentional, and that they were committed in anger or jealousy."

"How's that?"

"The clerk was so sure that JoBeth's behavior was genuine, a mother sincerely distraught over her children. Remember, he said no one else but a grieving mother would act like that."

"But the judge gave Dunning that one," John-Two observed. "He sustained the objection."

"Yes," Al agreed. "But the jury heard the testimony. It could take the edge off the accusation that JoBeth intentionally took the children to the lake to drown them. Juries like remorse and we gave them some today. They can't bring it to the deliberations directly, but they'll remember. Also, if the murders had been planned before she went to the lake, she would have come up with a better alibi. I think we can use that in the closing statement."

John-Two nodded. Sarah could see him mulling over the idea, imagining himself before the jury, making his point. "Anything else?"

"What about the timing?" Sarah asked. "She was aware enough to say she had arrived at the Maitlins' later than she actually showed up. Won't the DA see that as a cover up?"

"We can counter that with confusion. MacGrath's testimony about her state of mind will back that up," Al suggested. "But the prosecution won't let his reference to the checker go by."

"Al, can you come up with some damage control?" John-Two asked.

"I'll think about it. Meanwhile, we'll keep hammering on her life experiences that left her incapable of distinguishing right from wrong, that she doesn't see the murders as an act of vengeance but as an escape from the problems she couldn't solve. Sarah, what do you think?"

"You did a great job today. And I agree with you that she came to a point where she felt she was worthless. She didn't want strangers raising the kids because she believed no one could love them the way she does. But I think you missed something."

"And that is?" Al leaned toward her and gave her one of his penetrating stares.

"Why didn't she stay in the car with them? If we can't explain that, we'll have a difficult time convincing the jury the act was not intentional."

"Fear of death?" John-Two asked.

"Self-preservation," Al volunteered.

"Fear and self-preservation are the most obvious," Sarah agreed. "But if we rely on that, it'll allow the DA to suggest that she selfishly remained alive while destroying her children. That would certainly upset our case that she was a loving mother driven to extremes by her tragic life."

John-Two smiled. "The young lady has a point. What do you think, Al?"

"Then tell us why she decided to live?" Al challenged.

"I haven't figured that out," Sarah admitted. "As bad as things were in her young life, her adult life won't elicit sympathy from the jury. But in my heart, I know there's a reason, a connection that will explain her behavior. I just haven't found it."

"We'd better come up with something quickly. The defense is up sometime next week," Al warned.

"When I see her again, I know I can get to the bottom of this." Sarah spoke firmly. "There's something she isn't telling me, but if I'm patient, I'm sure it'll all come out. Give me a chance."

"What makes you so sure?" Al asked.

"Call it woman's intuition." She smiled at him, almost winked. He averted his eyes and sniffed. That's okay, by now she was accustomed to her father's derision. If she could take it from her father, she could take it from Al.

"It can't hurt." John-Two turned to Janet. "Set up an appointment for Sarah to see JoBeth on Friday. The prosecution is due to complete its case on Thursday and the judge will recess until Monday. Dunning is sure of his case so he won't want to drag this thing on too long. Plays it in the courtroom like he does on the golf course, nice and smug. Al, are we ready for Monday?"

"We're starting with the sheriff, then we'll move to Howard Maitlin."

"Tomorrow the prosecution is putting Phillip on the stand. That should be interesting," John-Two observed. "Any thoughts on that?

"If they play it according to the book, they'll make a dog and pony show out of his testimony," Al said. "You know, the man who'll never get over the loss of his beloved children."

"That might be a difficult one to counter," John-Two said. "He'll have the jury's sympathy for sure. Well, that's it for tonight. Everyone get a good night's sleep and be at the courthouse early." He put the Chivas Regal back in his drawer. Janet took the glasses to her office. Sarah followed her.

"Why don't you come over for dinner tonight?" Janet asked Sarah. She set the liquor glasses on a serving tray and left them for the cleaning lady.

"Are you sure you want to bother? You've had as long a day as any of us."

"Laura's home cooking; all we have to do is sit and eat."

The idea appealed to Sarah. It had been tough saying good-bye to Chewie. She dreaded going home and not being greeted by her. Her mother would want to talk about the dog's final moments and her father would act as though Chewie's death was no big deal. He'd probably say something insensitive, like she was just a dog. Eating with Laura and Janet would be a pleasant distraction. As she dialed home, Al and John-Two headed for the door. John-Two put his hand on the younger attorney's shoulder and asked, "Is your wife coming up for the closing statements?"

Sarah turned to stone. The two men left. The door slammed. Everything happened in slow motion: their voices dragged, her comprehension of what John-Two had asked, the office door closing and Janet's voice came to her over a long distance.

"Sarah, John-Two forgot this briefcase. Could you catch up with them and give it to him. I'll close up."

She came out of John-Two's office and handed the briefcase to Sarah. Numbly, she hurried after the two men, her brain awash in a mesh of thoughts. Married? Was he talking to Al? Had she heard right? Outside, the men were standing by the front door, having a few last words.

"Forgot something," she called out, handing the brief to John-Two. Her lips were thick and leaden, her words slurred. She closely watched John-Two's face to see if he understood what she said. A long time passed before he finally answered. The sidewalk swayed while she waited.

"Thanks, young lady. You keep thinking on that idea you have. See what you can come up with." He took the briefcase and walked off. "See you tomorrow in court."

Al opened his mouth as if he had something to say, took a few hesitant steps toward her, then turned and resolutely walked off. Sarah stood alone. She could hear "son-of-a-bitch," but didn't know if she uttered the words because couldn't feel her lips move.

Chapter Fourteen

Ellen touched her daughter's shoulder lightly. "Stay out too late last night?"

Sarah sat up, reached for her glasses, glanced at the clock radio, and placed her hand on her forehead, as if expecting a raging fever.

"Not feeling well?" Ellen asked.

"No, no. I'm okay. I—got up too fast."

She drew a deep breath and swung her legs over the edge of the bed, burying her toes in the sheepskin rug, searching for Chewie. Empty. She pulled her knees to her chest and huddled back under the covers. The dog, gone. Al. How could she face him today? Thinking about it made her head ache. Raggedy Ann and Andy stared at her from the chair beside the bed; the intensity of their beady eyes unnerved her. She tossed a pillow at them.

"Dad gone?" she mumbled. Things would be less stressful if he wasn't around.

Ellen opened the blinds. "Left early. Some big meeting or other. Have coffee before you dress. It'll get you started."

Sarah tried to clear her mind of the previous night's events, but it was no use. John-Two's words hovered like bees around her brain, taunting her with the fact that she had been seduced by a married man. She'd taken for granted that he was single. Lived alone. No ring. No mention of a wife or family. How was she to know? Why hadn't John-Two or Janet warned her?

Janet's caution the night they had dinner returned. Sure, Al was a private person. This went beyond privacy. But, she should have been more cautious, remembered one of her father's rules: if you don't ask the critical questions, you can't blame anyone but yourself. She had been careless. She had ignored Janet's caution and the obvious clue, a vasectomy. Was she angry or sad? Maybe some of both.

The night before, Sarah had negotiated her way through the dinner with Janet and Laura with studied politeness, fearful that any sound or movement on her part might reveal her frame of mind, that a wrong thought might be followed by tears or, even worse, a misplaced word could release the emotions building up inside. For the entire evening, she had perched on the edge of her chair like a school girl waiting for the bell to ring, half-listening to the table-talk, contemplating escape, and watching for the appropriate time to take flight. The food touching her lips was her only contact with the real world, but she had no idea what she had eaten.

One thing she did remember about the night before. Laura had returned to the previous afternoon's conversation, reexamining the element of fear that might be present in cases of infanticide. "What," she had asked at the dinner table, "did JoBeth have to fear? Many of the awful details of her life had been not only known long before the deaths of Daniel and Casey, but thoroughly discussed by the town's residents. Was there something else?"

What pushed JoBeth over the edge? Not Phillip. She was resigned to fact that her marriage was over. Dating? It wasn't Bendhurst. He was long gone, and according to the gossip, not missed. She probably never expected that much from him, anyway. Her stepfather? Hardly likely. Not much more could be added to that sordid affair. Something else they didn't know? Her job? Was she about to lose it? Surely not. Sam would never fire her. Must have been something she couldn't get over. Some hurt even her stepfather couldn't ease. Or was it that the sum of everything was so weighty that something had pushed her over the edge.

It was an overcast, humid and dreary morning. She leaned against the edge of the bathroom sink and raised the window shade. Outside, the clouds backed up against the mountains, promising but stubbornly withholding the much-needed rain. It was the kind of day when you couldn't decide whether or not to take an umbrella. She wanted to hide, stay in bed, and forget everything. But her return to Eight Mile Junction had become more than an escape; it had become a quest to find the truth behind the murders. She couldn't give up now. She showered and dressed. Downstairs, she called the office.

"Janet, tell John-Two I'm going directly to the jail this morning. And thanks for last night. It was a treat."

"What time do you expect to be in?" she asked.

She wanted to scream at Janet that she would never enter that office again. She wanted to say something nasty, like it was none of her business, but she couldn't blame Janet for what happened. Somehow, she'd have to find a way to face the day.

"Probably after lunch."

"See you." Janet hung up.

And when I get in, that bastard better stay out of my way. Good. Be angry. You're entitled. She poured herself another cup of coffee, sat at the table, and picked up the newspaper. No reason to get all whacked out over that creep. She shook the wrinkles out of the paper and held it in front of her face, hoping to discourage her mother's questions.

"I've never known you to read the sport's page," Ellen observed sweetly.

Sarah folded the paper and tossed it aside. The worry lines around her mother's eyes had deepened. She was concerned, but Sarah couldn't talk to her about what had happened. The wound was too raw. She buried her nose in the cup, letting the steam rise and dampen her face. It felt purifying.

"Perhaps you ought to take a day off."

"I'm okay. Just tired. I stayed out too late last night, that's all."

Sarah fingered the red Chinese hibiscus floating in a cut glass bowl, her mother's centerpiece for the day. The silky smoothness of the petals tempted her to bury her nose in the inviting recesses of the flower, to inhale its fragrance, but she knew its enticing appearance masked the absence of any anticipated sweetness. The flower's empty promise whispered betrayal. Betrayal, that's what it was all about, like the clouds that promised but withheld the rain, the affirmations of love for JoBeth that ended in a Judas kiss, and the overtures by Al that smashed her unfulfilled fantasies.

"What's on your agenda for today?" her mother asked. "Anything exciting happening?" Ellen began to tidy the breakfast table.

"Court's recessed. I'm going to visit JoBeth again."

"I can't imagine how awful it would be to be in jail, unable to be with her family and friends. That poor girl. How's she doing?"

"Holding up. Some days are better than others.

"Give her my best. Home for dinner tonight?"

"I'll call you."

On her way to the jail, Sarah retraced the steps she and Al had taken on their way to his apartment that night, reopening both tender and painful feelings. How could she have let herself be seduced? Her first impression of him was correct. He thought only of himself, not her, not his wife, not anybody. She clenched her fist and walked faster. What a fool she had been. She walked past the jail and continued almost to Millside before she realized she had gone too far and had to turn back.

When JoBeth was escorted into the interview room, she greeted Sarah with her old smile, her dimples appearing for the first time since Sarah's return. There was even a small sparkle in her eyes and the familiar tilt of her head made her little chin stand out like when they played chubby bunny, seeing who could stuff the most marshmallows into their mouth without swallowing. It lightened Sarah's mood.

"How's it going? Need anything?"

"No, they're treating me just fine. Why I'm getting to feel right at home in this place. Funny thing about that, ain't it? Who'd a thought I'd be at home in jail?"

Sarah didn't respond; she was mired in her own troubles. Was she that different than her friend? Maybe she had been like an insect, excreting pheromones, signaling her desires to Al. The idea that nature had taken over and everything had been out of her control was both repugnant and strangely comforting. Not her fault. She wished she could leave it at that, but she had an uncomfortable suspicion that he had seen the same pathetic need for love in her face that she had seen in JoBeth's, and he had taken advantage of the moment.

"Why are you here today?" JoBeth asked.

Her voice jolted Sarah. "I thought we could chat a bit." That sounded out of place in a jail. Chatting belonged to girlfriends at a slumber party, not in this grim interview room. Where to start? The beginning? "Do you remember the day we met?" she asked JoBeth.

"I think it was at school. Do I look good in orange? I never favored this color much before I came here. But I do believe that I'm beginning to look better in these clothes."

JoBeth resisted a visit to her earlier memories, but Sarah recalled that first day at the lake as if it had happened only a short time ago. The memory of her own reluctance to come to the lake, the heat, the sound of students' laughter, and most fondly, JoBeth's complete acceptance of her, crowded together into a pleasantly vague collage.

"Don't you remember that first day at the lake?"

"Why did you come on back here to Eight Mile Junction this summer? Was it for me?"

"It was," Sarah answered.

"But why? We hardly know each other anymore. I would've thought you had forgotten all about me, being up there in that big city with all those important people and having all those interesting things to do."

"I guess I didn't believe the JoBeth I knew could purposely drown her children. I wanted to find that it was an accident; that you lost control of the car and you were helpless to stop it from plunging into the water."

"Whatever made you think that?" JoBeth asked. She looked at Sarah in disbelief.

Her blunt response shook Sarah. She looked away. "I still hope that explains what happened," she whispered.

"That's not the way it was at all. Daniel and Casey were going to have to die, you know. Their momma couldn't protect them from what had happened to her. Those kids had already lost her, and there was no one here on earth to love them or to take care of them."

"What are you talking about? You're still alive."

"The JoBeth you knew died some time ago."

Panic gripped Sarah's throat. Had her friend lost her mind? If what she was saying was true, than the murders were intentional. "I don't understand. What are you saying?"

"Sometimes the thing that makes people who they are just dies away. The actual fact is that a person can be destroyed by the all the things they did. I didn't mean to be bad. It just turned out that way. Even though I might be walking around, I'm not really living, not the kind of living you know about. I'm just pretending that nothing has changed when it really has, so I just go on and on and try and try. But no matter how hard I try, no good ever comes of it. I knew in my heart that it ain't never going to work out for me.

"Who was it that destroyed your life? Was it Phil? Your stepfather?"

"It wasn't any one thing or any one person. It's all those things I did and all those things that was done to me by people I trusted and thought loved me. I used to hide it, but now I want everyone to know, and then I want to die and be with my children. Maybe after the trial is over, you'll know everything and you'll understand."

"JoBeth," Sarah said sternly. "I want to know what made you do this horrible thing."

She looked at Sarah kindly. "There's no more I can tell you. After all this is over, remember the way it was when we were young and how much I loved you. That's all I ask." She signaled the deputy that the interview was over.

When Sarah entered the office, she glanced toward Al's office door. It was closed. Hiding in shame, she hoped. She willed him to feel her mind-darts of anger through the door's wooden panels.

"Oh, Sarah, good morning," Janet said as she emerged from John-Two's office, both hands full of files. Motioning back toward his door with her chin, she said, "He wants you to do a quick interview with Audrey Salisbury late this afternoon."

"Who's that?" Sarah asked.

"She's a nurse at the Malcom Hornsby Medical Center, the hospital where JoBeth's children were born. She'll come to the office around four."

"How's she connected with the case?"

"Audrey and Phillip might have been lovers before he met Jaynelle. Al found something in the last discovery batch he received from the DA. One of the nursing assistants mentioned that, after Daniel's birth, Phillip and one of the nurses became pretty tight. Al asked JoBeth and Audrey's name came up."

"What do you know? Innocent Phillip." Sarah resisted the impulse to go tut, tut, tut. Not surprised. Actually, nothing could surprise her after last night. Even John-Two, pillar of the community, had something to hide. Was her father the only man in the world able to remain loyal to his family? "I'll see what I can get out of her."

She aced the first test, got past Al's door on her way to the library, acting as though nothing had changed. A list of witnesses for the defense had been placed on her desk. Her eyes wandered idly over the names, stopping abruptly at her father's. When did they decide this, and why hadn't anyone told her?

She remembered the conversation Al had with her father the night he came to the house. Something about JoBeth's job performance. More than the actual conversation, Sarah remembered her pleasure when Al had placed her father in an awkward position and how gleeful she'd been at father's discomfort. But was it Al's defense of Sarah or the topic of JoBeth's promotions that raised Sam's hackles. Her mother had interrupted, suggesting she and Al go downtown for the evening. Sarah had been thrilled at the time, glad to escape her father's scrutiny, and pleased to be able to spend time with Al. Now she wished her mother hadn't interfered. Things might have turned out much differently.

Don't make too much of it. Al most likely needs a character witness, and her father would give a great performance on the stand. He'd tell the jury how quickly JoBeth rose in the organization. She filed the list, still wishing someone had told her they had decided to call her father to the stand. Al's a shit but he knows what he's doing. But, despite her faith in his judgment, she couldn't dispel the grating feeling that some ulterior motive underlying Al's decision.

She leaned back and her eyes came to rest on the shelves holding volumes of laws accompanied by even more volumes of decisions and cases. In the end, the library of laws was attended by an even greater library of intellectual thought. Like the Torah and the Talmud. What was meant to be solid and immutable was rendered permeable by the interpretations of lawyers and scholars. She remembered her mother's admonition about Jewish religious thought: if two scholars lived in the same community, there would surely be three synagogues.

She smiled and turned toward the notes she had taken during the morning meeting. Could JoBeth have murdered her children because she thought she was dead already? That didn't make sense but if it was truly what she believed, there was nothing the courts could do to her. The trial was over before it started. Sarah was eager to talk to John-Two and Al about this. But first, she'd have to restrain her feelings about Al. They had carelessly poisoned their work environment. Now she had to live with it. Act as though the whole thing meant as little to her as it did to him. She clenched her teeth and returned to the transcription.

Precisely at four, Audrey Salisbury entered the library. She was a rather gangly woman with dyed black hair that hung loosely about her shoulders. Despite her youthful hair style, she looked to be in her mid-40s. She dropped stiff-backed into the library chair. Her mouth and eyes exhibited a contrived blandness, suggesting that years of attending the sick and damaged had taught her to be impassive. She gave Sarah a disparaging look. "I'm not sure why I'm here."

"We're preparing JoBeth's defense. John-Two thought you might help."

"Why would I?"

Wrong first move. Sarah had mistakenly started with a knight instead of a pawn. She picked up her pen, raised her eyebrows, signaling Audrey that it was time to get down to business.

"Let's start with your job."

"I'm a pediatric nurse."

"Is that how you met Phillip?"

"Look, I haven't seen him in years." She brushed her hand over her brow, as though she was wiping away a memory she didn't want to recall.

"Phillip testified for the prosecution last week, but that was before we suspected that you and he might have had a relationship. If that's the case, we may bring him back. It depends on what you have to tell us."

"What if I refuse? You're asking me about something that happened a long time ago. Not much I remember and, what I do remember, I don't want to talk about."

"We can call you to the stand as a hostile witness and, under oath, you'll have to testify." Sarah sat back in her chair letting the threat hang between them. When she spoke again, it was with a softened voice. "We'd rather not do that. It might be unpleasant for you. What you tell us today may call Phillip's testimony into question. All we want is for you to cooperate. If it goes as planned, we may not have to put you on the stand."

Audrey looked around the library. Sarah guessed Audrey didn't have to be told the consequences of her decision. If she didn't cooperate, she might be subpoenaed and have to testify before everyone about her relationship with Phillip. Messing around with a patient's husband might put her future at the hospital in jeopardy. If not her job, certainly her reputation. By cooperating, she might be able to remain in the background, a bystander instead of a participant. It didn't take her long to decide. "Go ahead, ask your questions," she said. "Just don't take this thing too far."

"Did you meet Phillip at the Malcolm Hornsby Medical Center?"

"Yes."

"And when was that?"

"When Daniel was born. He was jaundiced, so Dr. Forrest hospitalized him. I met Phillip when he came to visit Daniel after work. It was around eight and I was just going off my twelve-hour shift. He asked me to go for coffee. Said he was worried about his son."

"Was JoBeth present when you met?"

"She'd already been discharged. She spent days with Daniel. Phillip came at night."

"How long did that go on?"

Audrey made a wry face. "Does it matter?" When Sarah nodded, Audrey continued. "For several days. I can't remember. Jaundiced babies usually respond quickly."

"And you talked about what?"

"Daniel, mostly. Phillip was worried, of course. This was his first child, and he was inexperienced. He thought jaundiced babies died, or that, if it was a long illness, it might cost everything they had and leave the baby seriously impaired. I reassured him that jaundice was a fairly common occurrence among newborns, that Daniel would be fine, and that he'd be going home in a few days."

"Did you meet after Daniel was discharged from the hospital?"

"Do I have to answer that?"

"No, not now but if you make us call you as a witness, you'll be placed under oath and you'll have to answer. Otherwise, you will be cited for contempt."

Audrey grasped the edge of the chair with both hands. Her purse slid to the ground; the dull thud startled her. The light from the ceiling fell obliquely across her face when she reached to retrieve it. She looked older than Sarah had first guessed, obviously older than Phillip. What had attracted him to her?

Clayton entered the library, preceded by the smell of cigar smoke. As soon as he saw Sarah was with a client, he retreated. Audrey sat, immobile, staring at her purse on her lap, clutching the edges of the seat with both hands. She seemed to be mulling over being placed in contempt, oblivious of the intrusion.

Sarah was not without sympathy. What a miserable situation for someone who had expected so much. Sarah cleared her throat to get Audrey's attention. "How did it get beyond coffee and talk about Daniel?" Sarah asked.

"He told me he didn't love his wife, that he felt trapped, and that he planned to leave as soon as Daniel was old enough to go to school. He wanted to find someone who understood him."

"When did it go beyond comforting to intimate?"

"After Daniel left the hospital, we began meeting at my place. That's when it happened."

"What happened?"

"When we--no," she corrected herself. "I fell in love. I believed he would leave his wife. He asked me to wait."

"So you agreed?"

"Yes."

"Wasn't four or five years a long time?"

"I thought he was worth it."

Audrey took out a handkerchief and held it tightly to her eyes. Sarah waited until she returned it to her purse. Audrey's eyes were dry, but very red. Sarah lowered her voice, trying not to sound accusatory.

"How long did the affair last?"

"At least two years, maybe longer. It took some time before I realized he never meant anything he said to me and much too long to come to my senses."

"When did you realize it was over."

Audrey clutched her purse to her chest. "I was at Gladys'." Her voice was ragged with sorrow. "When Phil and I got serious I started having my hair done once a week. One Saturday JoBeth came in and I could see she was pregnant again." Audrey rubbed her eyes as if she was trying to erase the image of JoBeth with her swollen belly. "I couldn't believe it." She lowered her voice to a whisper. "I knew then that he never meant to leave her. I left the shop before Gladys finished my hair and I never went back."

"Did she know about you and her husband?"

"I suppose so."

"Why is that?"

"In this town? No one has a secret for long."

"What happened after you ended the affair?"

"I went back to my usual life and later, after Casey was born, he took up with the youngest Hollenbeck girl. He didn't even try to hide that one. They walked around in public like two lovebirds, even though he and JoBeth were only separated."

"How did that make you feel?"

"Stupid. I felt as though the whole town was laughing at the old woman who thought she landed a young husband." Her lips quivered. She rubbed them with a strong hand, as if trying to wipe away the painful words she had just spoken.

"And how do you think all this made JoBeth feel?" The question was unfair, but Sarah couldn't resist asking.

"Is that all?" Audrey's voice was harsh and her face stoical, as if she was resigned to carrying the burden of that humiliating experience as retribution for her behavior. She stood, angrily rigid, waiting for Sarah to dismiss her.

After Audrey left, Sarah prepared for the next day's meeting with John-Two and Al. Could she handle being in the same room as Al? Stop thinking and let it happen. She opened a file on her computer and labeled it.

As she typed, the tragedy of it all kept returning to her mind. Audrey must have been thrilled by Phillip's attentions. Already on the verge of never marrying, the unanticipated relationship with a younger man probably turned her colorless life into a rose garden in its second bloom. He must have wanted what she was best able to give: nurturing, comfort, and sympathy. She would have been content in such a relationship, she the caregiver occasionally titillated by the excitement of clandestine sexual encounters. What a shock it must have been, seeing Phillip's wife, the one he promised to leave, pregnant. She, too, must have felt betrayed.

But if his marriage was so unsatisfactory and he was getting what he needed from Audrey, why did Phillip get his wife pregnant again? Didn't he realize that it would contradict everything he'd been telling his lover? Or hadn't his dalliance with Audrey ever meant anything to him? Now, what was left? Two women used and cast aside and another, Jaynelle, waiting on the sidelines, seeing herself as the winner, ever-present in the courtroom and blowing little kisses at her wounded lover. And he, sitting as though enthroned on the stand, pleading with the jury to see him as much of a victim as Daniel and Casey. Well, Audrey had given them enough to discredit Phillip's self-portrayal as a dedicated husband and father.

But would John-Two and Al see Phillip as she saw him? She knew what she would do if she was in charge of the defense. She'd pillory Phillip. She'd get him on the stand and make him out to be the self-indulgent womanizer he was. Like Howard, he had used JoBeth. She may not have been what he was looking for, but was good enough while he looked. Sarah began to tidy her desk for the evening. Improper thoughts for an aspiring attorney. Better watch out, might lose her perspective.

Al's office door was closed but the light, seeping from around the frame, let slip that he was still present. Janet had left for the evening and John-Two's office was dark. The cleaning lady had not yet come in. She and Al were alone. She wanted to knock down the door, stand before him with an accusing finger pointed at his guilty face, scream so he could feel her bewilderment and anger.

She drew a deep breath and steadied. Too dramatic. He'd give her his look that said she was being irrational, probably start writing on his legal pad and pretending she wasn't there. She'd better wait. This was the wrong time. The office, the wrong place. Let him stew, let him wonder what she was thinking, be the one doing the guessing for a change. Might do him good. She'd confront him, but not now. Wait until she was stronger, more sure of herself.

The walk home was invigorating. The clouds had finally fulfilled their promise of rain, and the recently laundered air smelled of fresh linens. She hoped her father would be in a good mood at dinner; she didn't want a confrontation. Coming home for the summer wasn't turning out all that great, but it was a decision she had to live with. She'd ride it out, do her best, and stick to her father's plan. She'd return to Evanston and pick up where she left off.

Perhaps if she confessed that she had second thoughts about spending the summer at home, her father might lighten up. Present it as a casual thought, not an item for debate. Just tell him that, looking back, this may not have been in her best interest. He'd like hearing he was right. She'd tell him that she'd be leaving for Evanston before the sentencing trial. Only a week or two more and then she'd be through with this mess. That's it, patch things up before she left for school. Assure him she was still on track. Like her mother said, a little compromising went a long way.

Her heart lightened and her step quickened, but she still felt as though she was in a handball game, her emotions smacking into one wall after another. This summer would be one to remember. She was still unable to gauge from which direction her feelings about Al would come nor how swiftly they would engulf her. No matter. She'd forget all this once she was back in at school.

St. Agnes was ahead on her left and, when she turned the corner, she could see that the front porch lights of her house were welcoming her home. Well, old girl, she said to the church as she passed, I'll be leaving soon. You've been a kindred spirit, the one thing that has remained stable this whole summer. I'll miss you after I leave. She turned up the driveway, hoping for a pleasant evening.

Chapter Fifteen

The first day for the defense, Al recalled Sheriff Grimes. He walked briskly to the witness box, nodding to the bailiff as he approached.

"Refresh my memory, Sheriff Grimes," Al began. "You testified earlier that you suspected the defendant might be implicated in the murders but, lacking evidence, you proceeded as if the kidnapping had taken place."

"Yes."

"As part of the investigation, you assumed that the defendant's car might have been abandoned by the kidnappers. But dredging that end of the lake at Star's Crossing had not been a consideration."

"Not early in the investigation."

"So, you might never have found the car if the defendant hadn't confessed that she went to Star's Crossing that night. Is that true?"

Al was standing at the jury box, his back to the jurors, a wave of black hair had fallen over his forehead. He pushed it away, letting his hand come to rest on the back of his head. He held it there as he waited for the sheriff to answer.

"At the time the defendant confessed, that was true."

"Then if she hadn't said anything, you might still be looking for kidnappers." Grimes shifted uneasily in his chair.

"Objection. That calls for speculation on the part of the witness."

Without waiting for the judge's decision, Al walked to the witness box and continued. "I want to ask you about the circumstances under which the car entered the water. Since there were no eye witnesses, no one knows exactly what happened that night, no one but the defendant. Is that correct?"

"I'm not sure what you're getting at, but I suppose what you say is so."

"Can you be more definite?"

"We have no eye witnesses, if that's what you're getting at."

"Furthermore, while the defendant confessed driving to the lake, she doesn't remember what happened after she arrived. Is that true?"

"Yes."

"Do we know, without a doubt, that the defendant drove the car into the water, jumping out at the last minute to save herself? Or, could she have exited the car, perhaps to take a breath of fresh air, and watched helplessly as it rolled into the water?"

"Objection, Your Honor. The defense is leading the witness."

"Your Honor, I'm trying to establish that the evidence might show that the automobile could have entered the water accidentally."

"Overruled. However, keep to the point counselor or I'll cut you off."

"Sheriff Grimes, is it true that according to the forensic evidence, the car entered the water slowly and floated for a while before it sank?"

Grimes hesitated, looked at the DA as if for direction, but Dunning's head was turned toward his assistant. Grimes shrugged. "Yes."

"Then the car didn't enter the water under high speed as it would if someone were trying to dispose of it quickly?"

"Objection, Your Honor. The defense is asking the witness to attest to something outside his scope of experience."

"Your Honor, the fact that a speeding vehicle would sink more quickly has already been established by forensics. Sheriff Grimes would be a party to those findings."

"Overruled."

"Thank you." Al turned to Grimes. "Is it plausible that the memory embedded in the distraught mind of the defendant and what actually happened that night could have been different?"

"Objection. The witness cannot attest to what went on inside the mind of the defendant.

"Sustained."

"Let me put it another way. Is it possible that the defendant could have stepped out of the car and, once the car began to roll into the water, was unable to stop it?"

"I suppose it's possible, but…"

"That's all."

Al nodded toward Sarah as he returned to the defense table. She glanced at the jurors to see if the sheriff's testimony had an impact on them. An older woman in the back row blew her nose and wiped her eyes with her handkerchief. Crying or nursing a cold. She couldn't tell. The remaining jurors stared stolidly at the witness chair, showing no emotion.

"Redirect?"

The DA approached. "In your discussions with the defendant, did she ever mention that she forgot to put on the safety brake when she left the car?"

"No."

"Did the defendant ever suggest in any way that the incident might have been an accident as the defense attorney suggests?" He waved his hand toward Al.

"No."

"No more questions."

The judge nodded toward Grimes. "The witness may step down."

When Sarah entered the courthouse the next day, Vera Maitlin was ascending the staircase ahead of her, leaning heavily on a cane. Margaret Standcroft was beside her, holding her arm. Sarah couldn't remember Vera ever using a cane and wondered if she had an accident or if the cane was an attempt to seek sympathy. Howard was testifying that day and she was certainly savvy enough to try to influence the jury.

Every seat in the courtroom was taken. Al was seated next to JoBeth but John-Two wasn't present. As she looked to see if he was anywhere in the courtroom, Sarah saw Clayton and Laura sitting together. Laura passed a note asking Sarah to join them for lunch. Sarah gave her a thumbs up. Janet entered the court room, hurried forward to the defense table, and whispered to Al.

Spectators crowded in, held seats for latecomers and squeezed together to make room for stragglers. Everyone in town wanted to hear what Howard had to say. Where were they when JoBeth needed help, the friends and neighbors she was sure cared for one another, the reason she was reluctant to ever leave Eight Mile Junction? Too late they were gathering, not as a community of supporters, but like vultures perched on the edge of their seats, waiting to hear her tale of degradation.

JoBeth looked as if she was about to cry. Al put his hand on her shoulder, pulled her toward him, and whispered in her ear, massaging her shoulder as he spoke. JoBeth's tension appeared to ease. Sarah stared at his hand and remembered the night when that same hand had caressed her. She shook her head to free herself of the thought but it stubbornly persisted, causing a small drop in the pit of her stomach.

Howard took the stand, his face was ashen, and his lips a thin blue-tinged line. He breathed heavily and periodically cleared his throat. He stared vacantly at the ceiling, watching the ceiling fans. Although the room was air conditioned, his forehead glistened with sweat.

Al began. "Mr. Maitlin, you're the stepparent of the defendant, is that not so?"

"Yes." Howard cleared his throat.

"How old was she when you married Vera Maitlin, her mother?"

"Six." He wiped his brow with a handkerchief, studied it as if he expected to see something, and then blew his nose loudly. Bending slightly forward, he pushed the handkerchief into his coat pocket.

"How would you describe your relationship with JoBeth?"

"Relationship?"

"What were your feelings toward the defendant?"

"Feelings?" His hand fumbled inside his coat, as if searching for something. It came out, shaking and empty. He closed his eyes before he spoke. "I loved her like she was my own daughter."

"You said loved her like a daughter. Can you describe to us how you showed that love?"

"I gave her the best of everything. New clothes. A bike. Anything she wanted, she got. Ask my wife. She'll tell you I loved that child." He pointed toward Vera. "There's her mother, ask her."

"Is that the only way you demonstrated your love for her?"

Howard hung his head and slowly rotated it, as if he had a stiff neck. When he raised his head, his eyes found Vera among the spectators and his mouth formed a weak smile. He looked at Al, raised his eyebrows, but didn't answer.

"Let me ask you another way. How did you show your love for JoBeth?"

"I kissed her, held her on my lap and cuddled her, like any father. Her natural daddy was dead. She needed a man to love her."

"That's all?"

Howard nodded.

"Let the record show the witness indicated yes." He turned back toward Howard, standing close to the witness box. "You never went to her bed at night when she was a child?"

Howard rubbed his mouth before speaking. "I can't remember doing such a thing," he mumbled. He took his handkerchief out and wiped his brow again. He had trouble returning it to his pocket.

"You never went to her bed, fondled her or coerced her into having intimate relations with you?"

"Coerced?" Howard croaked. His face reddened; a sob preceded his words. "I loved her," he said with conviction. "I never coerced anything."

"Your Honor," Dunning interrupted. "I object. Mr. Maitlin isn't the one on trial here. Mrs. Ruland is. What does this have to do with the murders?"

"The defense is trying to show the defendant's frame of mind when the incident happened. And," Al continued, "it supports the case that, rather than committing an intentional act, the defendant succumbed to a series of events directly bearing on what happened that night."

"Continue," the judge directed.

Al turned back to Howard. "Did the defendant ever accuse you of having sexual relations with her?"

"She made a mistake. Ask her mother." He pointed toward Vera again, his forefinger trembling. "She'll tell you it was all a mistake. JoBeth was a child. She didn't know what she was saying."

"Were you called to school to answer the defendant's allegations that you were molesting her?"

"Nothing came of it. Ask her. Ask her. There she is." The words tumbled out of his mouth, his voice was close to hysteria. But he didn't slip. Al was unable to get him to admit to molesting his stepdaughter when she was a child.

"And did you continue to have sex with your stepdaughter, even after she was married?"

"Objection, Your Honor. The witness has testified that they never had sexual relations with the defendant."

"Sustained."

"Did you take your stepdaughter to a motel with the intention of having sexual relations with her?"

"No, no," he sobbed.

Vera leaned toward Margaret and turned her face into her shoulder. Margaret put both arms around her cousin. Sarah couldn't tell if Vera was crying or hiding her face in shame.

Al walked to the defense table, pulled out a bundle of papers, and showed one of them to Howard. "Is this your signature on this invoice for a motel room?"

He looked at the forms and mumbled yes.

"Your Honor, these are invoices from 15 motels with Mr. Maitlin's signature. The motel clerks identified pictures of Howard Maitlin as the motel guest." Al held up the papers. "The signatures on these invoices have been verified as his. The motel registers were signed, Mr. and Mrs. Maitlin. Was it Vera Maitlin who accompanied you to these motels?

"Mrs. Maitlin was not one to go to motels," he whispered.

"Was JoBeth with you when you went to these motels?"

"I, I can't remember." Howard grabbed the rail beside the witness chair. He looked so frail that Sarah was sure he would have fallen if he hadn't steadied himself.

"If the defense calls the motel staff as witnesses, how will they testify?"

"They'll say she was with me."

"By she, you mean?"

"JoBeth."

The courtroom hummed. JoBeth held her face in her hands. Sarah surveyed the jurors again. Several moved uneasily in their chairs. The testimony was having an effect, at least on some of them. What the effect was, Sarah couldn't imagine. But the likelihood of it evoking sympathy for JoBeth was probably minimal. Going to motels with her stepfather wasn't going to bring any cheers from the jurors. Howard had to confess to his behavior toward her as a child or this part of the testimony might not serve the defense's case.

As the judge gaveled for silence, John-Two entered the courtroom and slid into the chair next to JoBeth. Sarah wondered what he had been up to. Al continued questioning Howard.

"Then you admit the defendant accompanied you to the motels not once, but many times."

Howard swayed and sobbed softly.

"Were these meetings a continuation of your sexual relations with the defendant that began when she first entered your household at the age of six?"

"Leave him alone," Vera Maitlin called out. "Can't you see he's a sick old man?

"Silence," the judge gaveled. "I'll have you removed from the courtroom." Then to the defendant, "Answer the question."

"Ruined her," Howard sobbed. "I loved her but I ruined her. What have I done? Oh God, what have I done? Forgive me."

The sound of Howard's sobs joined JoBeth's as she dissolved into tears. Howard coughed. His face contorted and turned a deep purple-red. Al asked for a recess and was granted one until the next day.

As the courtroom emptied, Sarah watched JoBeth being shepherded back to her jail cell by two deputies. Barely able to put one foot in front of the other, she stumbled along as though she had no will, crying softly into the handkerchief she held to her face. Her muffled sobs teased Sarah's tear ducts, making her eyes moisten. What had been meant to further the defense, had brought JoBeth to the edge of a complete breakdown.

At the office, Janet motioned to Sarah that John-Two and Al were in the conference room. "Go right in," she said.

John-Two pointed to a large brown envelope. "This was slipped under the office door last night after I left." He handed the envelope to Al.

"What's this all about?" Al asked as he spread the contents on the table.

"It's the minutes of the meeting recording JoBeth's complaint against her stepfather."

"Great! Have you gone over them?" Al asked.

"Thoroughly. That's what I've been doing all morning. Take a look at it, Al. We'll meet here later this afternoon and decide what we'll do with it."

"Good enough." Al left the room.

John-Two turned to Sarah. "Something I want you to do. Get on the telephone and track down the person who delivered the envelope. Get the names of the school's administrative staff at the time this meeting was held. The person who delivered this is probably someone who was at this meeting and, if we're lucky, still lives in town or nearby."

"And if I find that someone?"

"See what you can get out of him. Or her."

Sarah's first call to the middle school receptionist revealed that Trudy Anders, the school secretary when JoBeth was in the seventh grade, was the most likely candidate. Now retired, she still lived in Eight Mile Junction. Sarah got her number from the phone book, called, and asked to see her.

"Oh dear me, now I remember you," Mrs. Anders greeted Sarah. "You were one of the brightest youngsters we ever had at the high school. Now look at you. All grown up. And a lawyer no less. My, my."

"Not an attorney yet, but I'm working on it. And I remember you, Mrs. Anders. You were a great help to students."

A spare, wrinkled woman, Mrs. Anders leaned on her walker, taking slow and unsteady steps as she led Sarah into the living room. She bent her knees gingerly, and fell back into an overstuffed chair next to the fireplace. A white ceramic cat slept peacefully on the hearth.

"You sit here, sweetie." She pointed to the chair beside her, folded the walker, and leaned it against the lamp table. Mrs. Anders raised her left leg onto the ottoman. "Swells if I don't put it up," she explained. A painfully red bunion on one of Miss Anders big toes squeezed itself between the straps of her sandals.

The curtains were pulled and the room was dimly lit. The walls were filled with pictures of the high school's graduating classes, and the mantel was crowded with framed honorary certificates for Mrs. Anders' service. Sarah tried to find her class among the pictures but they had been hung randomly.

"Mrs. Anders, did you deliver the package to the Williams' law offices last night?"

"Not really," Mrs. Anders said. "Can I get you some tea?" She leaned forward as if to rise from her chair.

Sarah held up her hand. "No, thank you," she said, imagining how long it would take for the older woman to walk from the living room to the kitchen. Keep her seated and focused.

Mrs. Anders sat back and waited, her eyes gazing myopically at Sarah through her thick lenses. The small stream of light that entered the room through the transom over the front door illuminated the dust particles in the air and made the red and blue sequins decorating her hair net flicker as her head bounced to a rhythm set by a slight tremor.

"Do you know who delivered it?"

Mrs. Anders averted her eyes, pushed some straggling hairs under her hair net, and adjusted her position. A rush of musty air rose and filled Sarah's nostrils. Before speaking, Mrs. Anders leaned forward in her chair. As if fearing someone would overhear her, she whispered, "I guess it wouldn't hurt if I told you, now would it?"

"Certainly not," Sarah assured her. This is like dealing with a kid. She looked at her watch.

"It was Louis Sterns, the next door neighbor's boy."

"How did he get those papers?"

"Why, I gave them to him," she said in a startled voice, as if surprised that Sarah hadn't guessed.

"How was it that you had those papers?"

"After the whole thing was settled, the meeting and all, Mr. Haverly, the principal, told me to destroy everything. He said there was no use in letting this stuff lay around. Might get into the wrong hands and ruin Mr. Maitlin's reputation. Vera put that thought into Mr. Haverly's head.

I didn't like it, that thought and all, but I didn't have the right to say so."

"Why didn't you destroy them?"

"It was so long ago, you know. But thinking back on what happened that day, I guess I felt that it was wrong. So I did the next best thing. I brought them home and hid them in the guest room under the mattress."

"So, you thought it might be wrong to destroy them. Why?"

"I felt sorry for that little girl. The whole thing didn't set right by me. Vera and her fancy ways, always protecting that fat old man. She'd a never looked at him twice if he wasn't rich, you know."

"Why did you decide to give the papers to Williams after all these years?"

"It's time someone stood up for what happened. Mrs. Jinnings, the school nurse, tried to. She told me how frightened JoBeth was the day she came to her office."

Mrs. Anders raised her hand to her cheek and mumbled a few words, then looked at Sarah with rheumy eyes. It took her awhile to gather her thoughts but, when she did, she spoke in a stronger voice. "When JoBeth told the nurse her story, Mrs. Jinnings demanded the principal do something about it. And she demanded, I can tell you. I could hear them talking in the principal's office and Mrs. Jinnings raised her voice to Mr. Haverly. Now that surprised me no end, you know. That wasn't like her at all. Oh, I could tell she was madder than a wet hen. I thought to myself at the time that there must be something to this to make her so gosh darned mad."

"Does Mrs. Jinnings still live around here?"

"My heavens, no. She died right after she retired. It was cancer. Liver, I think. Terrible thing, you know. So many of them go with cancer these days. Makes a body wonder."

"What about Mr. Haverly? Is he around?"

"He left town some years ago, I can't remember how many. Retired and moved to Florida, or was it Alabama? Some place farther south of here. I heard they went into one of those gated communities where all the folks with money go."

"What happened at the meeting?"

"Nothing, really. Mr. Haverly said it was a private family matter. JoBeth went back to class. No one ever mentioned it again."

"Miss Anders, we may ask you to come to court and testify to what happened that day."

"Oh, my dear, I couldn't do that." Mrs. Anders held her knee in both hands and massaged it, then lifted it off the ottoman. "Gets cranky if it sets too long."

"You could help JoBeth get the justice she never got as a child."

Mrs. Anders shrugged. "I have to live in this town, you know. Everyone would find out that I disobeyed the principal. Oh no, I couldn't have that. It would ruin my reputation, my years of service to the school. That's exactly why I had those papers delivered in secret. I told that boy not to say anything and he promised. That's why I gave him a quarter. Hush money. Like the detectives on the television."

"What if we called you as a hostile witness?"

"No." She was adamant. Then she asked, "What does that mean?"

"It means that you are testifying but you don't want to."

"Horse-pukkey," she said as she pulled her walker to the front of her chair and unfolded it. Sarah let herself out as Mrs. Anders headed for the kitchen.

In the conference room, papers were spread across the table, and the two attorneys were examining them. When Sarah walked in, John-Two looked up. "Well, young lady?"

"Found her. It was Mrs. Anders, the school secretary at the time JoBeth made the complaint against her stepfather. The principal told Mrs. Anders to destroy her notes from the meeting, but she didn't. She took them home and hid them."

John-Two snorted.

"Good work," said Al. He kept his eyes buried in the papers.

"Would she make a good witness?" John-Two asked.

"She isn't willing to testify. She's afraid if she admitted disobeying the principal, her reputation will be ruined."

"We'll see if we need her before we worry about it. So, what've we got here?" John-Two asked rhetorically.

Al picked up the first pile of papers and took the lead. "This evidence begins the day JoBeth made her claim. It contains notes of the complaint compiled by the school nurse and minutes of the succeeding meeting with the Maitlins. According to the school nurse, JoBeth came to her office and told her that her stepfather had been hurting her and that she'd bled after their encounter the night before. The nurse examined her head, arms, legs, and upper torso, thinking the child had been physically abused but couldn't find any skin breaks or abrasions. She asked how her stepfather had been hurting her, and JoBeth told her he had been sticking his fingers and his big thing in her. The nurse went to the principal and demanded they have a doctor examine the child. " Al handed John-Two the papers. "It's in the nurse's handwriting, but it's easy to read."

John-Two handed the papers to Sarah. "Was that before or after they called in Vera and Howard Maitlin?" he asked.

"Before. Because JoBeth was a minor, the school couldn't authorize an examination without Maitlin's permission. The nurse suggested a court order, but there was no follow-up."

"Did anyone suggest calling the police or child protective services?" Sarah asked. She tried to make eye contact with Al, show him she could rise above her personal life, but he avoided her, directing his comments to John-Two.

"There's no record of contacting anyone other than the Maitlins'."

"So then what happened?" Sarah asked.

"The principal directed Mrs. Anders to ask the Maitlins to come to school. Evidently Vera showed up first, Howard a little later."

"Where was JoBeth?" Sarah asked.

"The secretary's notes show that when Vera arrived, she asked for JoBeth. The nurse told her that her daughter was resting on the cot in her office. There's no record that Vera asked to see or to go to her." Al held up Mrs. Anders' notes recording the attendance and read. "Mr. Haverly, the principal, Mrs. Anders, the school secretary, Mrs. Jinnings, the school nurse, and the Maitlins were at the meeting. The rest we pretty much know. Howard denied the accusation and Vera assured everyone that her daughter had a vivid imagination, and that she had frequent sexual fantasies. Vera pleaded with the principal not to ruin her family life and her husband's reputation by following up on her daughter's childish stunt. She explained the bleeding by saying that JoBeth had begun menstruating a few days before."

"Did anyone at the meeting suggest that JoBeth be examined by a doctor?" Sarah asked.

"Not at the meeting. If anyone did, it wasn't recorded." Al said.

"Do you think the principal told Mrs. Anders not to include such a request in the notes?" Sarah persisted.

"We'll never know unless we put her on the stand," John-Two said. "Now, what do we have that we can present in court and whom can we call to testify? Can you convince the old lady that it's her civic duty?" he asked Sarah.

"If we did, she would be a reluctant witness. She could easily get away with saying she can't remember."

"The school nurse and principal, are they still around?" John-Two asked.

"The nurse died and the principal retired and moved south somewhere, Florida or Alabama. Mrs. Anders wasn't sure."

"I'll ask Janet to follow up," John-Two said. "It might take a while but if we can find him, we can ask for a delay."

"What about Vera?" Sarah asked. "She seemed very willing to give up her daughter to save her status and her husband's reputation. Get Vera on the stand and ask her why she never had her daughter examined by a medical doctor at that time of the complaint. If she continues to deny the molestation charges, ask her why she didn't take JoBeth to a therapist to find out why she had such vivid sexual fantasies."

"She's got something there," John-Two agreed. "Maybe Vera is the key or, if not the key, the weak link. Our young lady is growing up. Going to make a fine trial attorney, don't you think Al? You and she could become partners." His eyes twinkled.

Al looked directly at Sarah for the first time. If there was a memory of their night together, it couldn't be detected in his eyes. "Although Howard hasn't confessed that he molested her as a child, we can document that JoBeth did make an accusation as well as the Maitlins' response to their daughter's charges."

"Howard testified that he ruined her, didn't he? Isn't that a confession of something?" Sarah asked.

"Dunning won't let that pass as a confession. He'll find another interpretation. We've got to get Howard back on the stand as soon as he recovers and wear him down until he admits that he's a pedophile. Depending on how much the judge is willing let us get away with, it might work. So far, he's been pretty lenient." A note of bitterness crept into Al's voice. "If Howard perseveres, insisting that it was only a childhood fantasy, the defense will be weakened. All we have is an affair with a consenting adult," Al continued. "Be sure the prosecution will hammer that home."

"How about Vera?" Sarah asked.

"If she comes off as a selfish witch, ready to sacrifice her daughter for the sake her own interests, it might go a long way toward establishing JoBeth's state of mind when the incident at the lake occurred," Al said. "Even if we can't prove he molested his stepdaughter, we can use Sarah's line of thought: show that as parents, they neglected a disturbed child who needed help."

"Get your stuff ready for tomorrow," John-Two suggested. "After you finish with Howard, get right at Vera. No mercy. Do you need Sarah's help tonight?"

Al put the notes in order and returned them to the file. He handed it to Janet. "Take good care of this." Then, to John-Two, "No, I got this," he answered without looking at Sarah. "We already have Vera lined up right after we finish with Howard. I believe her testimony will have the greatest impact on the jury if we can show Howard's weaknesses followed by her vindictiveness. If Sarah's right, JoBeth's mother will help us by showing her sinister side."

"Be sure to work in her statement that Phillip left her daughter because she was pregnant and not pure when they married," John-Two reminded Al. "Get that "used goods" sentiment out of her."

When Sarah got home, her mother had posted a phone message from Jameson on the refrigerator door. Could she call him about coming to his house for dinner again the next weekend?

She wasn't ready for another evening at the Hillyard's. Not enough time had passed to put that dismal night behind her and not enough time for Arnold to come up with a new bag of tricks to add some humor to the evening. She put the message aside, planning to call and beg off in the morning before she went to court, but had a change of mind. She dialed and when Arnold answered, she asked him to tell Jameson that Sarah was calling.

"Knock, knock." Arnold said.

"Arnold, please, go get Jameson."

"Come on, Sarah," Arnold insisted. "Knock, knock."

Sarah played along. "Who's there?"

"Hairy."

"Hairy, who?"

"Hairy finger." Arnold laughed. "Get it, Sarah?"

"Very funny, Arnold. Now go get Jameson."

"It's Sarah," she said when he answered. "Thanks for the invite but we're busy at the office this weekend. The trial is at a critical place, so I can't come for dinner. But court recessed early and I'm free tonight. Can we meet at the Agusta for a drink? How about nine?"

As she walked down Main Street toward the hotel, Sarah felt pretty good. Both Al and John-Two had listened to her at the meeting, and her interview with Vera was going to become a major part of the defense. And Jameson--she felt a little guilty about that. Meeting him at the Agusta wasn't because she wanted to see him. She wanted out of another dinner with the Hillyards and, as an added plus, Al might stop by later to see Miss

Fancy Pants Waitress. A great chance to show him that she wasn't sitting home and wasting any thoughts on him. Her shamelessness nudged her conscience, but she pushed it away.

Chapter Sixteen

"*L*et the record show that the defense witness, Howard Maitlin, is resting at home under doctor's orders and unable to continue testifying." After the bailiff addressed the court, he handed the doctor's confirmation to the judge. He scanned the paperwork before handing it to the clerk. "Call your next witness," he instructed.

"Vera Maitlin."

Vera leaned heavily on her cane as she walked forward. The clerk held her arm as she climbed the step and settled into the witness chair. She patted his arm, turned and smiled broadly at the jury.

JoBeth bit her lip as she glanced back at Sarah and, raising her eyebrows quizzically, formed the word "why." Sarah gave a thin smile. Vera's intemperance was going to be hard on her daughter. As illogical as it was, Sarah knew that even most derelict mothers earned the love of their children. JoBeth was no exception.

Al addressed the courtroom. "Let the record show that this witness is testifying under duress."

"Proceed."

Al stood close to the witness stand and leaned in toward Vera. "Mrs. Maitlin, did your daughter, JoBeth Ruland, accuse her stepfather, Howard Maitlin, of sexual abuse when she was in the seventh grade?"

"Your Honor," Dunning interrupted. He unbuttoned his coat and leaned both hands on the desk as he spoke. He had moved so quickly, it appeared as though he might leap across and approach the bench. Instead, he leaned heavily on his clenched fists and growled, "What does this have to do with the murders of the Ruland children?"

"Are you objecting?" the judged asked the DA

"Can we approach the bench?" Dunning asked.

"If you don't have an objection, let's get on with the case."

"No ojection."

The judge nodded toward Vera. "Continue."

"That's all bygones now," Vera said. "Everyone in this town knows about Mr. Maitlin's good reputation. Anyway, what do you know about it?" She eyed Al malevolently. "You weren't even here."

"You must answer the question," the judge directed.

She screwed up her nose and shook her head. "It was only one of her silly fantasies." She paused and stared at the purse she held on her lap, absent-mindedly began opening and closing it. The cadence of the snap could be heard throughout the hushed courtroom. "Nothing ever came of it." Her eyes slid over her daughter, avoiding JoBeth's intense gaze.

"We had to go to school to straighten that whole thing out. It was a trying day, let me tell you, but it turned out to be a waste of our time."

"Who was at the meeting?"

"I don't remember."

Al walked to the defense table and brought forward the evidence of the school meeting that Mrs. Anders had delivered to John-Two's office. "This envelope was delivered to the Williams' law office the night before last. It contains the minutes of the meeting held to review the defendant's complaint that her stepfather had molested her."

Vera watched as Al approached the stand. She shrugged her shoulders and looked away, as if it were no concern of hers.

"According to the signatures on the attendance sheet, in addition to Mrs. Anders, the school secretary who recorded the proceedings, the meeting was attended by the principal, Mr. Haverly; the school nurse, Mrs. Jinnings; Mr. Maitlin, and yourself." He showed Vera the notes, pointing to the list, each name neatly printed followed by the attendee's signature. "Can you testify that these persons attended the meeting?"

Vera fumbled with her purse and pulled out her bifocals. To bring the words into focus, she lifted her chin and looked down through the lower half of the lenses.

"I--ah. I was told all this would be destroyed," Vera stuttered. "We all agreed on that." She took off her glasses and looked at the judge. "Since nothing did come of the meeting, Mr. Haverly said there was no need to keep this stuff laying around—they could be taken the wrong way."

"As you can see," Al said, "the minutes have been preserved. Can you verify that these persons were in attendance?"

"I suppose so."

Al turned toward the bench. "I'm entering these minutes into evidence." He turned back to the witness. "To whom did the defendant make the allegation of abuse?"

"I don't remember," Vera whispered. The purse was silent. Vera's hand fiddled with her eye glasses. They fell to the floor.

Al waited for Vera to retrieve her glasses. "Was it the school nurse, Mrs. Jinnings?"

"Maybe. As I said, it was a long time ago." She glanced at the judge. "But yes, I guess it was the school nurse."

"Did anyone at that meeting suggest that the defendant be examined for sexual abuse?"

"Before we arrived, the school nurse wanted to call in a doctor but they needed Mr. Maitlin and me to say it was okay. And it's a good thing, too. If she had had her way, that nurse would have had the whole town gossiping over nothing. My daughter made up that spiteful story about Mr. Maitlin doing something to her to make her bleed. I told that nurse that JoBeth had started to menstruate and that was all there was to it."

"Did anyone suggest child protective services be contacted?"

"No one suggested that. They knew she was a little liar."

JoBeth called out, her words sobbed into a jumble. The judge gaveled. "Continue," he ordered. JoBeth crumbled into her seat.

"Are you testifying that everyone at that meeting already knew that the defendant was a liar?"

"Yes, I am." Vera began to open and close the latch on her purse again.

"And how did everyone at the meeting know that the defendant was lying?"

"I told them about her sexual fantasies. From the time we moved into Mr. Maitlin's house she had them at one time or another. She was jealous of me, wanted to ruin my life. She told me there was a lion in her wardrobe and he came out at night and did, well, no Christian woman can repeat none of what she said."

"Did she tell you that the lion came into the bed and molested her?"

"Yes."

"Did you believe her or did you dismiss her knowing that, if you found it was true, it would destroy your marriage and your social standing?"

"Heavens no, I never believed that story of hers. She didn't even have a wardrobe in her bedroom."

Al took a deep breath before he asked the next question. "Were you aware that your husband frequently left your bed at night?"

Vera's eyes widened and when she spoke, her voice was tinged with anger. "You don't have to tell me anything about my husband. I know he got up at night and roamed around. He's a poor sleeper. He took to going downstairs to smoke. Sometimes he'd doctor himself up with a little brandy. I could smell it on his breath when he came back to bed."

"Now that you know your husband and the defendant were lovers and went to hotels, are you still sure that while he was up a night, he wasn't abusing your daughter?"

"I object, Your Honor." The DA stood and walked toward the bench. "Mr. Maitlin's behavior is not on trial here. I keep asking the court, what does this have to do with the murders?"

"Everything, Your Honor," Al countered. "The defense is trying to establish the series of events that contributed to the defendant's state of mind at the time of murders."

"Overruled. Make your point and let's get on with it. Do you have any further questions for the witness?"

"Wait, Your Honor," Vera called out. She stood up in the witness box and faced the judge.

"The witness shall remain seated," the judge cautioned her.

"Still standing, she pointed her cane toward her daughter as she spoke. "The hotel business was probably her idea. Put her on the stand and ask her."

JoBeth held her hands in front of her face, and pushed forward, as if to stand. John-Two placed a hand on her shoulder. She looked at him, mouthing words that Sarah couldn't hear. He shook his head and JoBeth lowered hers, cradling it in her hands.

Vera continued without looking at her daughter. "It's just the kind of thing she would think of. I know my daughter and her nasty habits."

"What kind of habits are you talking about, Mrs. Maitlin?" Al asked.

"You know, sex. She tried to come between me and my husband from the day we moved in. Following that darling man around like a little puppy dog, hanging on him, trying to get his attention when he was talking to me. He put up with her because he loved me. And don't you forget that she was pregnant when she got married. Doesn't that tell you something about the kind of person she is?" Vera's looked at Al, her lips drawn up in a mirthless smile, as though she had one-upped the defense attorney. "That tells you everything, doesn't it?"

"That's all, Your Honor."

Ian Dunning stood before Vera. "Tell me, Mrs. Maitlin, when your first husband Orrin Bellinger died, what happened?"

"Lord, everyone in this courtroom knows that business already."

"We'd like you to tell us for the record."

"We were thrown off our farm and it was sold to pay our debts, that's what happened. Not that there was enough money left to pay much of anything. Mr. Bellinger wasn't one for making money, not like my present husband."

"Then what happened to you and the defendant?"

"Mr. Maitlin took us in, spared nothing."

"Now think back carefully, and remember you're under oath. Can you testify that, to your knowledge, your husband never sexually abused your daughter when she was a child?"

"I swear to that."

"There was never a time you suspected anything?"

"Never. We were close as two people can ever be. I'd have known if anything like that was going on, so let me tell you, nothing was."

"How about now that you found that your husband was taking JoBeth out of town to motels. Didn't that shake your confidence in him?"

"I already told you. It was her idea." Vera pointed toward her daughter as she spoke. "Men are weak. It's up to women to keep the Lord's commandments. And my daughter doesn't have enough sense to keep one of them. If she did, she wouldn't be here now, would she?"

"That's all."

Vera left the witness stand without looking at the defense table. Sarah tried to assess how much of an impression Vera's testimony made on the jurors. Despite her disillusionment with Al, she had to admit he had done a masterful job. He had shown the jury that Vera was willing to sacrifice her daughter for material gain. But reading their faces was like reading tea leaves; you needed a great deal of imagination to know what was going on. Could Vera's testimony have given the jury any insight into the wretched life her daughter had led? Or did it merely underscore the opinions they already had formed?

That afternoon, Al recalled Phillip Ruland. He had "pudged" out since the days when JoBeth described him as her Prince Charming. Al reminded him that he was still under oath. "Earlier, you testified that you left your wife because your marriage wasn't going well. Is that correct?"

"Yes."

"Can you refresh the court's memory about the reasons you left the defendant?"

"Objection. That testimony is in the record. The defense is harassing the witness."

"Then may I take the time to have his testimony read? My questioning depends on the juror's remembering the details accurately."

"Withdrawn."

The judge directed Phillip to respond.

"I told the court that she was a lousy housekeeper, and that she spent money on things we couldn't afford. When I came home at night, she would be at her mother's house or some girlfriend's place, not home where she belonged." He nodded toward his former wife as he spoke, as if to make certain the jurors knew he was talking about her.

"Did she neglect the children?" Al asked.

"Oh no, she never did that. The fact is that it was in her nature to be mothering no matter what. But dinner was never ready because one or the other of them was always needing something. And if one of them took sick, forget it. I might as well have rented a room at the Agusta. I'd a got more attention from the help there than I ever got at home."

"So you became disillusioned. How soon after you married would you say that happened?"

"After our daughter was born. It was as if there was no place for me in that house anymore. It's an awful feeling when a man gets to being lonely in his own home."

"And that was after Casey was born? You're sure of that."

Phillip nodded.

Al walked to the defense desk and picked up a note pad. He faced Phillip and asked, "Do you know Audrey Salisbury?"

Phillip jerked his head aside, as if avoiding a blow. When he answered, his voice was cautious. "I believe she was one of the nurses over at the hospital where Daniel and Casey were born."

"When did you first meet her?"

"After Daniel was born."

"That was your son and first child. Is that correct?"

"Now that I think back on it, that's right."

"How well did you get to know Ms. Salisbury?"

"She was a great help to me and my wife at the time. Knew a lot about newborn jaundice." Phillip glanced toward Jaynelle. She puckered her lips, as if giving him a kiss. He fingered his collar and gave her a lop-sided grin.

"Did JoBeth ever talk to Ms. Salisbury after she was discharged from the hospital?"

Phillip glanced around the courtroom. "I surely think she did."

"But didn't JoBeth visit Daniel during the day, and Ms. Salisbury work the night shift?"

"I believe that's so," Phillip whispered.

"Then JoBeth wouldn't have spoken to Ms. Salisbury. Isn't that right?"

"Right."

"So, it was only you and Ms. Salisbury that discussed Daniel's condition."

"Yes."

"Did you talk to Ms. Salisbury about anything other than Daniel's condition?"

"Not that I can recollect right off."

"Did you ever meet her outside the hospital?"

"Maybe once or twice in the parking lot."

"You never met Ms. Salisbury anywhere other than the hospital or the hospital parking lot?"

"Not that I can recollect."

"Never at her apartment on 1632 East Street?"

"I don't have any remembrance of that address."

"You never met Ms. Salisbury's landlady, Mrs. Wallace Nalley?"

Phillip remained silent. Al continued.

"If the court please, I have a signed affidavit from Mrs. Nalley testifying that the witness visited Ms. Salisbury several times a month between January 1992 and December 1994." He entered the affidavit into evidence. "According to Mrs. Nalley, the visits lasted on and off for about two years. Would you say every one of those visits were about Daniel's condition?"

Phillip shrugged, "I needed someone to talk to," he spoke directly to Jaynelle. "Couldn't talk to my wife, what with her taking up with the children all the time and leaving me out."

"So, Ms. Salisbury became your confidant for two years. During that time, were you ever intimate with her?"

Phillip glared at Al. "That ain't none of your business."

"Answer the question," the judge instructed.

"You could say that."

Al pressed, "You could say what?"

"That we became intimate with each other every once in a while. That's what you want me to say, isn't it?"

"Then it would be correct to assume that you became disillusioned with your marriage quite some time before Casey, your daughter and second child was born, is that true?"

"I didn't mean it to be that way." He held out his hands as if pleading for understanding. "All I needed was a friend, someone to talk to. It was Audrey that kept inviting me to her place. She wanted more from me than I wanted to give. I was being put in a bad position."

The courtroom observers snickered; the judge gaveled.

"In fact," Al continued, "it was less than one year after you married the defendant that you had already begun to take an interest in another woman. Is that correct?"

"If you say so."

"Then your previous testimony about your discontent with your marriage was not entirely truthful. Would you say that was correct?"

"Yes. But that ain't got nothing to do with what happened to my children."

"What impact did you think your affair with Ms. Salisbury had on your wife?"

"I don't rightly know. Like as not, she didn't care much. I told you, she wasn't interested in me or keeping house."

"Why do you think you wife, JoBeth Ruland, murdered your children?"

"Objection. That calls for speculation."

"Do you think your indifference had a negative impact on the defendant and led to the murders?"

"She wanted to punish me for having some happiness. That's all there is to it. She wanted to take them away from me."

"That's all." Al returned to the defense table.

"No questions," the DA stated.

Sarah scanned the jury box, hoping to see some indication that the jurors saw Phillip's concerns had always been about himself, not his wife or his children. The juror's faces were impassive. In the end, Phillip's trysts with Audrey Salisbury, if not commendable, might be judged forgivable by the jurors because his testimony made it appear that it was he who suffered, he who needed to look elsewhere for companionship?

Kenny Bendhurst was called to testify next. It didn't help the defense when he showed up with chains wrapped around his lower legs and in a sleeveless shirt that revealed tattooed arms. The metal-spike bracelets around his wrists and ankles made it appear that he was ready to go into battle. Since Sarah had seen him last, his pony tail had been exchanged for a Mohawk: a two-inch spike ran from his forehead to the nape of his neck, the remaining scalp was shaved clean. He looked even more bizarre than when Sarah last saw him.

The spectators stirred as he swaggered into the courtroom. The difference between his appearance and Phillip's fastidiousness probably weakened the argument that the defendant was looking for a replacement father for her children. As hard as Al tried to show Bendhurst was another who used and dumped JoBeth, the witnesses' rejection of Daniel and Casey because they were not blood kin elicited knowing nods from the jury. Clearly, it was something they could relate to. In the end, his opinion that JoBeth had put the children to sleep for their own protection was uninspiring.

When Dunning cross-examined, he tore into Bendhurst's testimony on JoBeth's motivation.

"So, Mr. Bendhurst," Dunning began. "You testified that the defendant wanted to protect rather than harm her children. Is that correct?"

"Yes, sir."

"Did she ever tell you that she had reason to protect them?"

"I don't getcha."

"Did JoBeth say why she had to protect Daniel and Casey?"

"Not exactly, sir."

"What did she say?"

"Something like she didn't want them to live the life she lived."

"But she didn't use the word protect."

"But that's what she meant."

"The witness cannot testify to what the defendant meant," Dunning countered.

"Strike from the record," the judge ordered. Then to the witness, "Answer yes or no."

"Yes, sir."

"Thank you, Your Honor." Dunning turned to Bendhurst. "Did you speak to the defendant after the events of March 19?"

"No, sir."

"Then your testimony is not based on fact, is it?"

Bendhurst slumped in his seat, ran his hand across his shaved head, and cleared his throat. "Well, like I said to that other lawyer, JoBeth loved them kids. And she was a good mother."

"On the basis of that, you figured out all by yourself that she was protecting rather than murdering the children. Is that right?"

"Objection. Counselor is twisting the witnesses' words."

"No more questions."

Bendhurst's chains jangled as he left the stand.

During Bendhurst's testimony, the jury sat immobile. Despite his unconventional appearance, Sarah worried that the jurors would find him a victim of JoBeth's aggressive neediness rather than seeing her involved, once again, in an unhealthy relationship that offered no benefits. The case seemed to have taken two steps back.

The next morning, Dora Channing testified first. She entered the courtroom like a schooner under full sail: a determined look on her face, and elbows extended as ballast. Sarah almost expected to see Chelsea and Max running along behind her. As soon as Dora settled into the witness chair, she looked toward husband and waved. Henson smiled his toothless grin, and waved back.

Once Al established Dora's credentials, he asked her about JoBeth. "When the defendant worked in your shop, what was her position?"

"Data entry specialist. Everyone starts there in my shop. No exceptions," Dora said sharply.

"Was she a good employee?"

"I don't know what you mean by good. Good, like was she a good girl?" She cocked one eyebrow, daring Al to respond.

Ouch, Sarah thought. This is getting off on the wrong foot.

"I'm speaking of her work performance," Al said evenly.

"Should've said that right off," Dora reprimanded him. Al grinned, appeared unperturbed, and waited for her to go on. "She knew her job," Dora continued. "Could enter data as fast as anyone I ever hired. She was a quick learner, that one. I'll say that for her." She nodded toward JoBeth.

"About how long did she work in your shop?"

"Ninety-six days exactly."

"After ninety-six days, what happened?"

"She was promoted to the Human Relations Office."

"Was that usual?"

"What usual?" Dora's abrupt response caught Al off guard. He hesitated before he rephrased the question.

"I meant, were the employees in your shop usually promoted so quickly?"

"First time in my twenty-two years with the company." Dora folded her arms across her chest and looked down at Al, daring him to ask the next question.

"What was her job in the Human Relations Office?"

"Might have been some kind of special assistant to the manager."

"Objection. Hearsay."

The judge peered at Al from over his reading glasses. "Sustained."

"Do you know how long she worked in Human Relations?"

"I expect it was some six months, but I'm not saying that for a fact."

"What happened then?"

"She went to the front office."

"What did she do there?"

"Nobody never figured that out as far as I could tell."

"Did you find out why she was promoted so quickly in such a short time?"

"There was plenty of talk, but I don't listen to none of that."

"What kind of talk?"

"I said I don't listen. Don't you listen?" She took a deep breath and brushed back her bangs.

Al smiled. "How long did she work there?"

"For a while. I lost track of her. Then I heard she was sent over to the warehouse and worked for the operations manager. Don't know nothing about that neither."

"Was that a promotion?"

Dora wrinkled her nose and grunted. "I already told you I don't know nothing about that."

"What was her job in the warehouse?"

"Never did find that out."

"So in less than two years, the defendant had four jobs. Let me ask you again, were you surprised at the frequency of the promotions?"

"I stayed in my shop, did my work, and minded my business. Things go along better that way." Dora set her lips in a tight line, her eyes unwavering. She might as well have told Al outright that she wouldn't answer any more questions.

"Thank you, that's all."

The prosecution had no questions but reserved the right to call the witness back at a later time.

After lunch, Sarah passed the Agusta Hotel on her way back to the courtroom. Her plan to have Al spot her with someone else had been a bust; he never showed. Dragging Jameson over to tweak Al wasn't very smart. In fact, it had been childish. Even if Al had stopped for a drink, he would hardly have felt threatened. What had gotten into her?

She reached the courthouse steps and waited for the afternoon session. Her father was being called first. Perhaps the afternoon's testimony would be more favorable for the defense. Bendhurst proved to be a dud, and Dora's reluctance to speak about the promotions satisfied no one. It may have even increased the jurors' suspicion that JoBeth's behavior was self-indulgent and self-serving. The prosecution wasn't going to let that go by.

Her father would give the defense a boost. He would say that JoBeth was an exemplary employee and let Al get to that elusive reason of why she had been promoted. Sarah settled in her seat, eager to see her father on the stand. It wouldn't be another battle of the Titans that had occurred during the dinner at her house. This time, they would be on the same page.

She looked around the courtroom for her mother but Ellen wasn't present. Surprising. Her mother wasn't one to miss a chance to support her husband. Probably running late. Sarah folded her jacket and laid it on the seat beside her, reserving the place for Ellen's late arrival.

Sam came to the stand wearing a navy blue pin-striped suit and a bright red tie. He looked impressive as he was sworn in--straight, tall, and confident. She had to admit, he was someone to be admired. CEO or Chicago mobster, Sarah mused, he could be equally successful as either.

Al established her father's residence in the community, position in the company, and JoBeth's employment in the executive office directly under his supervision. Sam testified that she was a bright and trustworthy employee. He emphasized that, as far as he knew, everyone was pleased with her job performance, and that, as her ultimate, if not immediate boss, he was privileged to sign her many promotions. His testimony was convincing, and Sarah was sure his word would carry weight with the jury. They already knew him as a benefactor to the community: Little League baseball, chairman of the United Way, president of the Rotary Club. Sarah wished her mother was there to share her father's performance and wondered what was keeping her.

"Yesterday," Al continued, "Howard Maitlin admitted that he met JoBeth at a number of motels over a long period of time."

"Yes, I read about that in the morning's paper."

"Did you know additional information about those clandestine meetings was uncovered?"

"I don't believe I heard anything else." Sam dominated the witness box. He wore a slight smile and a contemplative look, as though rehearsing his next move.

"When we circulated JoBeth's picture among the motel owners and staff, they told the investigator that when she came, she was often accompanied by a man other than Howard Maitlin."

"I hadn't heard that." Sam changed his position in the chair, crossing his leg so that he was leaning to the right. He placed his elbow on the rail.

For a few seconds, it looked as though the two men were trying to stare each other down, like two dogs circling, but not quite ready to enter into a fight.

"What was your relationship with JoBeth?" Al demanded.

"I was her employer." He looked down at his suit jacket, picking off an imaginary piece of lint.

"Is that all?"

"Come out with it. What exactly are you getting at?" Her father was trying to intimidate Al. The best defense is an offense. The good old football stuff.

"When we found that another man was involved with the defendant, we made a return visit to the motels with a police artist. The artist drew a likeness of the other man described by the motel staff. As it turned out, all the drawings led us to the same man. Do you know who that is?"

"No, I couldn't say I do."

The muscles in Sam's jaw tensed. Sarah's heart beat wildly as Al walked toward the defense desk. She didn't like the way this was going.

"Do you recognize this man?"

Al held up a black and white drawing, faced the courtroom spectators as he walked with deliberate slowness to where the jurors sat. What started as a small inhalation of breath erupted into a whispering frenzy, then a loud buzz of excitement. Sarah stared stupidly at the drawing. Something must be wrong. The drawing resembled her father. She wanted to yell at Al, ask him what the hell he was doing. Afraid to look in her father's direction and certain that everyone was turning towards her, she bowed her head and pretended to be looking for something in her briefcase.

The judge gaveled. "Order," he commanded. "Order, or I'll have the courtroom cleared."

Al walked to the witness box, holding the picture so that Sam could see it. "Would you say the face in this picture resembles yours?"

Sam shrugged. "It's a pretty generic picture. Could be anyone."

"Then you're saying this picture does NOT look like you?"

Sam replied testily, "It could be anyone who resembles me."

"If called to the stand, would the motel staff be able to identify you as the person who accompanied the defendant to the motel?"

Sam glared at Al. "Why don't you have them testify?"

"The defense will do so, if necessary."

"Let me save the court some time. The picture." Sam paused and drew a deep breath. "Certainly looks like me."

"Enough so that you could be easily identified as the person in this picture?"

"Yes. But what does my private life have to do with this trial? I came here as a witness for the defense, not to be prosecuted for what is outside the jurisdiction of this court."

"Let me repeat. You were the other man who came to the motels with JoBeth. Is that correct?"

"Yes."

"It can be suggested that you were more than JoBeth's employer. You were also her lover. Is that correct?"

"Yes."

Sarah's face flushed, and she hung her head as though his shame was hers; she sat drowning in a pool of disgrace. Tears came and she let them slide down her cheeks. She longed to race out of the courtroom but couldn't because of the commotion it might cause. She sat, miserably listening as the father she loved and respected was dismantled.

"Is that why JoBeth' promotions came so rapidly? You were rewarding her for favors?"

"That's insulting, young man."

"And when you got tired of her, you farmed her out to yet another job at the warehouse."

"I wouldn't say I tired of her," Sam said defensively.

"You were finished with her?"

"Objection, badgering."

"That's all."

The DA called for a conference and the two attorneys approached the bench. While the spectators were distracted by the scene at the bench, Sarah hurried out of the courtroom, headed down the stairs, blinded by tears. She tried to erase her father's words and, at the same time, make sense of what she'd heard. It was like fighting on both sides of the same battle. It guaranteed that no matter what happened, she was going to come out seriously wounded. This can't be happening, she kept repeating, but deep down she knew that the man she had always looked up to was a fraud.

Habit guided her to the door and out onto the street. She turned toward home, but when she got there, she couldn't bear the thought of going inside and facing her mother. Instead, she got into her car and fled to the lake, to the place where she first met JoBeth, the place where her friend's dreams had sunk to the muddy bottom.

All the clues had been there, but she hadn't been paying attention:

her father badgering her over her decision to come home and work on the defense team, Dora's intimation that there was something amiss, JoBeth's hint that someday Sarah would know and understand, and Al cornering her father that night, zeroing in on the promotions. And she stupidly thought Al was defending her. How embarrassing. She gave a bitter laugh. And, of course, her mother must have known. If she hadn't known, at least suspected what Al was getting at that night. That's why she suggested that Sarah and Al go downtown rather than continue the conversation. She must have sensed things were moving in a dangerous direction. She wanted to spare her husband. Or, Sarah thought, maybe she wanted to protect me.

Sarah parked the car and walked to the lake, sat on the concrete ledge bordering the boat ramp, and looked out over its surface crowded with the dark images of the surrounding trees. The sun had slipped into an ocean of darkening clouds, and the last of the day's weakened light had stolen much of the color from the landscape. Sarah wondered if the water had a memory of closing over the car the evening JoBeth let it roll down the ramp. If it did, the lake kept its secret well. The crows, which a few minutes earlier had been noisily calling out to each other as they inspected one roosting place after another, had quieted and were replaced by the whip-poor-wills' whistling call from the edge of the woods.

The distinctive sound of the evening birds brought Sarah back to the summers when she and JoBeth came to the lake after supper to talk about school, and clothes, and boys. Back then, the lake had not yet become a sinister reminder of things better forgotten. It was a popular place where families gathered in the early evening, gossiping, the ends of their cigarettes blinking on and off in time with the fireflies. The rise and fall of the tree frogs' croaking had accompanied the children's voices as they called to each other in the twilight. It was always pleasant during those evenings, everyone patiently waiting, hoping that air would come across the lake to cool the place where they sat.

So much had changed since then. Her father, the man in control. The one who always made all the decisions. The person she had looked up to from as far back as she could remember; the one who had guided her every decision, who had made her what she was today. He was no better than the Maitlins or any of the others who had taken advantage of JoBeth's damaged psyche and exploited her vulnerability.

And what was she? A cut-out doll; her dress, her behavior, her goals, everything had been dictated by him. He was probably home right now, waiting for her to return so he could tell her how to feel, how to react to the day's events, how to carry on with her life, sure that he could still manage everything. One thing was certain, this would be her last night in Eight Mile Junction. She never wanted to see this town or her father again.

A shallow wind stirred the leaves that had fallen from the trees and sent a shiver across the surface of the water. Sarah rose from the boat ramp, brushed off her trousers and walked to the car. As she drove onto the main road, she passed the kudzu-covered shack. If she hadn't remembered that it once stood there, she wouldn't have known that a house was buried under the mass of vines. It had been abandoned and forsaken, left to suffocate under the frenzy of greenery that engulfed it. Would anyone remember those who had once been lived within the hidden walls of the house? And after the trial, would anyone remember the JoBeth she met that first summer's day at the lake?

Instead of going home, Sarah checked into a motel. As she stood at the front desk, she wondered if this was the one to which Howard or her father had taken JoBeth. She took the key, walked to her room, dropped onto the bed, and stared at the ceiling, trying to make sense of what was left of her life.

Later that evening, she drove to Millside and parked in front of Al's apartment. She wanted to vent her anger and frustration on somebody, and he was the perfect choice. It wasn't only the married thing. It had become bigger than that. His orchestration of her father's disgrace was something she had to deal with before she left town. If he was surprised to see her when he opened the door, he didn't show it. He simply said, "I'm sorry."

Sarah rushed across the threshold and stopped at the beanbag chair; it evoked shame and rage. Quickly, she looked away, not letting the powerful memory of that night distract her.

"Sarah, I'm sorry," he repeated. He walked toward her with his hands out, as if he expected her to take hold of them.

"Sorry?" she asked, retreating to the table. "Tell me what are you sorry for? Sorry for treating me like a fool this whole summer, sorry for screwing me when you knew you were married, sorry for using me to get at my father?"

"So that's got you all riled up? Having sex with a married man? Grow up, Sarah. Or do you want to be daddy's little girl all your life?"

"You're a selfish, lying bastard that uses people. You're no better than my father or—or—or Howard." She was on the verge of tears, furious with him and herself. She wanted to dig at him with her nails, hurt him; she wanted to hurl something at him, anything to disrupt his smug exterior. But if she did, she knew he would take it all in, give her that superior look that always made her feel incompetent. She held her hands behind her back and clenched her fists.

"Hear me out about that night. I want to explain..."

"Explain what? That you deceived me?"

"You made your own decisions," Al said calmly. "You returned to Eight Mile Junction on your own, and came to Williams for a job. And I do believe you enjoyed the sex. Did I ever force you do anything you didn't want to do?"

He was right, of course. She had insisted on making her own choices. But shit, what was happening here? Why was she seeing it from his point of view? Isn't that how her father always got her to agree? His unruffled self-assurance fueled her anger.

"Worst of all," she stammered, "you used me to meet my father, to get him on the stand, to humiliate him, and to devastate my mother."

"I could have brought him to the stand without coming to your house for dinner or without taking you to bed. Early on I suspected that he had been JoBeth's lover. It was your work that tipped me off. Remember Dora's interview? Besides, little lawyer lady, do you think your father deserved any better treatment than the others who ruined JoBeth with their selfishness? Didn't you come back to Eight Mile Junction to understand what happened to the friend you once knew? You should be home screaming at him, not here venting at me for exposing him for what he is."

"I hate your continual condescension." He grinned and reached out to her. She pulled back. "You could have at least told me what you were planning to do. Didn't I have a right to know?"

"Look how you're acting. We decided we had to keep your father's part in all this a secret. We weren't sure you could be neutral when we decided to put him on the stand and confront him. You told me yourself that you were dependent on him because he was the one who directed your life. We couldn't take the chance."

"You see. There it is. You've treated me like a clueless child ever since I got here and you're still doing it."

"Not true. We used your survey, the interviews, and brought some of your ideas into the trial. You know you influenced the defense strategy. If fact, you performed far beyond what I expected from the geeky, near-sighted, curly-headed law student that showed up at the office that first day." He gave a short laugh.

Sarah wasn't placated. It had become a contest, and she wasn't going to let him get the best of her. "And I suppose you screwed me for my own good."

"Well, there's some of that, too." Then, as if to retract the words, he said, "I'm really sorry it turned out like this. The seduction might have been unwise, but the attraction was there between us. Admit it. Besides, my wife and I..." He shrugged and looked away.

"You're kidding yourself. Save it, you jerk." Jerk, she said to herself. What kind of stupid word was that? Finding a stronger voice she yelled, "Save it you heartless, son-of-a-bitch. And go to hell." She slammed the door as she let herself out.

Chapter Seventeen

When Sarah woke the next morning, it took several minutes to remember that she had spent the night in a motel. Then, yesterday rushed back. Her father's disgrace. The scene with Al. Her life in turmoil. She groaned and reached for the telephone. Better get on with it. She dialed the office. While she waited for Janet to pick up, she pushed the rumpled bedcovers aside, and dug the gunk left from last night's tears from her eyes. She had slept in her underwear and felt grimy.

In the morning light, the motel room was much shabbier than it had appeared the night before. One side of the window curtain hung haphazardly from the rod and, under the air conditioner, the water-stained paper peeled away from the wall. The artist's drawing of her father came to mind. Little doubt, it had a strong resemblance to Sam's face. Watching Al parade the picture around the courtroom had to be the worst moment of her life. Janet answered the phone.

"Janet, please get me in to see JoBeth before she leaves for court this morning."

"Right," she answered. Her voice carried the unspoken question of why. "Do you want me to tell John-Two?"

"I don't really care. Just tell him I won't be in court today, and call me at this number to confirm when you get the visit set up." She read the digits on the motel phone to Janet. She'd know that it wasn't Sarah's home number, but she didn't explain.

"Will do."

"And have the janitor put a couple of boxes in the library. I'm leaving for Evanston."

Janet drew a sharp breath. "Does John-Two know?"

"I'll tell him when I get in."

The news wouldn't wait that long; Janet would get word to John-Two long before Sarah got to the office. She hoped that her decision to leave wouldn't interfere with seeing JoBeth.

She drove directly to the jail. Only Hillyard's Pharmacy was open. Bernie was swabbing yesterday's dust off the barber shop window, a closed sign hung crookedly on the door of Gladys' shop, and the porter at the Agusta was sweeping the carpet that ran from the front door to the curb. Traffic was slowly funneling into town. The leaves on the trees, only a few days before at the peak of their summer glory, were beginning to lose color and curl at the edges giving fair warning that the long days of summer were past. It seemed years instead of months since she had returned to Eight Mile Junction and first walked this way. The street hadn't changed, but she had.

When JoBeth entered the interview room, she looked spent, too preoccupied to give Sarah even a weak smile. The trial was wearing her down.

"I'm sorry about your father," JoBeth said as soon as she was seated.

"Never mind my father. I haven't come to discuss him or apologize for him."

Sarah reached across the table and took JoBeth's hand. The deputy either ignored the gesture or wasn't watching. Sarah didn't care. She squeezed her friend's hand; JoBeth held on tightly.

"I didn't understand," Sarah said softly. "I didn't know how far you had been pushed or how desperate you were."

"It would have been easier for me to go with the children on that night, but I told myself that I had to stay behind. I wanted everyone to know what was done to me, how my life had been ruined by what I had done." For a moment, JoBeth couldn't go on. "You understand, don't you? I hadn't planned on it being this way."

"I'm beginning to." The children's deaths were intentional, but not for the reasons the jury would find. Some things are too difficult to understand, too difficult to explain. But Sarah feared that the exposition of JoBeth's life would not bring understanding, certainly no sympathy. Instead, her conviction and subsequent punishment would clear away the threat that the residents of Eight Mile Junction were somehow implicated in the messy affair. The town's façade of southern gentility would remain untarnished.

"I'm willing to die for what I did."

"I know." Tears spread across Sarah's cheeks. She wiped them with her hand.

"Don't cry, Sarah."

"Why didn't you tell me about my father?"

"I didn't want to be the one. You came all the way down here to help me, it didn't seem right for you to be knowing what had gone on between him and me. I asked Al not to put Sam on the stand. I told him it would be for no good reason, that nothing would ever come of anything he said, but Al insisted."

"Al did the right thing. His job was to defend you, not look after me."

"You always loved your father so much. Oh, Sarah, believe me, I didn't mean to ruin that. I never thought you'd find out. You lived so far away when I started at the factory. Can you forgive me?"

"Don't worry about that. You have yourself to think of. I can take care of myself."

Sarah wanted to say God bless you, or I'll pray for you, but couldn't do that even though she knew the words would bring her friend comfort. She groped for the right words, but none came. I love you JoBeth were all that she could muster. Perhaps that was all that anyone could offer, the only thing left to give to her friend.

"It's enough for me that you understand." JoBeth reached into her coveralls and pulled up her bra strap. "These damn things don't ever want to stay up." She gave Sarah one of her old laughs and signaled for the deputy.

Sarah pulled a tissue from her purse and blew her nose, sitting for a while before she left. What a shitty world, she thought to herself. She wouldn't see JoBeth for a long time, if ever again. From the jail, she went to the office. As soon as she entered, Janet came out from behind her desk and put her arms around Sarah's shoulders.

"I'm so sorry it turned out this way."

Sarah wanted to ask her what she meant, wanted Janet to explain her part in keeping Al's marital status and her father's implication in the case a secret, but she already knew the answer. Janet, like Trudy Anders, had her place to protect. They both knew where their loyalties resided.

"Did the janitor come up with some boxes?"

"They're in the library. John-Two will be back before lunch. He wants to see you. Please, don't leave before he returns." She needn't have worried. Sarah had something to say to John-Two.

It didn't take long to pack. One box for the legal work she had completed for the firm to store in the archives, and one for personal items. She marked the box with her notes and reports with the date and listed the contents, then looked about the library, her home for the past several months. The law books on the surrounding shelves had their backs turned to her. They had no knowledge of how she was feeling and no inclination to find out; they were only interested in facts. Feelings get in the way. But Sarah knew that the law books wouldn't have the final say. Despite legalities, she was sure that the jury's attitude more than the letter of the law would influence the outcome. JoBeth would be sacrificed for the town's collective guilt. There wasn't going to be any happy ending. JoBeth would surely go to jail for a long time.

A sharp rap on the doorjamb announced Clayton. He stood just as he had so many months before when she first met him, looking down at her with a benevolent eye.

"So, Sarah, is this it?" he asked, nodding toward the packed boxes.

"Mmm," she said, not trusting herself to speak.

"Leaving something behind?"

He took a cigar from his inside jacket pocket, broke the tip, and lit it. A puff of smoke curled languidly before catching an air current and heading swiftly for the vent. Clayton walked into the library and pulled a chair over to Sarah's desk.

"Like a heart or something?"

Sarah tore her eyes away from the smoke wending its way to the ceiling and looked at him. So that's it. He knew about Al. His smile was full of empathy, and he looked so damned fatherly that Sarah wanted to put her head on his shoulder and cry.

"How did you know?"

"Small town, Sarah."

"He never told me he was married."

"Oh, did someone forget to tell you that men can be self-serving bastards?"

"Did you know he was married?"

"Yes, but I didn't know he was going to mess around with our new asset."

He threw his head back and blew what started out as smoke rings but turned into small, round clods. Sarah couldn't stop the smile that slipped onto her lips.

"I feel like such a sap." She put her elbows on her desk and held her head up with her hands.

"You're not leaving because of that, are you?"

"Not so much that as my father and what he did to JoBeth. It seems as though I've worked myself into the corner. Can't face Al and can't stand to see my father."

Clayton nodded. After a brief silence, he said, "You've had quite a time for yourself, haven't you?"

Sarah sniffed and blew her nose. "How could my father do that? He took advantage of his position and her vulnerability. Him, of all people."

"I repeat--did someone forget to tell you that men can be self-serving bastards?"

"I've always looked up to him. He never gave me a reason to doubt that there was anything other than a virtuous, caring man residing under that hard-driving exterior. After today, I don't think I can ever forgive him for what he did. Not only to JoBeth, but to my mother."

"Don't look that far ahead, Sarah. Forever is much too long. Put some distance between you and your father. You'll find forgiveness."

She nodded, her head sliding up and down between her hands. She straightened and folded her hands on her lap.

"And your mother? Will she leave also?" He stacked a neat pile of ashes in the paper clip tray.

"Oh, she'll stay with him, make the best of it. Strange, isn't it? My mother's most generous qualities are her worst enemy. She doesn't know how to be vindictive, only how to forgive and make things right. I can honestly say that I never understood her."

"Mothers, God bless them. I said that to you that once already, didn't I? Forgive me, I'm an old man repeating himself."

Sarah laughed aloud in spite of herself.

"And what about JoBeth? Did you find the answer to why she did it?"

"I think so," Sarah said. "She tried to reshape her life, but each time she tried and failed she returned to the same formula she followed in high school--find a man, fall in love, live happily ever after. When it didn't work, Howard was always near, waiting to catch her, dragging her further into the mire of guilt and self-hatred. Finally, there was no way out."

"Tragic."

"I think Dora Channing said it best. Kick a dog long enough, he'll be bound to turn and bite you."

"The folks in the hollow have a way of putting things. A lot of unspent wisdom up in those hills."

"JoBeth was looking for justice. She wanted everyone to know how she was used by the folks she loved. I guess a trial was the only way to expose them."

"Won't fly in a court of law, but it ranks high in the ledger of human understanding. You're a smart girl, Sarah. Maybe you should have been a sociologist instead of a lawyer." He added to the pile of ashes.

She looked down at her hands. They were clenched, holding on tightly, as if the only thing they had in the world were each other.

"I learned something this summer, and it wasn't about the law and how it works."

"And what was that?"

"Betrayal and what it does to a person. Before that day in court, I was my father's bright and successful daughter, his version of the perfect person. The day I found out the truth about him, I left the courtroom, feeling totally naked and so damaged I couldn't go home, couldn't face anyone. Really, I'm no better than JoBeth, just luckier."

"It's good you're leaving Eight Mile Junction," Clayton said. "Take from this town what you learned and make a new life, one that's your own."

"My father would call it running away. He'd tell me to stay and face up to it. He wouldn't say take it like a man, but he would imply it."

"What do you care what he thinks? Let him stew a bit. He'll come around."

"I suppose so, but I can't imagine how long that will take. He's a stubborn man who really believes he can manage everything. If I stay, he'll take up running my life as though nothing happened."

"He won't want to lose you. No matter what happens, you'll still be precious to him."

"Oh, Clayton." Sarah rose and put her arms around him. "I'll never forget what a good friend you've been." She kissed him on the cheek, giving it tiny little pecking kisses until he pushed her away, laughing. He smelled of cigar smoke and Old Spice, just like a relic.

John-Two was in the outer office taking the mail from Janet. When he saw Sarah, he immediately spoke. "Young lady, all I can say is that I'm sorry it turned out like this."

"For once I want to hear you call me by my name, Sarah. Just once." From the corner of her eye, she could see that Al's office door was closed.

John-Two's voice was low, almost a whisper. "Sarah, I can't tell you how sorry I am."

"Suddenly, everyone is sorry. Is it because I was so naïve? Because my father's an ass and betrayed his family and his position in this town? Is it because you thought I was not trustworthy enough to have your confidence? Let me come to the court, be taken unaware by the news that my father was our client's lover. Or are you sorry because right from the beginning you used me and thought I wouldn't notice?"

The only sound in the office were Janet's rapid taps on her keyboard. He looked sadly at Sarah, nodding his head in short little jerks. Her anger subsided when she saw his loss for words. It drove a wedge between her words and her fury.

"Don't be sorry," Sarah continued. "I learned something this summer, thanks to you. Something I might not have learned elsewhere. I may even look back on this and see that you did me a big favor. Let's leave it at that."

John-Two hung his head to the side and shuffled his feet. Made him look like a big oaf. "I hope so," he mumbled. "Yes, I hope so," he repeated

"I'll send you my address so you can forward my check." She picked up her box and walked out. The door to Al's office remained closed. At least she'd saved them the expense of giving her a farewell party.

She put the box into the trunk of the car and, for the last time, got behind the wheel. At home, she parked the car in front of the house where she first saw it, and went directly to her room. Her mother followed and stood in the doorway.

"Where were you last night? I was sick with worry." Ellen looked tired, older, more like the housekeeper in her apron and slippers than the woman who was the beneficiary of all the good things her father promised moving south would bring. Vera wasn't the only one who had aged that summer.

"I was okay." She purposely didn't say where she had slept. It wasn't that she meant to be spiteful; she no longer had to account to her mother for everything. She bent and pulled her suitcase from under the bed.

"Where are you going?" Ellen pointed to the suitcase. "Back to Evanston?" It was an idle question, but her mother didn't seem to know what else to say.

Sarah took out the children's quilt she had purchased her first week back in Eight Mile Junction. She gently refolded it and replaced it in the bottom of the suitcase. She'd never shown it to her parents. Just as well. They'd never understand how a little girl's handiwork helped her take her first steps toward examining her life.

"Are you leaving because of your father?"

"Did you know about JoBeth?" Sarah sat on the bed, reached for her mother, drawing her down beside her. She put one arm around her shoulder and held her tightly. Ellen leaned heavily against her daughter.

"A woman always knows when something is going on, doesn't she?" She hung her head, as if ashamed. "I suspected, but didn't know who it was until the night Al came to dinner. When he kept asking your father about the promotions, I made the connection between JoBeth and him. Until that moment, I was so happy. You were here with us, that nice young man, the Sabbath."

Nice young man? If she only knew. No sense unloading that on her. "That's why you sent us out, wasn't it? You wanted to protect Dad. And me."

"I didn't want any unpleasantness I wanted the evening to end as it began, full of warmth and happiness."

"Why didn't you tell me you suspected something?"

"How could I? You were always your father's finest prize, and you adored him from the time you could talk. I didn't know how you would take it or even if you would believe me."

"You must have known I would find out."

"Yes, but I let someone else tell you. I couldn't even find the courage to come to the courthouse that day. You had to face it alone while I stayed home, waiting for the explosion. I was such a coward."

Sarah hugged her mother, stroking her shoulder as she would a hurt child. Ellen continued to lean heavily against her daughter.

"Never mind me, what about yourself?" Sarah asked.

Ellen drew back and took Sarah's face in her hands. "You and your Dad are my life. If I let go of you and him, I let go of everything. There would be nothing left for me." She looked at Sarah, her eyes pleading for understanding. As they sat, holding each other, the telephone rang.

Ellen jumped up. "Let me get that. It might be your father." She looked back at Sarah as she hurried toward the door. "He'll need me more than ever now."

Sarah sat on the bed, listening to her mother's words float up the stairwell. She couldn't hear what her mother was saying, but it was pleasant listening to the sounds. So familiar, so much a part of the past.

My mother isn't much different than Vera. Preserve the family, make everything appear normal. Unlike Vera, Ellen had only sacrificed herself. But if it had been different, would Ellen have sacrificed me? Sarah hated the thought but knew no one could say for sure until that critical moment, when a life-changing decision had to be made. She finished packing, snapped the suitcase closed, and looked over her room one final time.

When she came downstairs, Ellen was preparing a sack lunch for the bus trip back to Columbia. "You might get a little hungry on your way to the airport."

"Thanks." She stuffed the lunch in her handbag and gave her mother a playful pinch on the cheek, pretending that everything was all right.

"What do you want me to tell your Dad?"

"Just tell him to return the car to Maitlin. The key is on the hook by the back door." She pulled her roller board toward the door, stopped, walked back to her mother, and put her arms around her.

"I'm a very lucky person to have a mother like you. I know it has been a tough balancing act standing between Dad's demands on me and my willingness to submit to his dictates. You tried to show me a gentler way. Thanks for that. I love you, Mom."

"Call me. I'll worry until I know you're safe, you know that. And Sarah, don't forget to fast for Yom Kippur."

"I won't."

Sarah smiled as she left the house. Her mother's connection with the rituals of her childhood had little meaning for Sarah. But her mother's insistence on keeping the past and its memories alive gave Sarah a feeling of warmth. She was glad she hadn't told her mother to get rid of the Raggedy Ann and Andy dolls and the high school stuff in her closet. She would know that her daughter had changed, and it was time to put them away. Sarah hurried toward the train station, giving St. Agnes her customary nod as she passed. "Hang on old girl," she whispered. "Don't let anyone push you off that corner."

Miles flew by as the bus traveled toward the capital. Past the Loblolly Pines, past the green signs that identified the location of little towns hidden away in the undulating landscape, past the mile markers announcing Columbia ten miles closer. Sarah tried to concentrate on the scenery, but only saw her faded reflection in the bus window.

What would be like to be back in Evanston, in her apartment, immersed in her studies? After all that had happened that summer, continuing on the track her father laid out was no longer possible. Becoming a corporate attorney had been his dream, not hers. But if not Evanston, what? She was overwhelmed by the risk. It would be easier to run away and hide. But where? Unlike her escape from the Molitar fiasco last spring, running home was no longer an option. The bus slid into the terminal at Columbia. The passengers stood in the aisle, retrieving their belongings from the overhead bins. She picked up her stuff and followed them off the bus.

When she stepped out onto the curb, a voice called, "Taxi, ma'am?" She raised her hand and almost said airport, but stopped and stared. "Taxi?" the driver repeated hopefully. She shook her head and reentered the bus station, heading directly for the pay phone.

"Hello, Aunt Bekkah?" she said into the phone. "This is Sarah. How would you like some company for a few weeks?"

"Why, Sarah. What a pleasant surprise. What's up?"

"Big changes," Sarah said. "Tell you when I get there. I'll call you when I get in sometime tomorrow."

At the ticket counter, the agent asked, "Where to, lady?"

"New York City," Sarah replied.

Thanks To

This novel began in Ellen Sussman's class, "A Novel in a Year," and progressed through many iterations with help from many others: additional classes taken with John Dusfesne, Michael David Lucas, and Zoe Keithley; editing by Vicky Mlyniec; and early draft readings by Anne DaVigo, Janet Rudenjack, Gwen Rigby, Marcy Place Sheehan, and Sandra Weiss. As much help as anything were the meetings with my Monday night prompt group in which many of my literary ideas are generated: Alice Carney, Gayanne Leachman, Virginia Kidd, and Teresa Thompson. I owe much to the legal advice given by Charles Bonneau, William Copper, and Bill West. It was Scott Evans' Blue Moon Writers Thursday night group that finally got this show on the road with their line-by-line edits of the manuscript: Emily Blodget, Jim Blodget, Dorothea Bonneau, Ronald Lane, David Sutton, and Howard Zochlinski. And finally, those who offered encouragement while I was filled with doubt: Judith Anderson, Mary Jo Bryan, Marilu Carter, Jennifer Chapman, Sue Hodgson, Nicky Neff, Bill and Linear Sleuter, Joan Sublett, and Lisette Walker. With deepest gratitude, I thank them all.

CPSIA information can be obtained
at www.ICGtesting.com
Printed in the USA
FSOW02n0843100517
34102FS